Bloodline Of A Serial Killer

written by

Jody Slyman

This book is a work of fiction. Any resemblance to actual events or persons, living or dead, is entirely coincidental.

"Bloodline Of A Serial Killer," by Jody Slyman. ISBN 978-1-60264-108-2.

Manufactured in the United States of America.

This book is dedicated to my friends, Amber Thieme and Nayda Santos. The two of you made me feel at home in a new town when I decided to start a new life. In the short time we have known each other, we have gotten to be such close friends. I cannot thank the both of you enough for everything you've done for me. I am honored to call both of you a friend. The two of you have my respect and most of all, my love.

Introduction

A YOUNG, BEAUTIFUL BRUNETTE in her mid-twenties walks around her small, one bedroom apartment. She is wearing a white cotton pajama top with small hearts all over it and cotton pajama pants of the same design. She has her shoulder length hair pulled back into a ponytail. Her captivating brown eyes look at the clock on the wall as it reads 11:05 pm.

The lady walks into her living room area. Along one wall is an entertainment center with a television and DVD player. On top of the entertainment center is a plant and a few pictures. In the middle of the room is a burgundy couch and to the left of the couch is a matching recliner. A couple of pictures hang on the walls and more plants dot the room as a fragrance of strawberry hangs in the air. In front of the couch is a small, brown coffee table.

The lady picks up the TV remote from the coffee table and turns on the TV. She flips the channels around until she finds what she is looking for. The show that covers unsolved mysteries and strange disappearances comes on. The lady turns up the volume.

The narrator of the show speaks, "Our next story goes

back 50 years. Tomorrow marks the 50th anniversary of when the manhunt was called off for Michael Newman, 13 year old son of prominent clockmaker, Thomas Newman, and founder of the O'Kelly Adoption Centers, Maureen O'Kelly-Newman." The narrator pauses then continues, "Seattle police believed that Michael Newman, due to incredible stress put on him by his father, ran away in the summer of 1949. The manhunt continued for six months until a bizarre murder in January of 1950 caused the police to have to shift their focus." Another pause and the narrator continues, "So, whatever happened to Michael Newman? The world may never know. His story is one of the great mysteries that haunt this countries past. Now, on to the next great disappearance."

The lady watches the show a little longer, then picks up the TV remote from the coffee table, "Wow, that is pretty wild how people just disappear."

She flips the channels and stops when the television comes to show the New Year's Ball in Times Square and the giant "2000" sign at the bottom of the pole. The lady sits back on the couch and a gray and white cat jumps up on the couch next to her.

The lady pets the cat, "Heathcliff, where have you been hiding. It's almost the year 2000."

At that time, the cordless phone on the coffee table rings.

The lady answers the phone, "Hello."

An older lady's voice, "Jackie, it's your mother."

Jackie replies, not very excited, "Hey mom, how are you?"

The mom replies, "I'm fine. It's you I'm worried about. It's the biggest New Year's celebration and your sitting at home all alone. You should be out there with some handsome guy."

Jackie sighs, "We're not going through this again mother, but if you must know, I'm not alone."

2

The mother gets a little excited, "Do you have a man there? Well, give me some details."

Jackie replies, "If I tell you his name, will you leave me alone?"

The mother responds, "For now maybe."

Jackie quickly speaks, "His name is Cliff. Now, have a Happy New Year mom."

The mother tries to speak, "But honey, what …"

Jackie hangs up the phone and looks at the cat, "Who needs a man when I got you, right Cliff."

Jackie pets the cat and watches the ball drop. She thinks about what her mom said. She does feel lonely from time to time, but she knows that she doesn't have much luck when it comes to men.

Jackie turns off the TV, "Well Heathcliff, I'm going to bed. Have a Happy New Year." Jackie gets up and walks towards the bedroom, "Maybe I'll meet Mr. Right this year."

Jackie walks through the open bedroom door and turns on the light. The single bed is across the room from the door. Along the left wall is a dresser and a desk. Each has a plant on it and some pictures. On the right of the room is a walk-in closet with the door closed. Her clothes lay on the floor from where she changed a few hours ago.

Jackie grabs the edge of the door and swings it in order to close the door. As the door starts to move closed, a figure comes from behind the door, moving quickly towards Jackie. The figure is dressed in a black turtleneck, black jeans and black boots. The figure also has on a dark blue jean jacket and black leather gloves. The intruder stands around 5'9" tall and holds a good build around 165 pounds. The person has a folded piece of white cloth in his right hand.

Jackie turns and a look of sheer terror comes to her face as the intruder moves for her deliberately. Before Jackie can scream, the cloth is placed firmly over her nose and mouth as a strong left arm wraps around her. Her terrified eyes lock on the unmasked face of the intruder. It is a man in his mid-twenties with short brownish hair with some blonde tip highlights, brown eyes and about a week of facial hair growth.

Jackie tries to struggle as the man drives her back with his momentum and down onto the bed. The chemical on the cloth starts to take effect. Jackie's vision starts to blur and fade in and out. She can feel her body get weaker and weaker. Jackie fights to stay conscious, fearful of what this man will do to her if she passes out. However, the chemicals are just too strong.

Just before Jackie passes out, the man calmly whispers, "Relax beautiful Jaqueline."

Then, everything in Jackie's world goes black.

Chapter 1

A LATE NINETIES, FOUR door Ford Taurus races down the busy New York street in the early morning, just after sunrise. The streets are covered with some slush and a small layer of snow covers the ground. There is a red flashing light in the windshield and a police siren sounding loud. The car weaves through traffic as the other cars move to get out of the way. The car turns sharp at a stoplight, leaving the main road and entering a residential area where numerous apartment buildings and condos line the street.

A couple blocks ahead of the Taurus there are numerous NYPD police cruisers, an ambulance and two CSI vans. The Taurus comes to a stop near the police cruisers. There are quite a few civilians standing around the yellow police tape trying to see what is going on.

A female, looking to be in her late twenties, gets out of the passenger seat. She stands around 5'1" tall and holds a nice build around 120 pounds. She has black hair that hangs just above her shoulders and brown eyes. She has on fairly tight blue jeans and sneakers with a blue turtleneck and a gray, medium weight jacket.

A second female, looking to be in her late twenties

also, gets out of the driver's seat. She stands about 5'7" tall and holds an athletic build of 135 pounds. She has blonde hair that just touches her shoulders and blue eyes. She has on tight fitting, stonewashed blue jeans, a white turtleneck and a blue medium weight jacket.

They can see their breath as they walk towards the police tape in the cold winter New York weather. The two ladies work their way through the crowd to a police officer standing at the police tape.

The officer looks at them, "Stop. This is an official crime scene."

The taller lady pulls out a badge, "I'm Detective Ashley Taylor and this is my partner, Detective Natalie Simpson."

The officer lifts up the police tape, "It's the second floor, down the left hallway."

The two detectives duck under the tape and start towards the six story, brick apartment building.

Detective Simpson speaks as they walk up the steps to the main door, "Looks like we're getting an early start this year."

Detective Taylor replies as they pass two more officers in the lobby, "You think they could have at least waited a day."

The two detectives walk up the stairs to the second floor. They turn right and start down the long, dark brown hallway. They see a "T" intersection at the end of the hall and hear some voices around one of the corners. They reach the end of the hallway and look left.

A few feet in front of them is another police officer talking to an elderly woman in a nightgown who appears to be really shaken up. About thirty feet down the hallway is two more police officers and twenty feet pass them is a man in his forties, dressed for the cold weather, taking pictures.

The two detectives walk over to the two police officers

and that is when they see why they were called so early on New Year's Day. They see Jackie's body, dressed in a white bra and panties, laying on her back next to the door of her apartment. Her legs are straight and together and her arms are laying next to her sides. She has a fluffy white pillow propped under her head. The man who looks to be in his late forties with graying hair and a mustache that stands about 6'1" tall and weighs around 190 pounds and is wearing jeans, a t-shirt and medium weight jacket, is taking pictures of the body.

The man taking the pictures speaks, "Just one more picture and I'll be ready to fill you in."

The man snaps his last picture and puts the camera down on the top of a large solid silver suitcase.

The man looks at the ladies, "Detective Taylor and Detective Simpson, we need to stop meeting like this."

Detective Simpson smiles, "Kevin, what does our favorite CSI have for us?"

Kevin walks over to the two detectives, "Victim's name is Jaqueline Kearny, age 25. The body was found by the neighbor, Mrs. Daniels." Kevin takes a breath, "The victim was strangled with what looks like some kind of nylon cord. I'll know for sure once I get the body to the lab for further analysis."

Detective Taylor speaks, "This whole scene looks like it was staged."

Kevin nods, "It was. The best I can say right now is the victim was killed around 2 am. The body was found right here at 6 am. Also, there are no signs of struggle, yet the victims wrists and ankles were bound at one time. My guess is that she was drugged. I've got a blood sample to test when I get to the lab."

Detective Taylor nods and Kevin continues, "But this is what is going to get you the most. Come look."

The three of them walk over next to the body and the two detectives see what Kevin is talking about.

Kevin speaks, "It looks like whoever did this wrote the letter 'M' on her stomach with a black marker."

The two detectives look at the three inch tall, black letter 'M' on Jackie's stomach as Kevin pulls out two large, clear evidence bags from his suitcase. The two detectives are unsure what to make of the letter on the body.

Kevin holds up the two bags, "I also found these."

The two detectives look at the bags and see a ripped piece of paper that reads "Government Adoption Form" across the top in one bag and the minute hand of a grandfather clock in the second bag. The paper and minute hand both look aged. This confuses the detectives even more. They know the clues mean something, but now to find out what.

Kevin speaks, "They were laying next to the body, right out in the open so whoever did this wanted them found."

Detective Simpson nods knowingly, "Looks like the killer is trying to tell us something."

Detective Taylor looks at Kevin, "We're going to let you get the body back to the lab. We'll be in the office all day once you get things together."

Kevin nods, "I can have the pictures by noon. The rest, hopefully by the end of the day."

Detective Simpson gives a quick nod, "Thanks Kevin."

Kevin walks off to get the body ready for transport.

Detective Taylor looks at her partner, "Well, lets check the apartment."

Detective Taylor walks in first. She looks around, not seeing anything at first. Detective Simpson follows her partner. Once they reach the living room, they see the first thing out of the ordinary.

Detective Taylor speaks, "Look. Why do you think this regular table chair is in the middle of the living room?"

Detective Simpson replies, "I'm going to check the bedroom."

Detective Simpson walks into the bedroom. She sees the bed somewhat messed up. At the end of the bed, piled on the floor, is Jackie's pajamas. Detective Simpson slowly walks around the room, taking in everything. She walks over to the closet and opens the door. She reaches in and turns on the light. She sees a bunch of cloths hanging up all around the walk-in closet and shoes line the floor. She turns to walk off, but stops and turns back to the closet. Detective Simpson notices two pair of shoes next to each other knocked over, not straight like the others.

Detective Taylor slowly walks around the living room. She hears something behind her that sounds like something was knocked off the coffee table. Detective Taylor turns quick, drawing her 40 caliber pistol from her holster and bringing it up. She lets her breath go as she sees Heathcliff standing on the coffee table and the TV remote on the floor.

Detective Simpson walks into the living room as Detective Taylor puts her pistol away.

Detective Taylor speaks, "Looks like we have a witness." She points to the cat, "Do you think he'll cooperate."

Detective Simpson smiles, "I wish he could. This whole crime scene has me puzzled."

Detective Taylor nods, "I know what you mean." She sighs, "We should get to the office in case Kevin finishes early. I don't think we're going to find anything here."

Detective Simpson picks up the cat and the two detectives walk out of the apartment. They walk over to the police officer and the elderly lady.

Detective Simpson speaks, "Mrs. Daniels?"

The elderly lady nods, "Yes."

Detective Simpson replies, "We are going to catch whoever did this. Could you take her cat for us?"

Mrs. Daniels takes the cat, "Oh Heathcliff."

Mrs. Daniels pets the cat as the two detectives start to walk off.

Detective Taylor turns back to the officer, "I want to see all the interviews once they are done. I want everyone in the building questioned."

The police officer nods and the two detectives walk off, still un-nerved by what they saw.

Detective Taylor is sitting at her neatly kept desk at the police station. The room is huge with numerous sets of two desks each lined up. It is mostly empty given the holiday. Detective Taylor's desk has a picture of her and her father on it, an inbox and outbox and a computer. It has three drawers on each side of the chair. There is a very sanitary smell in the air from the constant cleanliness of the workplace.

At that time, a young police officer walks up holding a large manila envelope.

The officer speaks, "Detective, I was asked to give this to you. They are pictures from this morning."

Detective Taylor nods and takes the envelope, "Thanks. How are the interviews with all the residents coming?"

The officer replies, "They are almost complete, but so far nothing has given us any leads yet."

Detective Taylor opens the envelope, "Good. Have them brought to us as soon as they are done."

The officer nods, "Yes detective."

The officer walks off as Detective Taylor pulls out the pictures. Then, Detective Simpson walks up carrying a couple bags of fast food.

Detective Simpson puts one bag down on Detective

Taylor's desk, "Well, I talked to the mother." She sits down at her desk which is facing Detective Taylor's, "Are those the pictures?"

Detective Taylor nods, "I was just about to start looking at them. So, what did you find out?"

Detective Simpson pulls out her notepad, "According to the mother, the victim was a loner. She hasn't had a steady relationship since her father died four years ago. She had very few, if any friends, but loved her cat, Heathcliff. The mother called the victim around midnight and the victim claimed to have a man there. The man's name is Cliff."

Detective Taylor nods, "Cliff, that's a start. Did the mother know any man by that name?"

Detective Simpson sighs, "No, but maybe the neighbors might know. Plus, once the officers are done at the apartments, I think we should have them start interviewing everyone she works with."

Detective Taylor replies while looking at the pictures, "Good idea." She stops at a certain picture, "I still don't understand the chair in the living room."

Detective Simpson thinks for a second, "Remember Kevin saying that the victim was tied up at some point. She was probably tied to the chair. But I'm pretty sure the attack happened in the bedroom."

Detective Taylor looks at her partner, "What makes you say that?"

Detective Simpson explains, "The covers on the bed were messed up, but not like someone was sleeping in them. Also, I found two pair of shoes in the closet knocked over. Given how neat everything else was, it stood out. Almost like the person was hiding in the closet."

Detective Taylor nods, "But in all these pictures, all I see is some pajamas on the floor in the bedroom, but no sign of any regular clothes. If the intruder was already in the apartment when she got home, you would think she went into the closet at least once. How did the intruder avoid being seen?"

They both sit quiet for a second and Detective Taylor continues, "The victim was wearing a bra and panties. I know I don't wear a bra in my pajamas and I'm not sure if anyone would. Which doesn't make sense why there are no clothes anywhere in the pictures. Plus, if there was a man there with her, you would think she would be in clothes. So again, where are they?"

Detective Simpson sighs, "Maybe the intruder took them."

The young officer walks back up, "Excuse me detectives."

Detective Simpson replies, "What is it?"

The officer places a couple of notepads on Detective Taylor's desk, "Here are the complied notes from all the interviews. We talked to the desk clerk at the apartment complex. There was no registered guest for the victim's room."

Detective Taylor questions, "What do you mean?"

The officer explains, "The security for the building is fairly good. All guests have to sign in at the front. That way if the building catches fire or something happens, then they know how many people are in the building and who they were." The officer takes a breath, "There was really only one other thing. The neighbor, Mrs. Daniels, said she stopped by the victim's apartment around 10 pm to drop off some brownies. She said she only stepped just inside the door, but she is sure that the victim was alone because she was already dressed in her pajamas."

The two detectives glance at each other and the officer asks, "Is there anything else?"

Detective Taylor shakes her head, "Yes. I want you to start finding who the victim works with and question them about how much they know about her life."

The officer gives a quick nod and walks off.

Detective Simpson is the first to speak, "So she was in her pajamas at 10 pm, but found this morning in her undergarments. It doesn't make sense."

Detective Taylor shakes her head, "Whoever did this put a lot of thought into it."

Detective Simpson speaks not really with an intent, "Well planned and executed, just like the time spent to stage the body. It's almost like ..."

Detective Simpson stops, but Detective Taylor can tell her partner is onto something, "Keep talking Natalie."

Detective Simpson continues, "With all this planning, the intruder must have known the victim's daily routine like clockwork. That's how he could avoid being seen in the apartment. The person must have watched her for awhile. Lets say she was alone because her cat's name is Heathcliff, and that could be the Cliff she claimed was there." She takes a breath, "A person comes by during the day and with all the excitement of New Years, the person slips by everyone unnoticed. The intruder lets himself into the apartment, knowing she is not home. He hides in the closet because maybe she doesn't go into the closet at night. Maybe she changes into her pajamas and puts her clothes up in the morning." She pauses, "I don't know. This is pretty far out in left field."

Detective Taylor pushes her partner on, "Keep going because it sounds like your onto something that makes sense."

Detective Simpson takes a drink and continues, "She goes into the bedroom after midnight because she wanted to see the new year in her own way and she gets attacked. The time of death is 2 am so that gives our intruder two hours to change the victim and tie her up. The body was found at 6 am so that gives the intruder plenty of time to stage the scene. If he knew the victim's routine that well, then he would probably know how to get in and out of the building unseen." She hesitates, "That's a stretch."

Detective Taylor just smiles, "No, it makes perfect sense. This wasn't just random or crime of passion. This was done to a picture perfect plan. Your ideas go along with the clues that were left. Whoever did this has a big plan in place and this was just the first step."

Detective Simpson stands, " I'm going to get with the front and have them put some of the information in the national criminal database. Given the strange clues and method of this crime, maybe it has happened before."

Detective Taylor nods, "I'll keep going over the pictures and the interview notes for anything we might have missed."

Detective Simpson gives a quick nod and walks off as Detective Taylor looks at the clock on the wall and it reads 1 pm.

Detective Taylor speaks to herself, "We got a long day ahead of us."

Detective Taylor starts going over the pictures again, looking for anything they might have missed.

Detective Simpson walks back up in about an hour and a half.

Detective Taylor is on the phone, "Thanks Kevin, we'll call if we need anything else."

Detective Taylor hangs up and Detective Simpson sits down, "What did Kevin have to say?"

Detective Taylor sits back, "He found traces of chloroform in the victim's body. He also confirmed that the victim was strangled with a quarter inch nylon cord, which was also used to bind the wrists and ankles. He figures that the victim was tied up before she was killed, given the marks on the wrists and ankles." She takes a breath and continues, "No fingerprints on the body or the paper and no signs of sexual assault."

Detective Simpson jumps in, "So the intruder looks, even undresses the victim, but doesn't touch. So it wasn't done for a sexual reason."

Detective Taylor nods and continues, "He said there was nothing special about the marker used, virtually untraceable, but there was something unusual about the paper."

Detective Simpson questions, "Like what?"

Detective Taylor explains, "Kevin thought it looked old so he did some date testing on it. He said it is roughly 75 years old."

Detective Simpson questions, not expecting an answer, "Why would someone leave a 75 year old piece of adoption form paper at the scene? What is this person trying to say?"

Detective Taylor sighs, "I don't know, but you know they have a meaning given the rest of the crime scene."

At that time, a female officer walks up with a few papers in her hands, "Detective Simpson, I have something on what you asked for earlier." The officer hands over the papers, "It doesn't make any sense."

Detective Simpson takes the papers and starts glancing through them, "Thank you officer."

The officer walks off and Detective Taylor questions, "Did we get some hits from the database?"

Detective Simpson doesn't respond at first. She just flips through the papers with a look of disbelief on her face.

Detective Taylor questions again, "Natalie, what is it?"

Detective Simpson replies hollowly, "This can't be right. We have 2 hits with a 100% match."

Detective Taylor gets a funny look, "A 100% match, that's not possible unless it is almost exactly the same in every way. Are they in New York?"

Detective Simpson shakes her head, "No. One is from

Kansas City, Missouri and the other is from Seattle, Washington."

Detective Taylor sits forward, "Looks like we have a possible serial killer making their way across the country." She can tell by her partner's look that there is more, "What else is there?"

Detective Simpson looks at her partner, "The one from Kansas City happened on January 1st, 1975 and the one from Seattle happened on January 1st, 1950."

Detective Taylor's stunned look says it all. Neither detective knows what to say, or even where to begin with this new information. They just stare at each other and then glance back at all the information on their desks as they both realize that they may have a serial killer case that dates back 50 years.

Chapter 2

A MIDDLE AGED COUPLE are walking around their two story townhouse. By the design and decorations in each room, it is obvious that they have money. The woman is dressed in a nice evening gown and the man is in a nice suit.

The man looks at his watch, "It's almost 5:30, we need to be going."

The woman nods and walks over to the bottom of the stairs, "I'll be right out." The man walks out and the woman yells up the stairs, "Carmen, your father and I are leaving for the country club!"

Carmen, a high school senior with flowing blonde hair and blue eyes, appears at the top of the stairs. Her beautifully attractive, petite frame is covered by gray sweatpants and a white tank top.

The woman speaks again, "We will be home around eleven. I have clothes in the dryer that should be done in 30 minutes. Can you fold them for me?"

Carmen smiles which would cause anyone to melt, "Sure mom, you and dad have fun."

The mother smiles, turns and walks out of the house.

Carmen walks back to her room. She has posters all over the walls. There is a big fluffy bed in the middle of the room with stuffed animals all over it. There is a desk on the wall opposite of a walk-in closet door and a chest of drawers next to the closet door. There is also an entertainment center with a TV and stereo.

Carmen sits back down at her desk and opens her physics book. She continues to work on her homework until she hears the faint buzz of the dryer. Carmen puts down her pencil and closes the book. She walks over to her closet door and opens it. She turns on the light and steps inside. Cloths hang everywhere and shoes are lying all over the floor. Carmen puts on her slippers and walks out, leaving the closet door open.

Carmen walks downstairs and down the hallway to the kitchen. She walks through the kitchen and into the laundry room. She grabs the laundry basket, opens the dryer and puts the clothes in the basket. Once she is done, she closes the dryer with her knee, picks up the basket and makes the trip back upstairs. She puts the basket on her bed. Carmen walks out of her room and across the hall to the bathroom. She starts some bathwater and walks back to her room. She walks over to the desk and takes off her sweatpants revealing her white panties.

Carmen looks up and notices her physics book is open. She appears a little confused as she closes the book again. She grabs her body wash off the desk and turns around. She walks over to the chest of drawers next to the now closed closet door. She pulls out her pajamas as a figure silently moves into the room behind her. As she closes the drawer, an arm wraps around her body and a piece of cloth covers her nose and mouth.

Carmen starts to struggle as fear comes across her face. Her muffled screams are lost in the empty house. She tries to get free, but she is just not able to. Her vision starts to fade and her world starts to go dim. Carmen fights to remain conscious.

The killer smoothly whispers in her ear, "Relax my beautiful, young Carmen."

Then, the lights in Carmen's world go out.

Detective Taylor and Detective Simpson are sitting at their desks late into the evening hours. Their Captain, a tall well built man in his fifties, walks up.

The Captain speaks, "It's past eleven, you two should get some rest."

Detective Taylor replies bewildered, "It has been two weeks. Two weeks and we have nothing to tell the mother, or the Mayor for that matter."

The Captain replies, "I'll deal with the Mayor. Have you gotten anything from Kansas City or Seattle?"

Detective Simpson sits back, "I've talked to both departments and they are giving us their full cooperation, but they both said it would take some time to pull all the records in their cases. Also, the officers that I talked to at both departments said that the case was larger than the one body, but they couldn't remember exact details so I went back to the database and widened the search. Hopefully we will get some more information back soon."

The Captain questions, "What about the detectives that worked the cases?"

Detective Simpson sighs, "Detective Conners in Seattle quit in January of 1951. Detective Gibson quit in January of 1976. Neither detective could deal with failing on the case and they have never been heard from since."

The Captain nods, "I'll make some calls in the morning to see if I can help come up with something."

Detective Taylor replies as the phone rings, "Thanks Captain."

Detective Simpson answers the phone, "Detective Simpson." A pause, "Kevin, what do you got for us?"

Detective Simpson grabs a piece of paper and a pen and scribbles down an address, "Okay, I got it. See you there."

Detective Simpson hangs up and Detective Taylor questions, "What did Kevin need?"

Detective Simpson looks at her, "Another body was just found. Kevin and his team is already on the way."

Detective Taylor and Detective Simpson stand up and the Captain speaks, "Keep me posted and let me know if you need anything."

The two detectives give a quick nod and hurry off. They each wonder what this crime scene will bring. Will it bring some answers or just more questions? They are both anxious, but nervous as well.

The two detectives pull up to the front of the townhouse where Carmen lives. Numerous police cars are present and officers are trying to keep the public at a safe distance. Detective Taylor gets out of the driver's seat and Detective Simpson gets out of the passenger's seat. The two detectives walk towards the front of the townhouse.

A police officer standing at the front door speaks when the two detectives walk up, "The body is upstairs detectives."

The detectives look around as they enter the house and walk towards the stairs. Nothing seems out of the ordinary to them yet. They walk up the stairs and they hear the clicking of the camera Kevin is using to take pictures. Both ladies sigh, not really wanting to see the newest outcome, but each hoping that this crime scene will give them some answers.

As they reach the top of the stairs, they see Kevin standing in the doorway of Carmen's bedroom. The two detectives walk up as Kevin finishes his pictures. The body is dressed in a white bra and panties, laying on the floor inside her bedroom. There is a pillow under the head and the arms are laying by the side of the body, just like the first body they found. The two detectives notice a three inch tall, black letter "N" on Carmen's stomach. Detective Taylor sighs, knowing it is the same killer.

Kevin snaps his last picture, "The young lady is Carmen Reynolds, age 17. She was drugged, tied up and strangled just like the last woman. The only clue left this time was the letter on her stomach."

Detective Simpson shakes her head, "First the letter 'M' and now the letter 'N', what is this person saying?"

Kevin sighs, "I don't know. Maybe the killer has a body planned for every letter of the alphabet and we just haven't found the earlier bodies."

Detective Taylor gives a lazy smile, "I wish it was that easy."

Kevin can tell that they have more information than what he knows, "Is there something you haven't shared with me yet?"

Detective Simpson sighs, "We are trying to keep it as quiet as possible, but get with us back at the precinct and we will fill you in."

Kevin nods, "I'm finished processing the body here."

Detective Taylor nods, "Go ahead and move the body to the lab. We are going to talk to the parents and process the rest of the house."

Kevin gives a quiet nod and motions for his assistants to move the body. Detective Simpson enters Carmen's bedroom as Detective Taylor heads back downstairs to talk with Carmen's parents.

Detective Taylor and Detective Simpson are sitting at their desks in the early morning hours waiting for Kevin to bring them the information from the crime scene two days ago. As they wait, the two detectives glance through the information from Jackie's crime scene.

Detective Simpson is the first to speak, "I don't think it is any coincidence that the paper and clock hand are 75 years old and the previous crimes are 25 years apart. I just wonder why the killer waits 25 years."

Detective Taylor replies, "We don't even know if it is the same person. I mean, if the killer was 18 in 1950, then he would be 68 years old now. It's possible, but a stretch."

Detective Simpson questions her partner, "Are you thinking more along the lines of a copycat killer?"

Detective Taylor nods slightly, "I would think more along that line than the same killer."

At that time, Kevin walks up with some folders full of papers and pictures, "Good morning ladies."

Detective Taylor smiles at Kevin, "Ready for another long day?"

Kevin gives a slight chuckle, "I guess so." He hands a folder to Detective Simpson, "The front desk wanted me to give this to you. I think it is more on the information from the database."

As Kevin sits next to Detective Taylor's desk, Detective Simpson starts looking through the papers.

Kevin opens the folder in front of him, "Sorry it took a couple of days, but I wanted to make sure we missed absolutely nothing."

Detective Taylor nods, "So, what do we have?"

Kevin sighs, "Unfortunately not much. No fingerprints in the house or on the body. Just like before, the girl was drugged, tied up, then strangled. Also, no signs of sexual assault." He pauses, "Now, why don't you share with me what you know?"

Detective Taylor replies, "After the first body, we ran the information through the database and got two hits. The only catch is that one is from 1975 and one is from 1950. Also, one happened in Kansas City and one in Seattle."

Kevin gets a shocked look on his face, "Wow, that is something. Three bodies, fifty years apart."

Detective Simpson interjects, "It's not just three anymore."

Detective Taylor looks at her partner, "What is it Natalie?"

Detective Simpson replies bewildered, "It appears that in 1950 there were 27 unsolved murders in Seattle that fit the M.O. and 27 unsolved murders in Kansas City in 1975 that also fit the M.O."

Kevin can't keep his response quiet, "Jesus, 54 prior murders that go all the way back to 1950."

Detective Taylor responds, "We need those case files from Seattle and Kansas City."

Detective Simpson nods, "We better let the Captain know about this."

Detective Taylor looks at all the information on the desk in front of her, "What have we gotten ourselves into?"

Detective Simpson and Kevin both let out a sigh as they stare down at the information on the desks.

Chapter 3

A RINGING PHONE ECHOES through the large three bedroom house in one of the nicer neighborhoods in Manhattan. A 5'3" tall 130 pound well built woman who appears to be in her early thirties with straight blonde hair that hangs down just past her shoulder blades walks into the kitchen and grabs the phone from the wall.

The woman speaks, "Hello."

A man's voice responds, "Shannon?"

Shannon responds with a smile, "Hey honey, so I take it you made it okay?"

The man replies, "Yeah, it took longer than expected, sorry for calling so late."

Shannon's blue eyes look up at the clock on the wall and it shows 10:20 pm, "That's okay, I just got back from dropping the kids off at your mother's house. She actually likes it when you go out of town because she gets to keep the kids for a couple days. All I'm going to do now is change and take a nice relaxing bath. After that, I …"

Shannon stops her sentence and quickly glances at the doorway from the kitchen to the dining room.

The man questions, "Shannon, are you still there?"

Shannon replies a little unsure, "Yea, I just thought I heard something coming from the other room."

The man speaks, "Just make sure you set the alarm and keep the phone near you."

Shannon smiles at her husband's concern, "I set the alarm as soon as I walked in."

The man replies, "Okay, well, I'll let you go. I love you."

Shannon responds caringly, "I love you too."

Shannon hangs up and slowly walks towards the dining room with the phone still in her right hand. She doesn't see anything in the dining room so she slowly walks into the living room. She looks around the living room, but doesn't see anything out of the ordinary.

Shannon shakes her head, "I must be losing my mind."

She takes off her tennis shoes, then removes the belt from around her tight fitting jeans and un-tucks her tight fitting, long sleeve t-shirt. She leaves the shoes next to the couch and tosses the belt on the couch and walks off down the long hallway towards the bedrooms. She gets to the end of the hall and opens the door on her left. She walks into a very large bedroom with a king size bed, two dressers and an entertainment center.

Shannon tosses the phone on the bed as she walks for the walk-in closet door, "I need a nice bubble bath."

Shannon opens the closet door. She turns on the light and looks around the closet. Once she spots her bathrobe, she steps into the closet to retrieve it. She pulls the bathrobe from it's hanger. She looks down and slides her feet into her house shoes. She steps back out of the closet and turns off the light. Shannon closes the door and walks across the room towards her dresser.

As she approaches her dresser she smiles at the 5x7 picture of her with her husband and two kids that is sitting on top of her dresser. She opens the top drawer. She shuffles through some clothes until she finds a pair of underwear. She closes the drawer.

As Shannon looks back up, her eyes widen in horror as the image of a man's face is reflected in the glass of the picture. Before Shannon can react, the killer wraps his left arm around Shannon as his right hand places the cloth over her nose and mouth.

Shannon starts to struggle, but the killer quickly spins her around and uses his weight to force Shannon down onto the bed and he lays on top of her from behind. Shannon feels the weight of the killer laying on her and the only thing she can think of is her family as she starts to cry. The chemicals start to take affect and Shannon's body gets weaker. She weeps and moans as loud as she can, fearing what this man has planned for her.

Shannon's vision starts to blur and she starts to fade out of consciousness. Images of her husband and kids flash through her mind as Shannon wonders if she will be killed, sexually assaulted or both.

Just before Shannon passes out, the killer whispers in her ear, "Relax beautiful Shannon, just relax."

Then, Shannon's world goes black.

Shannon's eyes slowly open and she tries to focus her blurry vision. Her body is still weak from the drug, but she realizes that she is sitting in one of her dining room chairs, but she finds herself in the middle of her living room. She looks down and sees that her wrists are tied to the arms of the chair with a green nylon cord. She tries to move her legs, but quickly realizes that they too are tied to the chair. With a cloth tied around her mouth, she knows she will never be able to make enough noise for anyone to hear her. She also takes notice that she is still in the same clothes she was wearing.

At that moment, she hears a man's voice from behind her, "Welcome back Shannon."

Shannon knows it is the same man that attacked her. The killer, dressed like before, walks around and stands in front of Shannon. Shannon sees the man's face clearly. Once she sees the unmasked face, she knows that there is no way this man is going to let her live. A few tears start to roll down her cheeks.

The man leans closer and wipes the tears away with his gloved hands, "Don't cry my beautiful Shannon. It will be over soon enough."

The killer kneels next to her and slowly runs his right hand up between her legs as he caresses her hair with his left hand. Shannon squeezes her eyes closed and lets out a helpless whimpering sound.

The killer speaks in a soothing voice, "You have nothing to fear. I am not here to have my way with your body. I am not a rapist." He pauses and his voice takes on a more evil tone, "I am simply a killer and you are nothing more than the next piece of my puzzle."

The killer stands up and moves around behind Shannon. She glances around and sees a bed pillow and a white bra and pair of white panties on the couch. The killer leans down next to Shannon's right ear and places both his hands in her groin area again. Shannon closes her eyes tight as the killer slowly moves his hands up her body. Once the killer's hands move over Shannon's breasts, he reaches his right hand into the left sleeve of his jacket and grabs hold of the nylon cord he has wrapped around his left wrist.

The killer wraps the cord once around his right hand and extends the piece of cord to 18 inches. Shannon feels the cord wrap tightly around her neck.

The killer whispers in Shannon's ear, "It is time my beautiful Shannon."

The killer pulls the cord tight and Shannon quickly

starts to fade again. This time, Shannon's world goes dark forever. Once he is sure that Shannon is dead, the killer removes the cord from around her neck and wraps it back around his left wrist. Then he carefully unties her wrists and ankles. Shannon's lifeless body slumps forward, but the killer catches it before it falls to the floor.

The killer gently lays Shannon's body on the floor. First, he slowly and carefully removes Shannon's shirt. Once the shirt is off, he removes her bra. Next, the killer slowly and carefully removes Shannon's pants. Once her pants are off, the killer carefully removes her panties. He gets up and takes all the clothes to Shannon's bedroom. He folds the clothes neatly and places them in the dresser and returns to the living room.

He takes the pieces of nylon cord that he used to tie Shannon up with and puts them in his jacket pocket. The killer then retrieves the bra and panties from the couch. He carefully puts the bra and panties on Shannon. Once done, he walks over to the front door and punches in the code to the alarm. The panel on the alarm switches from the word, "armed" to the word, "off". The killer walks back over to Shannon's body. He pulls a black marker out of his inside jacket pocket. He writes the letter "O" on Shannon's stomach and returns the marker to his pocket.

He grabs the pillow from the couch and drags Shannon's body out the front door and onto the porch. He straightens Shannon's legs and places her arms next to her body. He puts the pillow under Shannon's head. Once done setting up the body, the killer leans in the doorway and locks the front door. He punches in the alarm code and rearms the alarm. He closes the door and walks off into the night.

In the cold, early morning of New York City, the usually quiet and peaceful neighborhood is in complete disarray. Shannon's house is cut off from the world by yellow police tape as a dozen police cars and two CSI vans line the street. A few citizens have arrived to see what all the commotion is. Kevin, dressed for the cold weather, is standing over Shannon's body taking pictures. After snapping a picture, Kevin hears two car doors close in the background.

A minute later, Detective Taylor and Detective Simpson, both dressed for the cold weather, walk up to Kevin.

As soon as Detective Taylor sees the body, she sighs, "The same killer."

Detective Simpson nods as she looks over the body, "The letter 'O' this time." She pauses, "Maybe Kevin is right, maybe we have an alphabet killer."

Detective Taylor looks at her partner, "I'm not going to say either way until we get those old case files and see what the clues were from those crimes." She looks back at the body, "But it is the only thing that makes any sense so far. I just don't know."

Kevin lowers his camera, "Victim's name is Shannon Little, age 34. Just like before, it appears she was drugged, tied up, then strangled. My team has gone through the house and as you can probably guess, we didn't get anything that will help."

Detective Taylor glances over and sees more citizens starting to gather, "Kevin, lets wrap this up as quick as you can and get the body out of here. The less exposure right now, the better."

Detective Simpson notices the wedding ring on Shannon's hand, "She was married?"

Kevin nods, "Yes, and with two kids."

Detective Simpson questions, "Is the husband around?"

Kevin replies, "No, he and the kids are gone. The neighbor called it in when he went for his usual morning walk."

Detective Taylor questions, "Where is he?"

Kevin glances around, "He is the older gentleman over there with that officer."

Detective Simpson speaks up, "I'm going to talk with him."

Detective Taylor nods, "I'm going to have a look around inside."

Kevin speaks up, "I'm done with everything here. If its okay, I'll move the body to the lab and get started."

Detective Taylor gives a quick nod, "We'll catch up with you back at the precinct."

Detective Simpson walks off to go speak with the neighbor and Detective Taylor walks into the house. Kevin has his team gather up all the equipment and place Shannon's body in the van.

Detective Taylor and Detective Simpson are sitting at their desks completely unaware of the commotion going on around them. Both of their desks are covered with the paperwork and pictures from Shannon's crime scene. The two detectives have been going over the information for the last day and a half and still have come up with nothing.

The Captain, dressed in his usual suit, walks up, "You two need to step back and take a break. This information is not going anywhere and all you're doing now is frying your brains."

Detective Taylor sits back in her chair, "I know we've been at it for awhile and should take a break, but I just can't pull myself away. The answers are in here, if we can just find them."

At that time, Kevin walks up, "Hey, guess what just showed up." He pauses and smiles, "The case files from Seattle and Kansas City. I've got my team bringing them into the conference room now."

Detective Simpson gives a fulfilling sigh and nod, "Finally, now we can start to tie things together."

The Captain nods, "Good, because I have been unable to track down either of the two previous detectives. Its like they just disappeared."

Detective Taylor nods slightly, "I'm not surprised. It had to be hard living with the fact that the killer got away with 54 murders."

At that moment, a female police officer walks up to the desks, "Excuse me Detective Taylor."

Detective Taylor looks over to the officer, "Yes."

The officer replies nervously, "There is a call on line one for you."

Detective Taylor replies, "Can you take a message? We are in the middle of something."

The officer replies obviously uneasy, "He insists on speaking to you." She glances around and lowers her voice, "He says he is the killer you're looking for and told me to tell you the letters, 'M', 'N' and 'O'."

The Captain quickly speaks, "We never released those letters."

Detective Simpson speaks astonished, "Jesus, it's him."

The Captain looks at the officer, "Are you recording the call and trying to trace it?"

The officer nods nervously, "Yes sir."

The Captain looks at Detective Taylor, "Keep him on the phone as long as you can."

Detective Taylor, with her hand slightly shaking, picks up the phone and presses the line one button.

A male voice, the voice of the killer, speaks, "Is this Detective Ashley Taylor?"

Detective Taylor replies trying to conceal her nerves, "Yes, who is this?"

The killer replies, "I know you're trying to trace this so don't play games and just listen."

Detective Taylor notices one thing about the killer's voice, it's young sounding, "What do you want?"

The killer replies as if he is reading a prewritten message, "Once again, just like clockwork, it continues. Perhaps you will have better luck than Detective Conners in 1950 or Detective Gibson in 1975. I don't know, from what I have read, their work was really good. The next victim will come soon. You should actually know the date. However, if you want it all to end, you must go back to the beginning."

Before Detective Taylor can say anything, the killer hangs up. Detective Taylor slowly and nervously hangs up.

The Captain questions, "So, what did he have to say?"

Detective Taylor has a puzzled look, "It was like he was reading off a message." She pauses, "But I think we just got our next clue."

The Captain looks at the female officer, "I want a printout and recording of the entire conversation and I want it now."

The female officer nods and hurries off.

Detective Taylor shakes her head and looks at her partner, "One thing I can tell you. There is no way the man on the phone can be the same man from 1975 or 1950."

Detective Simpson questions, "Why is that?"

Detective Taylor replies, "His voice sounded way too young. If I had to guess, I would say someone in their twenties." She pauses, "Who is this guy?"

The two detectives, the Captain and Kevin all stare at the paperwork on the desks and each one wonders the same thing. What in the world do they have on their hands?

Chapter 4

IN THE EARLY MORNING hours, Detective Simpson walks into the empty and quiet office. She is carrying a thermos of coffee and a sack of food. She stops at her desk and checks for any messages. At that time, Detective Taylor walks in, also carrying a thermos of coffee and a sack of food.

Detective Simpson looks over to her partner, "Morning Ashley, I see you're ready for another long day of frustration."

Detective Taylor lets out a weak and tired smile, "That's for sure Natalie."

As the two ladies start for the conference room, Kevin walks into the office. He too carries coffee and a sack of food. Detective Simpson opens the door to the large conference room. There is a large table in the middle of the room with ten chairs around the table. At the far end of the room, across from the door, there is a large cork board on a wooden stand. A photo of each of the three victims is posted on the board. The table is covered with stacks of case files divided up into files from 1950, 1975 and the present. In one corner near the door is a refrigerator and the other corner near the door is a table with a notepad and phone on it.

Detective Simpson turns on the lights, "Lets see if today is any better than the last five."

Detective Taylor lets out a sigh, "Now that we got everything sorted out, I think we will start making progress."

As the two ladies put their food in the refrigerator, Kevin walks into the room, "Good morning ladies."

Detective Simpson smiles, "Good morning Kevin. Thanks for coming in early with us."

Kevin offers a helpful smile, "Hey, I want to solve this case as bad as you two."

Kevin closes the door, puts up his food and the three of them walk over to the table.

Detective Taylor grabs a transcript of the phone call she received, "I think we should break down the phone call and analyze it. I think it is going to give us the most clues to start with." She pauses, "Kevin, you take 1950, Natalie, you take 1975 and I'll take our cases."

Kevin and Detective Simpson both nod and walk over by the corresponding case files.

Detective Taylor reads the first line, "Once again, just like clockwork, it continues." She pauses, "So, what is the killer trying to say here?"

Detective Simpson and Kevin look at the information on the table in front of them, both in deep thought.

After a minute, Kevin looks up, "It directs us to the first body and one of the clues." He picks up an evidence bag from the 1950 part of the table, "The minute hand of a grandfather clock."

Detective Simpson glances over her evidence bags and picks one up, "Exactly, the same clues as the first body in each case. So the clock has meaning."

Detective Taylor nods slightly, "But what meaning?"

Kevin shakes his head, "Maybe another line in the call

will shed some light on it."

Detective Taylor nods, "The next two lines go together." She pauses, then reads them, "Perhaps you will have better luck than Detective Conners in 1950 or Detective Gibson in 1975. I don't know, from what I have read, their work was really good."

Detective Simpson quickly speaks, "Those lines tell us that it is not the same killer." Detective Taylor and Kevin both look puzzled and Natalie continues, "You see, he names the Detectives, but he says from what he has read, not seen. That tells me that the killer knows about the previous cases because he has read about them."

Kevin nods slightly, but questions, "That does make sense, but the crimes are so exact, its like the killer would have to have access to the case files to have that much detail."

Detective Taylor nods in agreement, "I would have to agree with Natalie, the voice on the phone was way too young sounding to be the same person from 1950."

Detective Simpson pushes Ashley on, "What is the next clue?"

Detective Taylor glances over the next two lines and a shocked look comes across her face. The other two can tell something is wrong.

Detective Simpson questions, "Ashley, what is it?"

Detective Taylor nervously reads the next two lines, "The next victim will come soon. You should actually know the date."

Detective Simpson and Kevin both get a stunned look.

Detective Taylor quickly questions, "When were the first three victim's bodies found in the prior cases?"

Kevin shuffles through some papers until he finds what he needs, "In 1950, the first three bodies were found on January 1st, January 15th and January 29th."

Detective Simpson holds up a piece of paper and reads it, "In 1975, the first three bodies were found on January

1st, January 15th and January 29th."

The three of them look up at the three pictures of the bodies posted on the cork board. Their eyes focus on the dates posted under each of the bodies. They look at Jaqueline Kearny, the first victim's picture and the date of January 1st posted beneath it. Then, the three move their eyes to Carmen Reynolds, the second victim's picture and the date of January 15th posted beneath it. At last, their eyes move to the picture of Shannon Little, the third victim, and the date of January 29th posted beneath it.

Kevin speaks with a hollow voice, "Jesus, the dates are all the same."

Detective Taylor, still staring at the cork board, questions, "When was the forth victim found?"

Kevin looks down at the paper in his hand, "The forth victim was found on February 7th."

Detective Simpson lets out a weak sigh, "That's tomorrow."

Detective Taylor breaks her stare from the board and looks at the others, "Then we better figure this puzzle out because we are running out of time."

The three of them look back at all the paperwork, pictures and evidence bags that cover the huge table and all three get a hopeless look on their face as they each come to the realization that another person is going to lose their life tonight and there is nothing they can do to stop it.

In the darkness of the cold city night, ten school buses pull onto the parking lot of the college gym. Basketball players, cheerleaders and students pour out of the buses, all shouting and cheering their latest victory over the rival school.

In the chaos, a senior cheerleader who stands about

5'3" tall and weighs around 118 pounds with a light complexion, strawberry blonde hair and brown eyes, starts across the parking lot towards a large sorority house.

Another cheerleader yells to the cheerleader walking away, "Hey Amanda! Are you going to be at the bonfire party?!"

Amanda lets out a smile that could melt the coldest of hearts, "Yea! Its my night to feed the pets so I'll meet you all there!"

The cheerleader waves and heads off for one of the many cars on the parking lot. As Amanda crosses the street, she is completely unaware of the shadowy figure that moves by one of the third floor windows.

Amanda walks up the front steps and unlocks the door to the large house. She steps inside, flips on the light switches next to the door, which turns on all the first floor lights, and sets her keys down on the table next to the door. In front of her is a staircase that leads up to the pitch dark second floor and a hallway. She closes the door behind her and walks through the open doorway on her left and into the large living area. She grabs the cordless phone from the wall and dials a phone number.

An older lady's voice answers, "Hello."

Amanda speaks jubilantly, "Hey mom, guess what? We won!"

The mom replies with a happy tone, "That's great honey. So, is there going to be a celebration party?"

Amanda walks over to the fish tank and feeds the fish as she talks, "Yea, a bonfire party. I just have to feed the fish and cats first."

The mom questions, "What time do you think you will be home?"

Amanda replies with a smile, "Probably when the sun comes up, like always. Don't worry, I'll call before you go to work in the morning so you know I made it home okay, like always."

The mom replies, "That's my girl. Okay, be careful and have fun."

Amanda continues to smile, "I will. Bye mom."

The mom replies, "Bye honey."

The two of them hang up. Amanda puts the phone down and the fish food. She walks through a doorway in the back of the room and into the kitchen. She goes under the sink and pulls out a bag of cat food. She fills up the bowl next to the back door, then fills up the water bowl next to it. Once she is done, she walks out of the kitchen and back through the living room.

Amanda walks into the foyer area where the stairs and hallway is at. As she reaches for her keys, she stops and looks up to the second floor at the top of the stairs. She sees the soft glow of a light from around the right corner at the top of the stairs.

Amanda yells, "Hello! Is anyone there?!"

Amanda gets a puzzled look like she could swear the lights were off when she came in, but she shakes her head slightly, puts her keys back on the table and starts up the stairs.

Amanda's eyes glance around quickly as she walks up the stairs, "Hello?!"

Her words are lost in the huge house. As she reaches the top of the stairs, she looks right. At the end of the hallway, about forty feet away, she can see that the lamp in her bedroom is on.

Amanda nervously speaks to herself, "That's odd. I don't remember leaving my lamp on."

Her eyes glance around as she slowly walks towards her bedroom. Her heart is pounding and her nerves are on edge. She walks into her bedroom and looks around. She doesn't see anything out of the ordinary, but she swallows hard and holds her breath as she walks over and taps the base of the touch lamp to turn it off.

The room goes dark and Amanda turns to leave. All

she can hear is her heart pounding in her ears. When she reaches the doorway, she stops and her whole body freezes in fear as the light comes on behind her. She physically starts to shake as a look of terror enters her eyes. She gets goose bumps as she swallows hard, holds her breath and slowly turns around.

As Amanda finishes turning back to the lamp, she lets out a frightened sigh as she sees a solid white cat on the nightstand next to the touch lamp.

Amanda lets out a slightly fearful chuckle, "Snowball, you practically scared me to death." She takes a couple deep breaths, "Okay guy, if you want the light on, you can have it on."

As Amanda turns back to the doorway, the figure of a man is right in front of her. Her eyes widen in horror, as the serial killer, dressed like before, wraps his left arm around her waist as his right hand places the white cloth over her nose and mouth. Amanda freezes in total fear as the killer turns and slams her hard against the wall next to the door and presses his body tightly against hers. Her whole body quivers with fear as her eyes look at the face of her attacker.

As the killer pulls Amanda away from the wall, she jerks and twists, breaking free from the man. Amanda turns quickly to the door and opens her mouth to scream. Before anything can come out of her mouth, the left arm wraps around her from behind and the right hand places the cloth back over her nose and mouth.

This time the killer turns and forces Amanda down onto the bed. As she lands face down on the bed, Amanda feels the entire weight of the killer laying on top of her. Tears come to Amanda's eyes and she starts to cry. A few seconds pass when she starts to feel weaker and her vision starts to fade in and out.

Just before Amanda passes out, the killer whispers in her ear, "Do not fear, beautiful Amanda."

Then, Amanda slips away into blackness. Feeling her body go weak, the killer stands up. He looks down at Amanda's body, dressed in her cheerleader outfit and he lets out a sigh.

The killer puts the cloth back in his jacket pocket as he speaks to himself, "I didn't expect that kind of a struggle from a little cheerleader." He looks up as if speaking to the ceiling, "You could have warned me."

The killer looks back at Amanda, breaks a slight smile and starts back about his business.

As the sun starts to break the horizon in the early morning, two cars pull up in front of the large sorority house. Five tired cheerleaders climb out of each car. As the cheerleaders walk up the front steps, the one that last talked to Amanda hears the phone ringing inside.

She unlocks the door, steps inside and flips on the light switches. The girl hears the phone in the living room and walks towards the ringing sound as the other girls all go their own way.

The cheerleader walks into the living room and answers the phone, "Hello, this is Becca."

Amanda's mom speaks, "Hello Becca, this is Mrs. Carr. Is Amanda there? She didn't call me this morning."

Becca replies in a tired voice, "I'm not sure. She never showed up at the bonfire party."

Suddenly, the sorority house is filled with two blood curling screams. Becca fearfully jerks from the noise and drops the phone.

In an hour, the house is taped off with crime scene tape

and about ten police cars line the street. The two CSI vans pull up. Kevin gets out of the driver's seat and the rest of the team gets out of the second coroner's van. Kevin walks around to the passenger seat and pulls out his silver case. The CSI team heads into the house to start processing the latest crime scene.

About thirty minutes later, a familiar Ford car pulls up. Detective Simpson gets out of the driver's seat and Detective Taylor gets out of the passenger's seat.

Detective Taylor speaks as they walk towards the house, "I hate to sound coldhearted, but maybe this scene will give us some better clues."

The two detectives walk up to the front door where a uniformed officer is standing.

The officer speaks, "The body is upstairs and to the right detectives. The head sorority sister is in the living room to the left."

Detective Simpson nods, "Thank you officer." She looks at Ashley, "I'll link up with Kevin if you want to talk to the girl."

Detective Taylor nods and the two of them walk into the house. Detective Simpson starts up the stairs and Detective Taylor walks into the living room.

Detective Taylor looks around and sees Becca sitting on the couch.

Detective Taylor walks up to the young girl, "Hello, I'm Detective Taylor."

Becca replies through the sniffles and tears, "I'm Rebecca."

Detective Taylor nods, "I know this is hard, but I have to ask you some questions."

Becca nods, "Okay."

Detective Taylor calmly questions, "First, do you know if anyone else was here last night that might have heard the attack happen?"

Becca shakes her head, "No, no one else would have

been here. We were all at a bonfire party last night."

Detective Taylor nods, "So why wasn't she there?"

Becca replies, "It was her night to feed the pets. She was going to meet us there."

Detective Taylor catches onto something, "What was that?"

Becca explains, "After we win a big game, we throw a bonfire party. One of us always goes to the house to feed the pets and meets up with us later because we are always gone until the next morning. Last night was Amanda's night."

Detective Taylor inquires more, "Does someone just volunteer or do you have a set schedule of who feeds?"

Becca sniffles, "We have a schedule?"

Detective Taylor stops writing, "Okay, just have a seat and I'll be back shortly."

Becca sits back down and Detective Taylor walks off to find her partner. Detective Simpson and Kevin are standing over Amanda's body. Amanda is dressed in a white bra and white pair of panties. She is laying on the floor just outside her bedroom door with her arms to her sides, legs straight and a pillow under her head. On her stomach is written the number "1".

Detective Taylor walks up, "So, what do we got?"

Kevin looks at Ashley, "Victim's name is Amanda Carr, age 22. Everything appears the same as the others. It appears she was drugged, tied up and then strangled."

Detective Taylor questions, "Is this her bedroom?"

Detective Simpson replies, "Yes, we are sure the attack happened in her bedroom. Why do you ask?"

Detective Taylor lets out a smile and speaks softly, "How would the killer know in a house this size that this was her bedroom?"

Kevin shrugs, "I don't know. A coincidence I guess."

Detective Taylor slightly shakes her head, "No, that would be too much of a coincidence."

Detective Simpson chimes in, "We know the killer must observe his victims."

Detective Taylor nods slightly, "Not observes, researches. He knows them inside and out. He knows all about them and any normal routines that they have."

Kevin speaks up, "I see what you're saying Ashley. He already has his 27 victims picked out because he has spent the time researching their lives and knows when each victim is available. Each victim has a normal routine that makes them available for the date that corresponds to the prior case dates."

Detective Simpson adds, "So he already has the next victim lined up. It's just a matter of when that day arrives."

Detective Taylor glances around, "I think there is something we might have to do, even though we have agreed not to yet."

Kevin looks at Ashley, "What's that?"

Detective Taylor gets a serious tone, "We might have to go public with the case. Warn everyone in the city about the serial killer. Warn them that if they have any normal routines to change them."

Detective Simpson slightly nods, "I can see your thinking, but I don't think this is the place to discuss it. We can talk to the Captain back at the station about that."

Kevin nods, "We are almost done processing the scene."

Detective Taylor nods back, "We'll talk to the rest of the girls and meet you back at the station."

Kevin gives a quick nod and returns to his work. The two detectives walk off.

As Ashley and Natalie walk down the stairs, Natalie speaks, "Well, we can rule out alphabet killer."

Ashley looks at her partner, "What?"

Natalie sighs, "That body has the number '1' written on it."

Chapter 5

DETECTIVE TAYLOR SITS AT the table in the conference room with her head down on the table. Detective Simpson is sitting across from her partner rubbing her eyes. Kevin is sitting at the end of the table near the board looking over some crime scene photos from Amanda's crime scene.

Detective Taylor looks up, "Why can't politics stay out of things. I mean, we talked to the Captain a week ago about going public and he still hasn't gotten an answer from the Mayor. We are running out of time." She sighs, "If the killer stays on track, the next body comes in three days."

Kevin sets the picture in his hand on the table, "There has to be something that we're not seeing. We know the whole alphabet theory is out."

Detective Simpson sighs, "Maybe the letters and numbers are just a decoy, meant to draw our attention away from the real clues like the phone call, the piece of adoption paper and the minute hand of the grandfather clock."

Detective Taylor looks down at the transcript of the

phone call she received. She glances over it and then looks at the transcript from the 1975 phone call. Once she reads the 1975 transcript she pauses for a second.

Detective Taylor speaks while looking at the two transcripts, "Look at this, the last line of the phone calls." She pauses, "Both in 1975 and ours ends with the sentence, 'However, if you want it all to end, you must go back to the beginning.'."

Kevin chimes up, "So, what is the killer trying to say? That we should look at the first clues more closely?"

Detective Simpson speaks up, "Maybe. I mean, there has to be some significance that the first two clues are a piece of adoption form paper and the minute hand of a grandfather clock."

At that time, the door opens and the Captain walks in. He is followed by the Mayor, a tall, heavy set man who looks to be in his mid-fifties. The Mayor does not look to be in a good mood.

Before the Captain can say anything, the Mayor swings the door shut and starts in on the detectives, "Are you crazy? You want to go to the public with all of this? You don't have anything, you don't know anything and all you're going to do is cause a panic." He takes a breath, "Tell me, are you any closer to solving this case?"

Detective Taylor stares coldly at the Mayor, "No, we're not any closer, but if going public throws a monkey wrench in the killer's plan, then it was worth a little panic."

The Mayor replies sternly, "I can't go to the press and tell them that we have four bodies and no leads, but everyone needs to change up any normal daily routines to avoid being killed. You must be crazy." He looks at the Captain, "What kind of detectives do you have running this case?"

The Captain replies, not too happy with the Mayor's comment, "My best detectives Mr. Mayor and I trust their judgment completely. They wouldn't suggest going public if they didn't have a good reason."

The Mayor points at the table, "Get me a lead! Get me a suspect and you'll get your press conference!"

The Mayor turns, jerks the door open and storms out of the room. The Captain calmly closes the door.

The Captain turns back to the others, "Sorry about that. Actually, it went better here than in his office. I'm surprised I have a butt left." He sighs, "So, without going public, do you have anything else to try?"

Detective Simpson sits back in her chair, "Honestly sir, no we don't. But we are not giving up yet. We'll come up with something."

The Captain nods, "Well, let me know if there is anything I can do."

Detective Taylor nods. The Captain turns and opens the door.

Before the Captain walks out, Detective Simpson speaks up, "Sir." The Captain turns back to them and Detective Simpson continues, "Thank you for supporting us."

The Captain smiles and gives a quick nod. He turns and walks out of the room and closes the door.

Kevin lets out a deep sigh, "Well, back at it I guess. Lets take a look at those first clues again."

The three of them shuffle through some papers and start the meticulous process of going over the evidence again.

The killer is sitting at a desk in a dark room, only lit by the small lamp sitting on the corner of the desk. He closes a notebook that he was reading. The notebook looks old and the pages look yellowed with age.

The killer sits back and smiles, "So, now they will

debate about going public with the case, thinking it will change the plan."

The killer reaches over to the ten oz. bag on the edge of the desk. He looks in the bag at the dirt inside.

He speaks to himself again, "Lets see if this helps."

The killer ties the bag shut and looks at the clock sitting on the desk and speaks to himself again, "I guess its that time again."

The killer stands up, puts the small bag in his pocket and turns off the light.

A well built 128 pound woman appearing to be in her late thirties that stands around 5'4" tall with auburn hair and blue eyes, waves goodbye to the last customer of the day as the customer walks out of the front door of the corner grocery store.

Before the door shuts, the customer waves back, "Goodnight Christie, I'll see you tomorrow."

The door shuts. Christie closes the register, walks over to the front door and locks it. She reaches over, grabs the steel bar door and closes it. She locks the padlock and walks back to the register. She grabs the money bag and heads for the office in the back.

Christie opens the door and flips on the light switch to light up the small office. She walks over to the desk, puts down the money bag and sits down in the rolling desk chair. The desk is covered with some financial papers and in the corner is the picture of a man in his seventies.

Christie smiles at the picture, "Well grandpa, another good day for the store."

She turns the chair around and unlocks the small safe that is behind her. She turns back, grabs the money bag and puts it in the safe. She closes the safe door and locks it. She turns quick to the office door as she hears the sound of a metal can hit the floor out in the store. Christie gets a nervous look as she opens the top, left hand drawer of the desk. She grabs the small can of mace with her right hand. She slowly stands up and inches her way over to the office door. She looks left out the office door towards the warm soda cans. Christie sees one of the cans on the floor.

Christie glances around nervously as she slowly walks towards the soda can. She holds the can of mace ready in her right hand. When she gets to the soda can she squats down to pick it up, completely unaware of the male figure now standing behind her.

The killer brings his right forearm up and shoves it into Christie's upper back. Christie is knocked forward and lands on her stomach. The killer places his right forearm on her upper back and uses his weight to hold her down. Before Christie can move due to extreme panic and fear, the killer grabs her right wrist with his left hand. He pins Christie's right wrist and hand to her lower back, rendering the can of mace useless. As Christie starts to let out a scream, the killer moves his right hand up and covers her nose and mouth with the white cloth as he lays his weight on her.

Christie tries to struggle and when she finds it useless, she starts to cry. She can feel her body get weaker and her vision starts to blur.

With a muffled voice, Christie manages one noticeable word, "Please."

The killer smoothly whispers in her ear, "Relax Christie, just relax."

Then, Christie's world goes black.

In the cold February morning, Detective Taylor and

Detective Simpson pull up to an all too familiar scene. As Detective Taylor parks the car near the two coroner vans, they see Kevin just inside the corner grocery store with his camera flashing. The two ladies get out of their car and start for the store. They duck under the police tape and pass two uniformed police officers as their hearts start to pound. They both start to break a nervous sweat as they approach the front door.

Detective Simpson quickly notices that the front door is undamaged and the bar door is standing open. Just inside the front door, on the floor laid out like the other bodies, is Christie's body. Both detectives blink as another flash goes off from Kevin's camera. Detective Taylor notices right away the letter "A" on Christie's stomach, but she also sees something that is not part of the ordinary scene. Detective Taylor makes out an object in Christie's left hand.

Kevin takes his last picture, "Victim's name is Christie Hughes, age 38. As you can see, the body is dressed and laid out like the others and appears to have been killed just like the other four."

Before Kevin can continue, Detective Taylor quickly speaks, "What is that in her left hand?"

Kevin smiles at Ashley's keen vision, "You picked it up right away too. I'm not sure, I wanted to wait until you two got here to look at it."

Detective Taylor and Detective Simpson both pull out latex gloves and put them on. Kevin pulls his latex gloves tight and moves over next to Christie's left hand. He gently rolls the left hand over so the palm is facing up and slowly pulls the fingers open. All three of them see the 10 oz. bag in the hand.

Detective Simpson reaches over and grabs Kevin's camera and hands it to him. Kevin takes a picture of the bag in the hand and places his camera down.

Detective Taylor squats next to Kevin, "Our next clue it would appear."

Kevin slowly takes the bag from Christie's hand. He unwinds the string from around the top and opens the small bag. Detective Taylor looks into the bag and gets a very puzzled look on her face.

Detective Simpson questions, "What is it Ashley?"

Detective Taylor looks up, "It looks like dirt."

The question just slips out of Kevin's mouth, "Why leave a bag of dirt?"

Detective Simpson sighs, "Well, we know it has some sort of significance."

Kevin ties the bag closed as Detective Simpson hands him an evidence bag.

Kevin places the clue in the evidence bag and seals it, "I'll analyze it back at the lab. I'll figure out where it came from."

At that time, a young woman in her late twenties standing about 5' tall and weighing about 115 pounds with black hair and blue eyes walks up, "Sir, we're done with the scene."

Detective Taylor speaks up, "Kevin, go ahead and get the body and everything else to the lab. We are going to look around some and we'll link up with you back at the station."

Kevin gives a quick nod and speaks to the young lady, "Jennifer, get the rest of the team and lets get things going."

Jennifer walks off to get the rest of the CSI team. Kevin gathers up his things as Detective Taylor and Detective Simpson walk into the store.

Detective Taylor and Detective Simpson are sitting at the table in the conference room, both staring at the pictures of the five bodies on the board. They both look like they have not slept for days. Their concentration is broken as the door opens.

Kevin walks in holding some papers in his hand, "Okay, ready for the next twist?"

He closes the door behind him and sits down at the table.

Detective Simpson questions, "So what is it?"

Kevin replies, "I analyzed the dirt over the last three days and I can tell you this for certain, this dirt is not from New York or even the northeast region of the United States."

Detective Taylor looks puzzled, "So, where is the dirt from?"

Kevin sits back and sighs, "Good question Ashley, I don't know yet. Jennifer is still analyzing all the chemicals contained in the dirt. We will have it soon."

At that moment, the door opens and the Captain steps in, "Hey, get ready. The Mayor has called a press conference to start in an hour."

Detective Simpson looks stunned, "What?"

The Captain smiles, "Apparently the fifth body has changed his mind. He has given me full latitude over the conference. I need briefed in 30 minutes. I want to know everything because I'm going to tell them everything."

The Captain walks out and closes the door. The three of them just sit and look at each other, somewhat stunned at the sudden change of events.

The afternoon, February sky is clear and somewhat warmer than usual. From the top of the city hall steps, Detective Taylor and Detective Simpson look out at all the reporters that have gathered for the press conference. Standing next to them is Kevin and the Captain. The

Mayor steps up to the podium and taps the microphone to make sure it is on.

The Mayor clears his throat and speaks, "Thank you all for showing on such short notice. I know all of you have heard rumors swirling around about a possible serial killer working in our city. I have asked Captain Sutherland to speak to you all about this. Please hold all questions until the end. Thank you." He turns to Captain Sutherland, "Captain."

The Mayor steps away and Captain Sutherland steps up to the podium, "Thank you Mr. Mayor and members of the press for being here." He takes a nervous breath, "No police officer likes to admit it when they are not getting anywhere with a case they are working on, but we must now ask for the citizens of this city for their help." He pauses, "Since January 1st, my two top detectives and CSI team has been working on a serial killer case. I do regret that the case is not going very well."

Captain Sutherland looks at the detectives and then continues, "To date, we have five bodies and no suspects. At each crime scene, the killer has left puzzling clues that as of today, we have not been able to solve." He pauses again, "As you know, we do not often share much information with an ongoing investigation, but we feel that this case requires extreme measures be taken." He licks his lips and continues, "The killer has left a very distinctive mark on each of the bodies, he has also left a piece of adoption form paper, the minute hand of a grandfather clock and most recently, a small bag of dirt."

Captain Sutherland nervously rubs his hands, like he is debating on if he should say what comes next.

Finally, Captain Sutherland speaks, "Also, after the third body was found, the killer placed a call to Detective Taylor and left a very specific message." He pauses, "We do know that the killer is very calculating and already has plans for his next victim. He targets people who have very distinct daily routines. So, we are asking everyone that if you have noticed anything out of the ordinary, please change up any daily routines you may have. Understand, we are not wanting to cause everyone to panic, we are confident that we will solve this case, but we are asking the citizens that if they know anything or have any information, please contact the police." He pauses, "We are almost out of time, but does anyone have any questions?"

It is surprisingly quiet given everything the Captain has just said. Almost like all the reporters are just as baffled as the police.

The Mayor, seeing his opportunity to make a clean escape, quickly steps up to the podium, "I'm sorry, that's all the time we have. Thank you again for showing up."

The Mayor turns, looks at Captain Sutherland, Kevin, Detective Taylor and Detective Simpson. He motions for them to follow him inside and the four of them follow the Mayor into city hall.

Chapter 6

IN THE PITCH BLACKNESS of a small, empty house, a man that looks to be in his fifties, sits down in a recliner and grabs the television remote from the table next to the chair. On the table, under the remote, sits a year long calendar with twenty seven specific dates marked on it. The man is about 5'11" tall and holds a decent 190 pound build with brown eyes and graying brown hair.

He turns on the TV with the remote in his right hand as his left hand places the glass of whiskey he is drinking on the table next to the chair. He turns the TV to a very specific channel and the national news comes on. He places the remote back down and picks up his glass of whiskey. The man watches a couple of news stories and sips his whiskey.

After 30 minutes, the anchor of the news station comes on.

The anchor speaks, "Now, as promised, we will play the news conference that was held today in New York City. The news conference about what the Police Captain has stated as a puzzling serial killer case."

The man freezes in his chair and his left hand starts to

tighten around the glass. He grabs the remote with his right hand and turns up the volume. He sets the remote down, takes a sip of whiskey and intently listens to the news conference. His body physically shivers as he hears Captain Sutherland describe the clues of the serial killer. Then, the man gets tears in his eyes when he hears the one thing that he knew was coming and a single tear rolls down his cheek when he hears about the phone call placed from the killer.

The man swallows hard as he doesn't want to believe what he has just heard. He picks up the remote and turns off the TV as more tears come to his eyes. His body nervously quivers as he chugs the rest of his whiskey and puts the glass down. He sits forward in the recliner, places his head in his hands and starts to weep.

Through the weeping, he speaks softly to himself, "It's started again."

Detective Taylor and Detective Simpson are sitting in the conference room looking over the massive amounts of paperwork and pictures. Again, both look like they haven't slept in days. At that time, Kevin walks in with Captain Sutherland. Kevin sits down. Captain Sutherland closes the door and sits down.

Kevin speaks up, "We know where the dirt in the bag came from."

Detective Simpson and Detective Taylor quickly look up and Detective Simpson questions, "Where?"

Kevin nervously answers, "Its from the Seattle area."

Detective Taylor sits back with a look of frustration, "Again, a reference to the past. The paper and minute hand of the clock are both 75 years old which is well before any of the killings and now, dirt from Seattle. What is going on here?"

Detective Taylor slams the papers in her hands down on the table startling everyone else.

Detective Simpson sighs, "Everything refers back, just like the last line in the phone call. Go back to the beginning to solve this puzzle or something like that."

Then, the four of them hear a knock on the door.

Captain Sutherland yells, "Yes."

The door opens and a female officer is standing there, "Sorry for interrupting, but I have a gentleman out here that says he might be able to help you."

Detective Taylor looks a bit surprised, "Please, send him in."

The officer nods and motions with her hand. The man that had watched the news conference on TV in the dark, empty house walks in dressed in black dress shoes, slacks, a dress shirt and jacket holding a hat in his hands.

Captain Sutherland stands up and holds out his right hand, "Hello, I'm Captain Sutherland."

The man nervously shakes Captain Sutherland's hand, but says nothing. His eyes are locked on the board at the end of the table with the pictures on it. The man's gaze lowers to all the paperwork on the table and the four others just look at the man in wonder.

Detective Taylor speaks up, "Sir, can we help you?"

The man blinks a few times as if coming out of a dream, "I'm sorry. So many memories."

Detective Taylor, Detective Simpson, Kevin and Captain Sutherland all look puzzled about this man.

The man takes a deep breath, "I'm Matthew Gibson." He pauses, "I see you have my case files from Kansas City and Detective Conners' files from Seattle."

The four of them are completely taken off guard and they all get a shocked look. At first, none of them can talk.

Finally, Captain Sutherland smiles, "Please Mr. Gibson, have a seat."

Mr. Gibson sits down, "I haven't been in a room like this in 24 years. I resigned and disappeared right after the funeral."

Kevin can't help but ask, "What funeral was that?"

Mr. Gibson sits back, "Detective Conners' funeral." He pauses, "He couldn't deal with failing in 1950 and came to help me after he watched a press conference on TV. When we were unable to solve the case in 1975, he couldn't handle failing again so he took his own life."

Detective Simpson replies caringly, "I'm sorry."

Mr. Gibson nods slightly, "Me too. I can't help but feel responsible and that is why I'm here. I promised to his grave that if it started again, I would do everything I could to stop it." He glances around, "So, what do you say? Lets get started and I'll give you some things that are not in these files. Things that only Detective Conners, myself and apparently the killer knows, and some of our theories that we never released."

Detective Taylor looks up at Detective Simpson and they both have a rejuvenated look on their faces as they realize that they could be very well close to solving the case now.

In a cold, dark room, the killer sits at his poorly lit desk as he is looking through an old notebook. He ever so gentle turns the page.

The killer speaks quietly to himself, "So they went public and no doubt you're right, the press conference will draw out Detective Gibson, just like it drew out Detective Conners in 1975."

He slowly turns to the next page and reads the old, yellowed paper.

The killer quietly speaks again, "No doubt he will give

them more insight into the clues, but his fate will be no different than that of Detective Conners, or his sister for that matter."

The killer gently closes the notebook and looks at the clock on the edge of the desk, "It's time once again. Time to give them the next piece of the puzzle."

In the cold, rainy night of the big city, a taxi pulls up in front of one of the city's exclusive five star hotels. The older gentleman doorkeeper walks over to the taxi with an umbrella. The man opens the back door of the taxi. A young woman looking to be in her early twenties with shoulder length brown hair and brown eyes gets out of the taxi. She stands around 5'7" tall and holds a trim yet busty build of 125 pounds with a light, golden skin tone. She is dressed in a very nice outfit covered by an expensive overcoat. One thing is certain to anyone looking, the young woman is absolutely beautiful.

The doorkeeper smiles at the incredibly beautiful young lady, "Good evening Miss Milan."

Miss Milan gives the older doorkeeper a heartwarming smile, "Good evening William."

William slips her a door key that looks like a credit card, "Everything is taken care of as usual Miss Milan. Now, lets get you out of this rain and I'll have the bellhop bring your bags up to the suite."

Miss Milan gives William a kiss on the cheek and smiles, "Thank you William, and please, I've told you to call me Vanessa."

William walks Vanessa over to the door, "Room service will be up in an hour. I know how you like to relax and watch your show first."

Vanessa gives him warm smile, "If you were not

married William, you would be mine."

William breaks a little smile, "Thank you. You sure know how to make this old man feel good about himself."

William opens the door and Vanessa walks inside the lobby. William motions for the bellhop to come get the bags from the taxi. The bellhop, a young man of eighteen years rushes out to the taxi with a covered luggage cart to get the bags.

Vanessa gets in the elevator and swipes her room key through the card reader next to the floor numbers and presses the tenth floor button. The elevator moves quickly and the doors open to the tenth floor. Vanessa steps out of the elevator and turns left without looking at the room number signs as if she knows exactly where she is going. She gets to the end of the hall and turns right. She walks another hundred feet and stops in front of a very nice mahogany door. She swipes the door key in the card reader next to the door handle and the door lock clicks.

Vanessa steps inside and flips on the light switches next to the door. The living area of the suite is lit up. Fine Persian carpet covers the floor. A huge, plush couch sits in the middle of the room and a matching chair sits next to it. Two nice mahogany end tables and one mahogany coffee table sit by the couch and chair. On the left wall is an entertainment center with a big screen television and expensive stereo system. On the right hand side of the room is a full bar. In the back is full sized windows with a sliding door that leads out to the large balcony. A doorway in the back left of the room leads to the bedroom and bathroom.

Vanessa takes off her sandals and leaves them by the door. She takes off her overcoat and leaves it hanging by the door. Vanessa walks over to the coffee table, leaving the door open. She smiles as she feels the soft, Persian rug under her feet. She sets her door key on the coffee table and sits down on the couch. She pulls out her cell phone and places it next to the door key.

A minute later, she hears a young man's voice from the hallway, "Miss, I have your bags."

Vanessa yells back, "Come in!" The bellhop rolls in the luggage cart and Vanessa speaks, "Just place them in the bedroom, thank you."

The bellhop takes the cart into the bedroom, unloads it and returns to the living area a minute later. Vanessa stands up and hands the young man a fifty dollar bill.

The bellhop smiles, "Thank you miss."

The bellhop walks out and closes the door behind him. The door automatically locks when it is shut. Vanessa walks over to the door and locks the deadbolt. She turns around and walks to the bedroom. As she walks through the doorway to the bedroom, she reaches over with her left hand and flips on the lights. In the middle of the room is a king sized bed. On the right is another plush couch and in the back right is the door to the walk-in closet. On the left is the door to the bathroom. The bedroom also has an entertainment center and two chest of drawers.

Vanessa grabs one of her bags, places it on the table next to the couch and opens it. She pulls out a pair of jeans, a t-shirt and some house shoes. She changes into the more comfortable clothes and walks back out into the living room. She grabs the television remote and sits down on the couch. She turns on the television, changes the channel to a comedy sitcom and sits back to relax.

She watches one episode and halfway through the second, there is a knock at the door.

Vanessa gets up and walks towards the door, "Who is it?!"

A male voice replies, "Room service!"

Vanessa looks at the little TV monitor next to the door and sees a man dressed in a food service uniform facing away from the camera and he has a food cart next to him.

Vanessa unlocks the deadbolt first. Then she grabs the

door handle, twists it down and slowly opens the door. The man turns to face the door and he is a clean shaven young man in his early twenties.

The young man smiles at Vanessa, "Your dinner as ordered miss."

Vanessa smiles, pulls out a fifty dollar bill and hands it to the young man, "Thank you."

The young man smiles, turns and walks off. Vanessa pulls the food cart inside and shuts the door behind her. She locks the deadbolt again and pulls the cart over to the couch. Vanessa enjoys the nice meal as she watches more television. Once she is done eating, she pushes the cart back into the hallway, locks up the door again, grabs her cell phone and heads for the bedroom.

She walks into the bedroom and flips on the lights again. She sets her cell phone on the bed and walks over to the bathroom. She walks into the bathroom and flips on the lights. It is a massive bathroom. A full counter with double sinks line the left wall with two chairs. An oversized sauna tub sits in the back of the room and a double sized, enclosed shower stands next to the tub and on the right is the toilet and another one person sink.

Vanessa walks over to the tub and starts to run some hot bath water. She grabs a bottle next to the tub and pours some of the bubble bath liquid into the water. She puts the bottle back, grabs the crushed velvet bathrobe hanging next to the tub and walks across the Persian rug back to the bedroom. She sets the bathrobe on the bed and undresses. She drops her clothes at the foot of the bed, puts the robe on, grabs her cell phone and walks back into the bathroom.

Vanessa shuts and locks the door. She hangs the robe next to the tub and steps into the hot bubble bath with her cell phone in her right hand. She sinks down into the tub up to her armpits with her arms sitting on the edges of the tub and she is facing the faucet. As the hot, bubble bath covers her body, she gets a relaxed look on her face. Vanessa flips open her cell phone and presses speed dial number one as she turns the water off with her foot.

The phone rings a couple times, then a female voice answers, "Hello."

Vanessa speaks lovingly, "Hey baby."

The young female voice replies, "Hey sweetheart. I take it your at the suite."

Vanessa smiles, "Oh yes. I'm enjoying my bubble bath right now."

The female voice replies sensually, "Um, I wish I was there to enjoy it with you."

Vanessa closes her eyes and smiles at that thought, "Me too." She pauses a second then opens her eyes, "So, your flight comes in at 7 am?"

The female speaks smoothly, "Yea, and I'll be curling up next to you by nine."

Vanessa takes a quiet breath, "I can't wait."

The female sighs, "I'll let you go. I have to be up early to catch my flight. I'll see you in the morning."

Vanessa smiles, "See you in the morning. I love you."

The female replies caringly, "I love you too."

The two young ladies hang up. Vanessa drops her cell phone on the rug next to the tub and sinks down into the hot water and closes her eyes. Vanessa soaks for another thirty minutes, then flips the latch with her foot to drain the water. She stands up, steps out of the tub, grabs the robe and puts it on. She picks up her cell phone and walks out of the bathroom back into the bedroom.

Vanessa walks by the closed bedroom door over to the table next to the couch and puts her cell phone down. She reaches into the suitcase and grabs her toothbrush and toothpaste as her foot brushes against her jeans and t-shirt that are sitting on the floor next to the table now. She returns to the bathroom and brushes her teeth. Once finished, she walks back into the bedroom. She walks over and tosses the toothbrush and toothpaste back into the suitcase.

Vanessa grabs a larger suitcase and sets it on the couch. She unzips the suitcase and opens it to reveal clothes on hangers. She grabs the clothes and sees her jeans and t-shirt out of the corner of her eye. She gets a slightly puzzled look and walks over to the walk-in closet. She opens the door with her left hand. She steps inside and turns on the light. She hangs up the clothes and turns around. She walks out of the closet, turns off the light and closes the door. She grabs her cell phone and walks over to the bedroom door.

Vanessa opens the bedroom door. She walks into the living room and puts her cell phone down on the coffee table, grabs the television remote and turns on the television again. She flips the channel to the entertainment news and sits down on the couch. She watches the program for ten minutes when the show fades out to go to a commercial.

Vanessa's eyes widen in horror as the reflection of a man appears in the television screen standing right behind her. Before she can act. The killer places the cloth over Vanessa's nose and mouth. With all his strength, the killer lifts her over the back of the couch. Vanessa lands hard on her back as the killer lays on her with all of his weight.

Vanessa's wide eyes start to tear up as she looks at the face of the killer. The killer presses the cloth more firmly over her nose and mouth. Vanessa squirms, but to no avail. She feels her body getting weaker. She starts to sob, fearful of what is going to happen to her.

With a muffled, sobbing voice, she pleads to the killer, "Please, don't."

The killer leans down and whispers in her ear, "Its okay Vanessa, just relax."

Then, Vanessa's body goes limp and her world is covered in darkness.

In the cold, wet New York City morning, the familiar Ford pulls up in front of the five star hotel and parks behind the two CSI vans. Detective Taylor gets out of the passenger seat, Detective Simpson gets out of the driver's seat and Mr. Gibson gets out of the back seat.

Mr. Gibson just stares at the front doors of the hotel as Detective Taylor looks at him. She can tell something is wrong.

Detective Taylor speaks empathetically, "You don't have to go in if you don't want to."

Mr. Gibson swallows hard, "No, I'm okay. It's just that I've lived with these nightmares for the last 24 years. I can still see the faces of all of my 27 victims."

Detective Simpson nods sympathetically, "We're going to catch this guy. He won't get away this time."

Mr. Gibson gives a false smile, "For your sake, I pray so."

Detective Taylor and Detective Simpson can tell that there is still more that Mr. Gibson has not told them, but that is going to have to wait for now. The three of them walk into the lobby. They see two uniformed police officers standing with the hotel manager. The three of them walk over to the officers and the hotel manager.

The hotel manager just shakes his head, "I just don't see how. This is our first crime since we installed our new security system two years ago."

One of the officers speaks to Detective Taylor, "The tenth floor, left off the elevator, then right at the end of the hall." He holds out a card that looks like one of the room keys, "Here, you'll need this access card."

Detective Taylor takes the card, "Thank you."

Detective Taylor, Detective Simpson and Mr. Gibson walk over to the elevators. They get on an elevator and

Detective Taylor swipes the card and presses the ten button.

Detective Simpson speaks, "This seems like a pretty secure place."

Mr. Gibson smiles at the comment, "You're going to find out real fast that no place is safe from this guy."

The elevator opens to the tenth floor and the three of them make their way to the crime scene. They can hear the clicking of the camera as they reach the door to the suite. Detective Taylor walks in first followed by Detective Simpson. Mr. Gibson takes a deep breath, then walks into the suite.

The three of them see Vanessa's body laying on the floor behind the couch. She is laid out and dressed just like the others with the letter "W" written on her stomach. Mr. Gibson closes his eyes and looks away, not wanting it to be true. Detective Taylor and Detective Simpson walk over next to Kevin who puts his camera down.

Detective Simpson speaks up, "She looks familiar."

Kevin sighs, "Victim's name is Vanessa Milan, age 22. She appears to have been killed just like the others. The only clue we found is the letter 'W' written on the body." He pauses, "She should look familiar, she is a very popular local catalogue model."

Detective Taylor speaks up, "If she is local, what is she doing here?"

Kevin motions to a young, attractive blonde across the room, "That's her girlfriend. She can fill you in on that."

Detective Simpson shakes her head, "The killer just upped the stakes. He had to know we would go public after the last victim to kill someone who is in the public eye."

Kevin questions, "How could he have possibly known we would go public after the fifth victim?"

Detective Simpson replies, "I don't know, but he had to know that killing someone like her could not be hidden from the news."

Mr. Gibson walks up, "Of course he knew. It's all part of the plan."

Jennifer walks up to Kevin, "We're finished processing the scene."

Kevin nods, "Get everything together and get the body ready for transport."

Jennifer nods and as she starts to walk off, Mr. Gibson turns to her, "Excuse me miss. Which direction is west?"

Jennifer stops for a second, then points towards the front door, "That way."

Mr. Gibson nods, "Thank you."

Detective Taylor leans over to Mr. Gibson, "Why is that important?"

Mr. Gibson lowers his voice, "We'll talk about it back at the station."

Detective Simpson speaks up, "Well, lets talk to the girlfriend, then get back to the station and get started."

Kevin picks up his camera, "I'll see the three of you there."

Detective Taylor and Detective Simpson walk over to the girlfriend as Kevin and his team exit with Vanessa's body. Detective Taylor keeps glancing over to Mr. Gibson as he slowly walks around the room.

Chapter 7

IN THE EARLY MORNING hours of the day, Kevin walks into the conference room holding a bunch of papers and pictures in his hands. Detective Taylor, Detective Simpson and Mr. Gibson are all sitting around the table looking over old case files.

Kevin closes the door and turns around, "I have all the information from the last scene and Jennifer is going to call me when she has the results from the other tests on the two previous dirt samples and the date tests on the other two pieces of adoption paper and clock hands."

Detective Simpson sighs, "Well, all the tests will do is confirm what we all believe."

Detective Taylor sits back, "We have to come up with something soon. The next victim is just a few days away."

Detective Simpson tosses the papers in her hand on the table, "There is no way we are going to crack this by the next victim." Her frustration starts to show, "How can this guy be so perfect at this?"

Detective Taylor speaks up, "We can't get that attitude. The cases are uncannily similar, but everything we need to solve the case is here. We just have to find it."

Mr. Gibson finally speaks up, "You haven't figured that part out yet, have you?"

Kevin questions, "What's that?"

Mr. Gibson sits back, "How your killer has everything so perfectly laid out?"

Detective Taylor peers at Mr. Gibson, "You asked a strange question about which way was west at the scene. What haven't you told us?"

Mr. Gibson speaks up, "I was like you two. I couldn't see how two cases 25 years apart could be so exactly the same until Detective Conners gave me his theory."

Detective Simpson questions, "What theory is that?"

Mr. Gibson explains, "We know it is not a simple copycat killer, everything is too exact, but still possible because all the information is in the case files somewhere."

Kevin interjects quickly, "A cop would have access to the files."

Mr. Gibson slightly nods, "True, but his theory went much deeper. He asked me to challenge the killer in 1975. He asked me to post something in the newspaper." He pauses, "So in the paper, I asked the killer to send me a certified letter and give me one detail about the bodies that only the killer would know about."

Detective Simpson questions, "What was it?"

Mr. Gibson reaches into his pocket and pulls out an old piece of paper, "This is the letter he sent. I never entered it in the case files so no one knows what it says except for Detective Conners, myself and the killer." He opens the paper and reads it, "I see that one of you has figured it out. The clue in which you are asking for is that all the bodies in 1950 and every body so far in 1975 has been laid out with the top of the head pointed to the west."

The two detectives and Kevin are completely quiet and Mr. Gibson poses them a question, "Now, how would the killer in 1975 possibly know that? It was never listed in any case files."

Kevin speaks a little puzzled, "Luck or coincidence?"

Mr. Gibson shakes his head, "Not a chance. A few bodies maybe, but every single one, I don't think so. The direction of the bodies was the hidden clue to prove it wasn't a copycat killer." He poses another question, "How would you have information from the past that is not listed anywhere in the public sector?"

The looks on the detective's faces shows that they still don't understand what Mr. Gibson is trying to tell them.

Mr. Gibson smiles, "It was so obvious, I didn't see it either because I was so frustrated, just like you are. Your killer has personal information from my killer who got the information from the 1950 killer." He pauses, "Don't you see it. It is the only possibility. The killers are passing the information down to each other probably through journals of some kind."

Detective Taylor finally speaks up, "What in the world are you saying, that some psycho in 1950 mailed his journals to another psycho in 1975 who mailed them to our psycho?"

Mr. Gibson smiles at Detective Taylor, "No. What I'm saying is that the information was handed down, like a father would pass something on to his son."

Kevin can't help but interject, "What?"

Detective Simpson quickly speaks, "Are you saying a family of killers?"

Mr. Gibson gets an eerily serious tone, "What I'm saying is that we are watching a serial killer bloodline take shape right in front of us."

The room goes deathly quiet as everyone takes in what Mr. Gibson just said. Finally, the silence is broken by the ringing phone.

Kevin walks over and answers the phone, "Hello."

Jennifer's voice comes on, "Sir, we have the results."

Kevin replies, "What is it?"

Jennifer explains everything to Kevin, then hangs up.

Kevin hangs up and turns back to the table with a puzzled look on his face.

Detective Taylor questions, "Was that Jennifer with the information?"

Kevin nods, "Yes." He pauses, "In 1975 the dirt left was from Seattle and the paper and clock hand date to approximately 1925 time frame. In 1950, the paper and clock hand date to about 1925."

Kevin stops and Detective Simpson pushes him on, "What about the dirt in 1950?"

Kevin gets a far away look, "The analysis shows that the dirt from best we can tell is from the Atlanta area."

Everyone sits back in their chairs as they all realize the same thing. Another city has just come into play. The four of them look back at the table. With what Mr. Gibson said running through their heads, they all wonder the same thing, is Seattle the start or now is it Atlanta in 1900 or 1925?

In the darkness of the city night, an African American woman looking to be in her mid-thirties, dressed in a nice female suit is sitting at a large wooden desk in a very large corner office at one of the major law firm buildings in Manhattan. She is a petite yet well put together 5'3" tall and weighs about 114 pounds with jet black hair and dark brown eyes. She looks more like a Hollywood star than a lawyer.

She looks up at the clock on the wall and it reads 8:40 pm. She starts typing on her computer when she hears a knock on the door.

The lady yells in a strong yet feminine voice, "Yes."

An older man in his sixties walks in, "Halle, what are you still doing here? The quarterly meeting ended nearly

40 minutes ago."

Halle smiles at her boss, "Just going through my email. I won't be too much longer."

The man smiles at her dedication, "Would you like me to wait and walk you to your car?"

Halle smiles at her boss, "Always fathering me. That's okay, I'll be fine."

Her boss replies, "Alright, be careful going home and I'll see you in the morning."

Halle replies warmly, "Goodnight Richard."

Richard walks out and shuts the door. Halle spends about ten more minutes checking her email, then she shuts down her computer. Halle stands up, grabs her coat from the coat rack and puts it on. She walks over to her office door and opens it. She flips the lights in her office off, locks the door, steps out of the office and pulls the door closed.

Halle walks down the hallway towards the elevator. She reactively reaches into her right jacket pocket. She stops and a puzzled look crosses her face as she digs around in the jacket pocket. She starts digging in her left jacket pocket, but is unable to find what she is looking for.

She turns back to her office and speaks quietly to herself, "When did I take my keys out of my pocket?"

Halle walks back to her office door, pulls her spare office key out of her pants pocket and unlocks the door. She swings the door open and flips on the lights. She heads for her desk completely unaware that the door didn't open the entire way. As she gets to her desk, she sees her keys sitting next to the keyboard of the computer.

Halle grabs the keys, "Wonder how I missed those?"

Halle turns and starts for the door. When she is about ten feet from the door, the door flies shut as the figure of the killer, dressed like before, moves straight for Halle. Halle's eyes show the shock and horror of seeing this strange man heading for her. Her body freezes for a moment, then she follows her first instinct when she turns away from the man.

Now with her back to the killer, the killer wraps his left arm around Halle's body and places the cloth in his right hand over her nose and mouth. The killer drives Halle towards her desk. Halle's upper thighs hit the desk and she is forcefully bent over the desk. The killer presses his body hard against Halle's body to keep her from moving. Halle starts to weep as her body starts to go weak.

Halle struggles to get the muffled words out, "Don't do this, please."

The killer smoothly whispers in Halle's ear, "Relax my beautiful Halle."

Those are the last words she hears before Halle blacks out.

Detective Taylor, Detective Simpson and Mr. Gibson step off the elevator and they see a uniformed police officer standing with Richard. The three of them can hear the faint clicking of Kevin's camera.

As they walk, Detective Simpson speaks, "I'll talk with the boss if the two of you want to check out the body."

Detective Taylor nods, "Sounds good to me."

Detective Simpson stops by Richard as Detective Taylor and Mr. Gibson continue down the hallway. Detective Taylor and Mr. Gibson stop near Halle's body which is laying just outside her office door. The body is dressed and laid out like all the others. Detective Taylor notices the letter "T" written on Halle's stomach.

Kevin walks up holding his camera, "Well, the victim's name is Halle Fisher, age 36. From the preliminary analysis, everything appears to be the same as the others, but once we get the body to the lab, we'll check it out just to make sure."

Detective Taylor sighs, "Please tell me that there is something more than just the letter. Tell me we actually got something else this time."

Kevin smiles, "We actually do."

Mr. Gibson looks surprised, "What is it?"

Kevin motions for them to follow him into the office, "Come look at this."

The three of them walk into the office a few feet and stop.

Kevin makes a blanket comment, "Nice office, wouldn't you say."

Detective Taylor looks around, "Yes, but what do you have to show us?"

Kevin looks at her, "Take a step back and look down."

Both Detective Taylor and Mr. Gibson step back and look down at the very expensive carpet. Their eyes widen as they clearly see their footprint indentions in the carpet.

Kevin explains, "The foam padding used under the carpet is very expensive and it holds shapes for a very long time. So, what we have found is a good imprint of our victim, her boss and an unknown person."

Detective Taylor gets a little excited, "The killer?"

Kevin nods, "It would appear so. We have made a cast of the footprint and taken the piece of carpet that gives us the clearest indention. Now all we need to do is track down everyone that was here yesterday, workers and clients, and see if we have a match."

Detective Taylor gives a small sigh of relief, "Finally, the killer's first mistake." She quickly looks at Mr. Gibson, "Unless …"

Mr. Gibson smiles knowing what she is going to ask, "No, we never got a clue like this in either of the first two cases."

Kevin speaks up, "We're done and ready to move the body if that is okay?"

Detective Taylor nods, "Of course."

Kevin motions to Jennifer and she starts getting the team moving. Kevin turns to walk out of the room.

Detective Taylor looks at Kevin, "Kevin." He turns back to her and she continues, "Good work. Excellent job."

Kevin just gives a warm smile, turns and walks out. Detective Taylor glances around the office.

Mr. Gibson looks at Detective Taylor, "A footprint is good, but its still a long way from solving the case."

Detective Taylor looks at Mr. Gibson, "I know." She gives him a slight smile, "But at least now we know he is capable of making mistakes."

Detective Simpson walks up, "Kevin told me on the way out. Is it true, we have a footprint?"

Detective Taylor nods slightly, "It would appear so."

The three of them look at each other and smile.

The killer is sitting at his desk as the only light that is on is the desk lamp.

As the killer writes in his journal, he speaks, "I know I took a risk and left them a clue with my footprint in the carpet."

The killer stops writing and looks over at a pair of boots, "But the size eleven boot print will yield them nothing but more headache."

The killer closes the journal and stands up. He walks over and picks up the size eleven boots. He walks out of the room and down a dark hallway into a small living room. The only light in the living room is coming from the fire in the fireplace. The killer walks over and tosses the boots on the fire.

The killer steps back and watches as the boots start to burn.

The killer looks down at the boots he is wearing, "Forensics will tell them a size eleven." He pauses and smiles, "At least I'm back to wearing my comfy size nines."

The killer lets out a satisfying sigh, turns around and heads back to his study.

Chapter 8

DETECTIVE TAYLOR, DETECTIVE SIMPSON and Mr. Gibson are sitting at the table in the conference room. All three of them have an exhausted look on their face, that of not getting much sleep coupled with great frustration.

Detective Taylor sits back and rubs her eyes, "I just don't see it. Whatever the killer is trying to tell us, I just don't see it."

Detective Simpson lets out a sigh, "And we are running out of time until the next victim. It is always a race against time with this guy."

Mr. Gibson shakes his head, "You cannot give in. The answers are here, its just a matter of putting it all together."

Detective Taylor looks at Mr. Gibson, "Why did you quit in January of 1976 and disappear? You seem so passionate about this. Why not keep working on it?"

Mr. Gibson gets a far away look, "The last victim and the last clue. I finally broke and couldn't take anymore. Plus, the killer stated that there was no reason to continue."

Detective Simpson questions, "What do you mean?"

Mr. Gibson looks at her, "Didn't you look at the last victim's of the two prior cases and the last clue left?"

Detective Taylor starts to shuffle through the papers in front of her and so does Detective Simpson. Almost at the exact same time, the two of them pull out an evidence bag.

Mr. Gibson sighs, "Those words have stuck in my head for 24 years." He pauses and continues as if he is reading the notes that were left with the last bodies, "You failed. The prizes will be removed until the next time. The work will go on in…" He pauses, "And then a fixed quarter from 1949."

Detective Simpson and Detective Taylor look at each other and give the other a slight nod as if to say, he is right. At that moment, the door opens and Kevin walks in with the boot cast in his hand.

Kevin shuts the door and turns to the others, "So, do you want the good news or the bad news?"

Detective Simpson sits back, "You mean it actually gets worse." She glances at Ashley, then back to Kevin, "Just shoot away with either one."

Kevin walks over to the board at the end of the table, "My investigator that was sent to Atlanta has not found any kind of records to tell us that this has happened before in the Atlanta area. So, the best we can tell is that Seattle is the first time."

Mr. Gibson slightly nods, "Well, that's at least a positive note."

Kevin smiles and places the cast in front of them, "Now, to burst your bubble. What do you see here?"

Detective Taylor stands and looks at Kevin, "A footprint?"

Kevin nods sarcastically, "Yes, but look closer."

Detective Taylor, Detective Simpson and Mr. Gibson all look at the cast for a moment. None of them see what Kevin is talking about a first.

Finally, Mr. Gibson speaks up, "There is hardly no indention at the toe of the print."

Kevin nods in approval, "Exactly."

Detective Taylor questions, "So what does that mean?"

Kevin explains, "Well, that means either our killer walks really funny, with all his weight on the heels and middle of the foot, or ..."

Mr. Gibson picks up the sentence, "He was wearing larger boots than normal."

Kevin nods again, "Exactly, his toes didn't reach to the end of the boot so he was unable to apply much pressure with that part of the boot."

Detective Simpson speaks up, "So the print is useless."

Kevin speaks up, "Not exactly. What we have put together is that the killer wears smaller than a size eleven and best we can say is larger than a size seven. We have also estimated his weight to around 160 to 170 pounds."

Detective Taylor sighs, "Well, that's something. Can we get an idea of how tall he is?"

Kevin lets out a chuckle, "Not from this print."

Detective Simpson questions, "If you had to take an educated guess?"

Kevin thinks for a second, then replies, "I would say, 5'8" to 5'10" tall."

Mr. Gibson smiles, "And he has blonde hair and blue eyes from California."

Kevin smiles, "Aw, this is science, not science fiction." He pauses, "We don't have a whole lot more, but more than we did have."

Detective Simpson sighs, "I know one thing, its not going to be the big break we need before the next victim."

Detective Taylor sits back down in her seat, "Well, lets get back at it."

The four of them start shuffling through the growing case files in hopes of finding the one thing that will break the case.

It's a cold night in the city. A young, oriental woman is standing behind the counter at an out of the way convenience store. She looks up at the clock on the wall and it reads 2:55. She stands about 5'2" tall and looks to weigh a trim 105 pounds. She has long blonde colored hair and dark eyes. She is wearing tight blue jeans and a sweatshirt with her work vest on over her top and she has on cowboy boots.

At that time, a young man walks in. He has on appropriate clothing for the cold weather and under his open coat, he has on a work vest for the store.

The young lady smiles, "Hey Michael. How are you at this grand 3 am?"

Michael returns the smile, "Hey Ayumi. I'm cold. The temperature has dropped and their calling for snow so be careful going home." He pauses, "Let me put my coat up and I'll be ready."

Michael walks to the back as Ayumi closes her register. Michael walks back up in a couple minutes.

Ayumi walks for the back of the store as Michael logs in on the register. Ayumi comes back in a couple of minutes.

Ayumi smiles, "Have a good day."

Michael smiles in return, "You too and be safe."

Ayumi gives a quick nod, "I will."

Ayumi pulls her car keys out of her pocket as she walks out the front of the store. The parking lot is fairly well lit in front, but it gets a lot darker as she starts around the side of the building where she is parked. She can see her breath as she walks. She holds her keys ready in her hand as she approaches her car. She is parked just about twenty feet from the dumpsters. Her eyes glance around as she walks by the front of her car.

When Ayumi gets to the driver's door, she hears a cat screech and glass break by the dumpsters. Ayumi lets out a quick scream and drops her keys on the ground. She looks over to the dumpsters and sees an alley cat standing next to a broken bottle. Ayumi lets out a sigh and bends down to pick up her keys. When she stands back up, a homeless man is standing there. Ayumi jumps back in shock and drops her keys again.

The homeless man speaks with a weak voice, "Can you spare some change Miss?"

Ayumi, with her soft heart pounding in her ears, smiles, "Sure."

Ayumi digs in her purse and pulls out a couple of one dollar bills, "Here you go."

Ayumi hands the money to the man.

The man gives a thankful smile, "Thank you young Miss."

The man turns and walks off. Ayumi watches the man disappear behind the dumpsters.

Ayumi speaks to herself as she bends down to pick up her keys again, "I hate working this late."

Ayumi grabs her keys and stands back up. She unlocks the driver's door and gets in the car. She quickly closes the door and locks it. She puts the key in the ignition and turns it. As the car tries to start, she looks up into the rearview mirror and sees the image of a person come up from behind her seat.

The killer quickly puts the cloth over Ayumi's nose and mouth and pulls her hard against the seat. Ayumi's eyes fill with fear and she freezes from terror and panic. As her vision starts to fade, Ayumi reaches up with her right hand and hits the car horn, but no sound comes out.

Ayumi feels her body grow even weaker and her vision is almost gone now.

The killer leans over the back of her seat and whispers in Ayumi's ear, "Relax now, my exotic Ayumi."

One more inhale and Ayumi's world goes dark.

Ashley Taylor sits up in her bed, breathing heavily and sweating from the nightmare she just had. She swallows hard and focuses her eyes. She looks over at the clock next to her bed and it shows 6 am. She throws the covers off revealing her leopard skin patterned pajama pants and her white top.

Ashley gets out of bed and slides her feet into her house shoes. She grabs her watch and looks at the date. She puts her watch down and grabs the year long calendar from the nightstand and notices that the date on her watch is circled on the calendar. Ashley lets out a sigh and sits back down on the bed.

At that moment, Ashley's cell phone starts ringing. Ashley drops the calendar and picks up the phone. She sees her partner's phone number on the ID.

Ashley answers the phone, "Hello."

Natalie's voice comes on, "Hey Ashley. Kevin called me. They have another body. I'm on my way over to pick you up. I'll be there in about twenty minutes. Kevin said he already picked up Mr. Gibson."

Ashley lets out a somber sigh, "I'll be ready."

The two detectives hang up and Ashley heads for the bathroom to quickly clean up and get ready.

Detective Simpson and Detective Taylor pull up in front of the store where Ayumi works. Detective Simpson gets out of the driver's seat and Detective Taylor gets out of the passenger's seat. The two of them see Mr. Gibson standing by the corner of the store.

Mr. Gibson nods as the two detectives walk up, "Good

morning ladies."

Detective Taylor questions, "He killed one in public?"

Mr. Gibson nods slightly, "No place is off limits for this guy. Kevin and his team has processed the body and the surrounding area, but I'll walk you through it."

The three of them walk over to Ayumi's car and they see her body laid out like all the others next to the driver's door. They see the letter "R" written on her stomach.

Mr. Gibson speaks, "The killer was in the back floorboard of the car. The victim got in the car and started it and that is when she was attacked."

Detective Simpson questions, "Did anyone hear anything?"

Mr. Gibson shakes his head, "Kevin told me that there is not much traffic around here early in the morning. Also, the killer disabled the car horn in case she tried to push it."

Detective Taylor glances around, "Once again, he shows how smart he is." She sees a standard dinning chair by the dumpsters, "I take it he tied her to that chair over there."

Kevin walks up behind the two detectives, "From the best we can tell, yes." He pauses, "The victim's name is Ayumi Kuriyama, age 23. She worked here part time and was a full time student. Everything appears the same as the others, but we will check it all out at the lab."

Detective Taylor nods, "You can go ahead and take the body, we are going to look around some and talk to the clerk."

Kevin nods and looks over at Jennifer, "Jennifer, go ahead and load everything up."

Jennifer gets the team moving and Kevin heads for his van.

Mr. Gibson looks at the two detectives, "I'll hang out here with you two."

Kevin and his team leaves as Detective Taylor, Detective Simpson and Mr. Gibson start looking around the area.

Detective Simpson questions while looking around, "What's the chance we'll find something?"

Mr. Gibson lets out a weak chuckle, "Zero."

In the early hours of the morning, Detective Taylor, Detective Simpson and Mr. Gibson are sitting at the table in the conference room at the station.

Detective Simpson lets out a sigh as she puts down some photos, "Two days since the last body and still, not even an idea at a lead."

Detective Taylor is looking over a few papers in front of her, "We'll find something."

At that moment, Kevin walks in followed by Captain Sutherland. Kevin puts his food in the refrigerator.

Captain Sutherland unfolds the newspaper in his hand, "Well, at least we didn't make the top story today."

Detective Simpson looks at Captain Sutherland, "How did that happen?"

Captain Sutherland sets the newspaper on the table, "It appears that Mrs. Maureen O'Kelly-Newman passed away last night. She is the one who founded the O'Kelly Adoption Centers."

Detective Taylor speaks up, "Look at this. All the writings on our eight victims are the same as the first eight victims in the two prior cases."

Kevin speaks up, "So, if all the writings are the same, then maybe it says something."

Mr. Gibson speaks up, "Not all 27 are the same. I had seen that too back in 1975, but the writings did change."

Detective Simpson chimes up, "It still seems strange to write something on the bodies, unless …" She pauses, "Maybe they do have a meaning."

Kevin pipes up, "Maybe they spell the killer's name."

Mr. Gibson lets out a smile, "That would be nice, if names had numbers in them."

Detective Taylor sighs, "Surely they have some meaning. Unless they are meant to draw our attention from the other big clues that has been left."

Mr. Gibson sits back, "The writings changed, but in the first two cases and so far in this one, the big, physical clues have been the same."

Kevin speaks up, "I think we should do some testing on the physical clues from the two prior cases. We already tested the adoption paper and the clock hand as well as the dirt, but perhaps we should test the other clues."

Mr. Gibson nods, "You know, that is not a bad idea. Maybe technology of today can give more insight than what we had back then."

Kevin stands up, "I'll call my team and get them ready."

Detective Taylor, Detective Simpson and Mr. Gibson gather the evidence bags from the 1950 and 1975 cases as Kevin gets on the phone.

Captain Sutherland speaks up, "I'll go to my office and call all the labs to let them know that your work is priority."

Detective Taylor nods, "Thanks Captain."

Kevin hangs up the phone, "Jennifer is rounding up the team so lets get these things to the lab."

Everyone exits the conference room and follows Kevin.

Chapter 9

IN THE DARKNESS OF his study, the killer sits at his desk with the low light of the lamp glowing. The killer is writing an entry in his journal. He smiles as he writes about how confused he has the police and how they are completely unable to put together the clues because of their frustration.

The killer puts down his pen and looks up, "You both were right. The answer is so simple and right in front of them, but the lack of physical evidence keeps them frustrated." He takes a breath, "It is nearly April and they are no closer than Detective Conners or Detective Gibson were."

The killer closes the journal and picks up a picture, "Time to give them the next piece to the ever growing puzzle."

The killer gives himself an evil smile and stands to leave. He turns off the light and walks out of the room.

The sun is getting lower in the sky over a lower middle class neighborhood. A car pulls up in front of the third house on the block. It is a small, two bedroom house with a decent sized front and back yard. The backyard is surrounded by a privacy fence.

A Latino woman gets out of the driver's seat. She appears to be about 5'5" tall and holds a healthy build of 135 pounds. She has flowing dark brown hair and brown eyes. She has on tan jeans and a blue, long sleeve top with a winter jacket. The woman appears tired after a long day of work.

The woman locks her car door, closes it and heads for the front door of her house. She unlocks the two locks on the front door and steps inside the dark house. She walks into a small living room and turns on the light. A couch, chair, end table, coffee table and entertainment center dot the room.

The woman sets her keys on the coffee table along with her purse. She walks into the kitchen to the left and turns on the light. She opens the refrigerator and grabs a bottle of water. She turns around and sighs as she sees the full trash can.

The woman puts her open bottle of water on the counter next to the bottle cap, "My work is never done. Someday I might find a man to do this for me."

The woman smiles as she pulls the trash bag out of the can and ties it closed. She walks over to the back door and unlocks it. She turns on the light to the outside of the back door. She walks outside and across the backyard to the dumpster. She can hear her neighbors, but with the tall privacy fence, she can't see anything. She puts the trash in the dumpster and turns back around.

The woman walks back into the house and locks up the back door. She walks over and picks up her bottle of water. Not noticing the cap back on the bottle, she twists the cap off again and takes another drink. She walks back into the living room and sets her water down on the coffee table next to her keys. She has a puzzled look as she glances around and spots her purse on the couch. She shrugs it off and pulls her cell phone out of her purse and checks for any messages.

The woman puts her phone down, takes her coat off and tosses it on the couch, covering her purse. She slides her shoes off and heads for the bathroom. She walks into the small bathroom, turns the light on and brushes her teeth. Once done, she turns the light off and walks back into the living room. She picks up her coat, completely unaware that her purse is back on the coffee table and takes her coat to the kitchen and hangs it up next to the back door.

As the woman walks back into the living room, she can see the bathroom light is on.

The woman gets a puzzled look, "I thought I turned that off. I must be losing my mind."

As the woman walks down the hall she passes her bedroom door. Once she is a few feet pass the bedroom door, the killer steps out of the bedroom into the hallway behind the woman. With her mind wandering, she is completely unaware of the killer moving quietly up behind her. As the woman reaches into the bathroom to turn off the light, the killer firmly wraps his left arm around her waist and his right hand firmly places the cloth over her nose and mouth.

Complete and total fear enters the woman's beautiful brown eyes. The killer spins her around and pins her to the wall in the hallway. The woman struggles, but the man holding her is just too strong. She can feel her body getting weaker. Tears fill her eyes and she tries to make whatever noise she can. As she gets weaker, she hears her house phone start ringing. She continues to struggle as the answering machine picks up the call.

The woman hears a man's voice on the machine, "Hey Constance, remember it's my time to drive tomorrow so I'll be there around seven to pick you up. See you tomorrow, bye."

Just before Constance passes out, the killer whispers

in her ear, "It's okay my lovely Constance. It will all be over soon."

Then, the chloroform becomes too much and Constance's world goes black.

Mr. Gibson is standing in the bathroom of the hotel room that he has been living out of since getting to New York City. He is still in his sweatpants and t-shirt that he slept in. He calmly washes his face and brushes his teeth. He has a far away look in his eyes, the look of knowing the inevitable is about to come.

Mr. Gibson turns the water off and stares into the mirror, "What are you doing? You wanted to break this case and you're right back to where you were 25 years ago. Think Mat, think. What have you missed?"

At that moment, Mr. Gibson hears a knocking at the door. He gets a sad look on his face as he knows the date and what this visit is going to bring. He walks over and opens the door to see Detective Taylor and Detective Simpson standing there.

Mr. Gibson can tell by the looks on their faces the next victim has been found, "How long ago?"

Detective Simpson replies down hearted, "An hour ago. Kevin and his team just got there."

Mr. Gibson gives a half-hearted nod, "I'll get changed."

Detective Taylor replies, "We'll be waiting in the car."

Detective Taylor and Detective Simpson walk off as Mr. Gibson closes the door and heads for his bedroom to change.

Kevin is standing on the front porch of Constance's house when the familiar Ford pulls up. Detective Taylor, Detective Simpson and Mr. Gibson climb out of the car. They spot Kevin and Jennifer and start towards them. As the three of them walk up the steps, they can see Constance's body laying in front of the front door.

Kevin gives a quick nod and gets right to the point, "The victim is Constance Lopez, age 31. It appears to be the same as before, but we will confirm that back at the lab. All that we could find was the letter left on the body."

Detective Taylor, Detective Simpson and Mr. Gibson walk over to the body and see the letter "A" written on the stomach.

Detective Simpson speaks up, "The killer just duplicated his first letter. This is the same letter as the fifth victim." She pauses, "I wonder if that has any meaning?"

Mr. Gibson replies, "There were duplicate letters in the first two cases also. The writings have to have some kind of meaning."

Detective Taylor glances around and notices more people starting to show up, "We better get the body out of here." She pauses, "You know what, I wonder how the killer gets the information for his journals if that is what he uses?"

Jennifer questions, "What do you mean?"

Detective Taylor continues, "The killer could very well be one of the citizens standing around at each crime scene."

Kevin nods slightly, "You know, I never thought of that, but it does make sense."

Mr. Gibson chimes in, "I have no doubt the killer is watching, but how are you going to single him out? Standing around a crime scene is not a crime in itself."

Detective Simpson speaks up, "Maybe we can start having a few officers carry video cameras and record the crime scene and accidentally catch shots of the crowd."

Mr. Gibson nods, "That's not a bad idea."

Detective Taylor speaks up, "We can run it by the Captain back at the station, but we better wrap it up here."

Jennifer gathers the CSI team and they all get the body and equipment into the van. Kevin and his team drive off as Detective Taylor, Detective Simpson and Mr. Gibson start looking around.

Detective Taylor, Detective Simpson, Kevin and Mr. Gibson are sitting at the table in the conference room. Each one looks exhausted from the long hours and days they have spent here since the last body was found.

Detective Taylor sits back, "The next victim is coming soon, we have to come up with something."

The four of them look up at the board at the end of the table with the pictures of the nine victims on it.

The stares are broken as Captain Sutherland walks in, "Anything yet?"

Detective Simpson shakes her head, "I'm afraid not sir."

Captain Sutherland nods, "Well, if we get another victim, I've set aside four officers to carry video cameras to the scene. Who knows, we might just get lucky."

Kevin sighs, "We could use a little luck right now."

Mr. Gibson sits back, "The writings on the body have to have some sort of meaning. The killer's plan is too exact for them to mean nothing."

Detective Taylor speaks up, "We could take all the writings from the two prior cases and see what we can come up with. Maybe they spell something like we were thinking before."

Kevin lets out a slight chuckle, "Are you kidding? Do you know how many possible combinations you are talking about with 27 characters, given they are all used? That is going to take some time."

Detective Simpson chimes in, "We can put all the characters in a computer and it shouldn't take long for all the possibilities to be computed."

Kevin nods, "True, but then you have to go through every single one of the possibilities and see if it matches with any of the other clues we have." He pauses, "That is the part that can take a lifetime."

Mr. Gibson speaks up, "I think we should try. Maybe one of the possibilities will just stand out. We won't know unless we try."

Captain Sutherland chimes in, "Get all the writings together. I'll tell the lab you are on your way."

Detective Taylor speaks up, "Natalie, you and Kevin take the writings to the lab. Mr. Gibson and I will stay here and continue to look at the rest of the clues."

Detective Simpson gathers up the paperwork she needs and she follows Kevin out of the room.

Detective Taylor looks over to Mr. Gibson, "Kevin is right about one thing, it will take some time and how many victims will we fail until we find what we are looking for."

Mr. Gibson replies, "You can't think about it like that. All you can do is keep plugging away at the clues."

Captain Sutherland speaks up, "He is right Ashley. If we start concerning ourselves with the next victim, the pressure and pushing yourself might cause you to miss something important."

Mr. Gibson speaks back up, "It might sound cold, but the only deadline we have is the 27th victim. After that, the game is over for another 25 years."

Detective Taylor nods, "We're going to catch him. I know it."

Captain Sutherland speaks, "Then I'll let the two of you get back to work."

Captain Sutherland walks out and Detective Taylor

and Mr. Gibson returns to analyzing the massive amounts of paperwork on the table in front of them.

Chapter 10

THE KILLER IS SITTING at his desk which is lit by the dim light of the lamp. He is making another entry in his journal.

The killer stops and sits back, "The two of you have been right. They are so concerned with each individual clue, that they are completely unaware that all the clues work together." He pauses, "They will no doubt try to break the codes in the writings on the bodies, but if they don't know what they are looking for, then the findings from the writings will be useless to them."

The killer starts writing some more in his journal. After a few more minutes, the killer puts down his pen and closes his journal. The killer picks up a picture and puts it in his jacket pocket.

The killer grabs two pennies from the desk, "Time for the next clue."

The killer stands up, puts the pennies in his pocket and turns off the lamp. The killer walks out of his room and into the darkness of the city night.

Detective Taylor, Detective Simpson, Kevin and Mr. Gibson are sitting at the table in the conference room. Each one is looking over the clues from the killings in New York.

Detective Taylor looks at Kevin, "Has the lab given us anything on the physical clues from the two previous cases yet?"

Kevin shakes his head, "No. It is going to take a little more time. The clues are old and we have to be absolutely certain of our findings."

Mr. Gibson looks at Detective Simpson, "Have we got anything back on the writings?"

Detective Simpson looks frustrated, "Not yet. There are so many possible combinations. We told the lab to start with possible names and work from there." She pauses, "We are thinking that somewhere in the 27 writings is the killer's name."

Mr. Gibson nods slightly, "It's a good possibility."

Detective Taylor looks at her watch and lets out a sigh, "It's too late."

Kevin looks at Ashley, "What do you mean?"

Detective Taylor shakes her head, "Look at the date on your watch."

The three of them check their watches and look up at the calendar posted on the board at the end of the table. A heaviness comes over the room as they each know it is just a matter of getting that phone call now. All four of them let out a collective sigh of having failed another victim.

Mr. Gibson finally speaks, "It's too late to change what is going to happen. All we can do is keep pushing forward."

The other three nod and get back to the business at hand.

At one of the all night television news stations, a beautiful petite woman who stands maybe 5'3" tall and weighs about 105 pounds with brown hair and brown eyes looking to be in her late thirties, walks out of a nicely decorated office. She is wearing a blue top and black slacks. She looks at her watch and it shows 1 am.

As the woman hurries down one of the hallways, an older man dressed in a suit walks up to her, "Great show tonight Karima. That story was great."

Karima smiles, "Thanks Mr. Watson, but can we talk about it tomorrow? I'm running late."

Mr. Watson nods, "Of course. I'll see you tomorrow night."

Karima hurries off towards the elevator. She gets in the elevator and pushes the button for the parking garage in the basement. The elevator takes her down without a stop. The doors open and a man in a security uniform is standing there.

Karima starts off the elevator as soon as the doors opened and the security guard shocks her. She lets out a slight scream.

The security guard smiles, "Sorry Miss Bakhtair, I didn't mean to startle you."

Karima gives the man a smile, "That's okay. I should have been paying more attention."

The security guard replies, "Would you like me to walk you to your car?"

Karima gives a thanking look, "That's okay. I'll be fine."

The security guard nods, "Well, I just finished walking through the parking garage and didn't see anything so hopefully you won't get anymore shocks."

Karima smiles, "Thanks, have a good night."

The security guard nods, "You too."

Karima walks off the elevator and the security guard gets on the elevator. Karima walks down the hallway to the solid door leading to the parking garage. She turns the handle on the door and pushes, but the door doesn't open. Karima gets a puzzled look, turns the handle again and hears the door click. She pushes the door open and steps into the dimly lit parking garage. She pulls her keys out of her pocket and keeps her finger on the panic alarm of her key chain.

The sound of Karima's heels echo through the parking garage. She glances around often and has the look of someone that hates being out this late at night. As she approaches her car, she hears the faint meow of a cat. She glances around, but doesn't see anything as she continues towards her car. As she reaches her driver's door, she hears the cat again, even louder this time.

Karima glances around. She can hear the cat, but is unable to locate it. Then the meow gets even closer. As Karima glances around the cat jumps up on the hood of her car. Karima jumps back and lets out a fearful sigh.

As Karima catches her breath, she looks at the cat, "What are you doing down here little kitty? How did you get in here?"

As Karima approaches the cat, it jumps off the hood to the other side of the car.

Karima smiles, "Where are you going little kitty?"

Suddenly, a strong left arm wraps around Karima's waist and a hand places a cloth over her mouth. Terror fills her eyes as the weight of the killer pushes her against the hood of her car. The killer pins her to the hood with all his strength and weight. Karima struggles, but her petite size is no match for the killer.

Karima starts to weep as the chemicals on the rag start to take affect. She can feel her body getting weaker. The muffled sounds of her panicked voice are lost in the parking garage.

The killer leans down and whispers in Karima's ear, "Relax my beautiful Karima. You will be on the news again soon enough."

The chemicals become too much and Karima's world fades into blackness.

Detective Taylor, Detective Simpson, Kevin and Mr. Gibson are still sitting at the table in the conference room. Each one has a look of being exhausted having been there all night.

Detective Simpson sits back and looks at her watch, "It's 6am, I would have expected a call by now."

Kevin speaks up, "Maybe the killer missed his target."

Mr. Gibson sighs, "I doubt that happened. This guy is way too good to miss a victim on the scheduled date."

Kevin replies, "Doesn't hurt to think positive. It could happen."

At that moment, the phone in the conference room rings. The four of them get a sickened look on their faces, not wanting this to be the call they were all expecting.

Detective Taylor gets up and answers the phone, "Detective Taylor." She pauses, "Hey Captain, what's up?"

Detective Taylor gets the all too familiar look on her face and the other three know right away what the call is about.

Detective Taylor nods, "Yes sir, we will get there as soon as possible."

Detective Taylor hangs up and turns back to the others.

Kevin stands up, "I'll get my team together. Where is the body?"

Detective Taylor sighs, "It's at the parking garage of the Channel 11 news building."

Kevin gives a slight nod and walks out of the room.

Mr. Gibson stands up, "Well, shall we?"

Detective Taylor nods slightly and she walks out of the room with Detective Simpson and Mr. Gibson right behind her.

In less than an hour, two CSI vans and a Ford Taurus are parked outside the entrance to the parking garage at the Channel 11 news building. Detective Taylor, Detective Simpson and Mr. Gibson are talking to some of the employees while Kevin and his team are inside going over the crime scene.

A short time passes and they hear Kevin yell, "Okay, you three can come in!"

Detective Taylor, Detective Simpson and Mr. Gibson walk into the parking garage. They spot Kevin and walk over to him. As the three of them get closer to the car Kevin is standing by, they spot Karima's body on the ground. The body is dressed and laid out like all the others.

Detective Simpson sighs, "Well, number ten."

The three of them stop next to Kevin and Mr. Gibson questions, "Where are the pennies located?"

Detective Taylor looks at Mr. Gibson, "What are you talking about?"

Mr. Gibson replies, "The tenth body in both prior cases had pennies placed over the eyes of the victim as well as a writing on the stomach."

Kevin speaks up, "The pennies are placed over the eyes. I haven't touched them yet. I wanted the three of you to see them first."

Detective Taylor, Detective Simpson, Mr. Gibson and

Kevin walk over by the body.

Kevin speaks, "The victim is Karima Bakhtair, age 37. As you can see, everything appears to be the same as the others. She appears to have been drugged, tied up, then strangled. However, we can't find her clothes or the chair she was tied to."

Detective Simpson looks down and sees the number "8" written on Karima's stomach, "No doubt the killer took them."

Detective Taylor squats down by the victim's head, "Is there any reason why one penny is heads up and the other is tails?"

Mr. Gibson shakes his head slightly, "Not that I'm aware of. I just know that they should be on the eyes and that the date of the pennies should be 1949."

Detective Taylor puts on some latex gloves as Detective Simpson questions, "Why 1949? The first killings didn't start until 1950."

Mr. Gibson replies, "That, I don't know." He pauses, "But I'm sure there is a reason he picked that year."

Detective Taylor gently lifts up the pennies, "Yep, 1949 on both."

Kevin holds out an evidence bag and Detective Taylor places the pennies in the bag. Kevin seals the evidence bag.

Detective Taylor stands up, "So, now we have two numbers and another physical clue that is an exact match of the two previous cases."

Detective Simpson adds, "Plus, the physical clue, just like the others, refers back to the first case in 1950. That's where the answer has to be."

Mr. Gibson gets a look to his face, a look of a light bulb coming on, "The first clues date to around 1925. The dirt is from the Seattle area except for the 1950 dirt being from Atlanta and pennies from 1949."

Kevin gets a puzzled look, "What are you saying?"

Mr. Gibson gets a serious look, "The answer has to lay

with Seattle and most likely with the time frame of 1925 to 1950. We just have to figure out what that is."

Detective Taylor nods, "We should get back into the office and start looking into that."

Kevin speaks up, "My team and I will take care of everything here if the three of you want to get back to the office."

Detective Taylor, Detective Simpson and Mr. Gibson walk off as Kevin and his team get the body and equipment ready to move.

Chapter 11

IN THE EARLY MORNING hours of the new day, Detective Taylor, Detective Simpson, Mr. Gibson and Kevin are sitting in the conference room at the police station. Each one has the look of another long day of frustration ahead of them.

Detective Taylor is the first to speak, breaking the stressful silence, "Okay, I think we all can see that the clues are pointing us to the case in 1950. Something about that case and Seattle holds the keys to unraveling this mystery."

Mr. Gibson speaks up, "We definitely need to look at Seattle's history to see what stands out that we can possibly match some of these clues up to."

At that moment, the door opens and Jennifer walks in carrying a large cardboard box.

Kevin looks at her, "What do you have Jennifer?"

Jennifer sets the box on the table, "We have the results back from the testing on the other clues."

Jennifer pulls some papers out of the box, "We already know about the adoption paper, minute hand of the clock, the bag of dirt and now the pennies." She pauses, "The next physical clue is this."

Jennifer reaches into the box and pulls out a clear evidence bag that holds a very old, black and white picture in it. The picture is clearly old and worn. The picture is of a man that appears to be well dressed and in his twenties with a small child, no more than two to four years old, sitting on his lap.

Jennifer holds the picture up, "This picture, the best we can tell was taken somewhere in the 1920's. We have no idea who the man and child in the picture is or where it would be from."

Jennifer puts the picture on the table and pulls out two clear evidence bags. In one bag is an old looking piece of paper that appears to be a blank birth certificate. In the second bag appears to be another old piece of paper that looks like a blank death certificate.

Jennifer continues, "We have found that the blank birth certificate is roughly from the thirties and the blank death certificate is from the forties."

Jennifer puts the two clear bags on the table and pulls out another clear bag with another picture in it, "This last picture is the most puzzling. We are not really sure when it was taken. The best we can tell is the one from Seattle was from the fifties and the picture from Kansas City was from the seventies." She pauses, "We also have no idea what this picture is suppose to be of. All we have been able to see is that it is a picture of a grassy opening in the woods. Both pictures look to be of the same spot, just many years apart."

Mr. Gibson speaks up, "No doubt the pictures are from 1950 and 1975, and of the same area." He sighs, "But what makes a grassy opening in the woods important? Every victim in all three cases have been found in the city."

Jennifer nods slightly and puts the bag on the table, "And of course, you all know about the letters from the last victim in the two previous cases about failing and the prizes being removed."

Detective Simpson shakes her head, "This is just so bizarre. Why these clues and the times that they correlate to?"

Detective Taylor sighs, "Okay, lets go with this. Jennifer, you and Kevin start looking into the history of the first case and Seattle. Natalie, keep on the computer guys and see if they have come up with anything that might go along with these clues." She pauses, "Mr. Gibson and I will stay here and keep looking over the clues and the evidence."

Kevin nods and stands up, "Lets go Jen."

Detective Simpson stands up, "I'll call if I get anything."

The three of them leave the room and Detective Taylor and Mr. Gibson get back to looking over the mounds of evidence and clues in front of them.

It is a cool spring morning in the city. The numerous school buses have pulled up in front of one of the city's junior high schools. As the kids pour off the school buses, a beautiful woman in her late twenties with deep red hair and incredible brown eyes, standing about 5'4" tall and weighing around 120 pounds is weaving her way through the crowd of kids. She is wearing a nice female suit that covers her sexy, trim body and she is carrying a few books. Another figure is also weaving his way through the crowd of kids, it is the killer, dressed like he always is and he appears to be on a collision course with the beautiful woman.

The woman looks to her left and at that moment, the killer bumps into her, knocking her books from her hands. The books fall on the sidewalk.

The killer speaks, "I'm so sorry. Let me help you."

The woman looks at the killer as he bends down and picks up the books. The killer stands back up and hands the books back to the woman.

The woman smiles, "Thank you."

The killer returns the smile, "I really am sorry about that." He pauses, "Music books I see."

The woman nods, "Yea. I'm the assistant music teacher here." She holds out her right hand, "I'm Alicia."

The killer reaches out with his gloved right hand as he gazes into Alicia's eyes, "Phillip." He smiles, "Nice to meet you, though I must say, you look familiar, like we've met before."

Alicia smiles again, "I get that a lot." She sighs, "I better go. It was nice to meet you Phillip."

The killer nods, "Likewise."

Alicia walks off towards the school entrance as the killer slowly disappears into the sea of students.

Another mind draining day has started for Detective Taylor, Detective Simpson, Mr. Gibson and Kevin as they sit around the table in the conference room. Each person is looking over some papers in front of them and writing down notes. It is deathly silent in the room, until Detective Taylor breaks the silence.

Detective Taylor sits back and throws her pen across the room, "Damn it! We have two more days before we lose another one."

The others jump in their seats from Detective Taylor's outburst.

Mr. Gibson speaks calmly, "We have to stay focused. Frustration is the killer's greatest weapon. He knows it will disrupt our thinking."

Kevin speaks up, "The two biggest things we have

found in Seattle's past given our time frame is the disappearance of Michael Newman which the police ruled a runaway and of course, the 27 unsolved murders." He pauses, "It is hard to find information from that long ago. Jennifer is checking into some more subtle stories that might have gotten under the radar to see if anything helps."

Detective Simpson questions, "Michael Newman?"

Kevin nods, "He was the son of Thomas Newman and Maureen O'Kelly-Newman. He disappeared in 1949, but due to the investigation into what happened, the police determined that the boy ran away because his father was just too unbearable to live with."

Mr. Gibson speaks up, "How old was the boy?"

Kevin pauses, "If I remember correctly, thirteen."

Detective Simpson sighs, "Sounds like you have had as much luck as I have." She pauses, "Without any variables to narrow down the possible combinations from the written clues, we could wallpaper the entire building with all the possible combinations."

Detective Taylor shakes her head, "I can't believe with all our technology, we can't get any kind of leads on who this is."

At that moment, Captain Sutherland walks in, "Well, things have gotten better. You should see the story the morning news just ran."

Detective Simpson questions, "How bad was it?"

Captain Sutherland continues, "A basic summary would be that the police have no idea at how to stop the killer and that we are just waiting for the next victim so we can get the next clue."

Mr. Gibson sighs, "I see the news media also hasn't changed in twenty-five years."

Detective Taylor speaks up, "We will stop this guy, no matter how many hours it takes us. The killings will stop this year."

Mr. Gibson smiles, "Now that's what I like to hear.

Shall we get back at it."

The four of them get back to analyzing the clues as Captain Sutherland leaves to answer his ringing phone in the background.

Alicia is walking down the near empty school hallway. The last of the students are making their way from their lockers to the school buses waiting outside. As Alicia walks by one of the side hallways, she hears her name.

A man's voice, "Miss Hannigan!"

Alicia stops and looks around. She sees the principal walking towards her. The man is about 6'3" tall and close to 250 pounds. He is dressed in a nice suit.

As the principal walks up, Alicia smiles, "Can I help you Mr. Newman?"

Mr. Newman smiles, "No, I just wanted to say that the music ensemble that you put together for the assembly today was really good. It was very inspirational."

Alicia looks a little embarrassed, "Thank you sir."

Mr. Newman replies, "Well, if you're headed to your car, I'll walk you there."

Alicia smiles which could capture anyone, "That's okay. I'm going to stop by the music room and work a little then head home."

Mr. Newman nods, "Okay. Again, great job and be careful going home."

Alicia nods, "I will."

Mr. Newman walks off and Alicia continues on to the music room. She approaches two large wooden doors and she pulls out her keys. Alicia unlocks the door and walks inside. She reaches over and turns on the lights as the door shuts behind her. The room is a huge open room with instruments everywhere. There is a separate room in the back that appears to be smaller. Alicia weaves her way through the instruments to the back room.

Alicia walks into the smaller room. It is an office with a desk, small table with a coffee pot on it and a bookshelf. In the back of the room is a wall locker. Alicia sits down at the desk and pulls a music book out of the right hand drawer. She opens the book and starts glancing through the pages. Then the lights flicker and go out. Alicia looks up quickly, a little surprised. She glances around the nearly pitch black room.

Alicia smiles, "Great time to lose the electricity."

Alicia stands up, not realizing the light on the front of the coffee pot is still on. She starts for the office door. As she walks through the doorway into the larger room, the lights flicker again and the killer is right next to her. Alicia's eyes widen as the killer wraps his left arm around her and tackles her to the floor.

As the two of them land on the floor, Alicia yells, "Help!"

The killer quickly places the cloth over her mouth and nose as the cry is lost in the sound proof room. Alicia tries to struggle, but the entire weight of the killer has her firmly pressed to the floor. Her body gets weaker as tears fill her eyes. With the sheer horror running through her mind, Alicia doesn't even recognize the face of the killer from a few days before.

Alicia wiggles some more, but the chemicals have made her too weak to struggle anymore. Her vision starts to fade in and out as she gets a swimmy feeling in her head. Alicia knows this is the end. Before she loses all her faculties, she hears the door handle to the room jiggle. She knows it is the janitor making sure all the doors are locked. Alicia knows that she didn't lock the door, but some how it got locked.

Just before Alicia passes out, the killer whispers in her ear, "Relax my beautiful, red headed Alicia. It will all be over soon."

Then, Alicia's world passes into darkness.

Chapter 12

AFTER A LONG DAY of work, Detective Taylor walks into her ground level apartment. It is a nice three bedroom, two bath place with a large living room and kitchen. She tosses her keys on the coffee table and walks into the kitchen. She turns on the kitchen light and walks over to the refrigerator and opens it. She opens the bottom drawer and grabs one of the many bud light cans. She closes the drawer and the refrigerator. She puts the can in her bud light coozie and opens it. She walks into her living room and turns the light on. She grabs the TV remote and turns on the television. Ashley changes it over to the local news.

Ashley sits down on her couch and starts drinking her bud light. She watches the news and drinks her beer for about ten minutes when there is a knock at the door. She puts her drink down on the coffee table, stands up and draws her pistol from her holster. She slowly walks over to the door and looks through the peep hole. Ashley breathes a sigh of relief when she sees Mr. Gibson.

Ashley holsters her pistol and opens the door, "Good evening."

Mr. Gibson smiles, "Detective Taylor."

Ashley steps to the side, "Please come in, and call me Ashley."

Mr. Gibson walks in and Ashley closes and locks the door, "Can I get you a beer?"

Mr. Gibson nods, "That would be nice right now."

Ashley goes into the kitchen and returns with a beer for Mr. Gibson and another one for herself. The two of them sit down on the couch.

Ashley looks at Mr. Gibson, "Having trouble sleeping?"

Mr. Gibson nods slowly, "For about 25 years." He pauses, "I see I'm not the only one."

Ashley nods in return, "Yea. It's hard to get the images of the victims out of my head cause I feel like I've let them down."

Mr. Gibson replies, "That's what makes you a good detective. It's what keeps you going in the face of what seems like an impossible case."

Ashley smiles, "Well, my parents always told me I was strong willed and hard headed, very stubborn when I latch onto something."

Mr. Gibson takes a drink, "Was your mom or dad in law enforcement?"

Ashley shakes her head, "No. I'm the first." She pauses, "How about you?"

Mr. Gibson nods, "A long line. My dad, my grandfather, all my uncles and even my brother-in-law."

Ashley questions, "You have a sister?"

Mr. Gibson nods slightly, "Yea."

Ashley continues, "So, does she live in Kansas City also?"

Mr. Gibson replies somberly, "No." He pauses, "She died in 1975."

Ashley replies caringly, "I'm sorry."

Mr. Gibson takes another drink, "Its alright. How could you have known about it." He pauses, "It is something I actually wanted to share with you."

Ashley replies, "Of course you can. If it helps to talk about it."

Mr. Gibson gets a more serious look, "It actually deals with the case."

Ashley looks at Mr. Gibson, "What do you mean?"

Mr. Gibson takes a breath, "She was the twenty-seventh victim in 1975. She was listed as Stacy Williams, but that was her married name."

Ashley has a look of disbelief, "The killer's last victim was your sister?"

Mr. Gibson replies, "That is another similarity in the cases."

Ashley questions after another drink, "What do you mean?"

Mr. Gibson stares at Ashley, "The last victim in 1950 was a woman named, Rebecca Conners." He pauses, "She was the wife of Detective Conners, lead detective on the case."

Ashley has a stunned look, "Oh my God."

Mr. Gibson sighs, "I thought I should tell you now. The last victim seems to be someone close to the lead detective of the case."

Ashley drinks the last of her beer and sets it on the table. The news has her quiet, unable to grasp all the possible people in her life that could be a target.

Ashley looks at Mr. Gibson and finally speaks, "Well, its not going to come to that this time."

Mr. Gibson smiles at Ashley, "I have to admit, you are definitely ..." He suddenly stops and looks over at the front door, "Did you hear that?"

Ashley stands up and draws her pistol. As Mr. Gibson stands up, they hear footsteps running off down the pavement. Ashley rushes to the door with Mr. Gibson right behind her. She quickly unlocks the door, throws it open, steps outside and looks around. The two of them can hear dogs barking in the background, but they know that it is too late.

Ashley lets out a sigh, "It was him, wasn't it?"

Mr. Gibson nods as he continues to glance around, "I would say, yes."

Ashley and Mr. Gibson walk back inside and she locks up the door, "I think it's time to get some rest. You can crash on the couch if you want."

Mr. Gibson nods, "That'll work for me."

Ashley walks into the bedroom and returns with a pillow and blanket. She hands them to Mr. Gibson and turns off the TV.

Ashley smiles, "Well, goodnight."

Mr. Gibson nods, "Goodnight."

Mr. Gibson lays down. Ashley turns off the lights and heads to her bedroom. However, both of them find that sleep is hard to come by.

Ashley sits up in her bed as her cell phone is ringing. She looks around, then reaches over and grabs her phone.

Ashley answers her phone, "Hello."

Detective Simpson's voice, "Ashley, it's Natalie. I just got off the phone with Kevin. We have another body."

Ashley sighs, "Where at?"

Natalie replies, "Manhattan High School. Kevin and his team are already on the way."

Ashley replies, "I'll get Mr. Gibson and we'll be by to get you."

Natalie responds, "I'll be ready. See you soon."

The two detectives hang up. Ashley, still in her t-shirt and pajama pants, walks into the living room. She sees Mr. Gibson already dressed and sitting on the couch.

Mr. Gibson speaks, "I'll be sitting here whenever

you're ready."

Ashley nods, "I'll be back out in a few minutes."

Ashley walks back into her bedroom and shuts the door. She walks into her bathroom to get cleaned up. She looks in the mirror and wonders what this crime scene will bring.

Shortly after the phone call, Detective Taylor stops the car in front of Manhattan High School. Detective Simpson gets out of the passenger's seat, Mr. Gibson gets out of the back seat and Detective Taylor gets out of the driver's seat. The three of them start walking towards the school and the numerous uniformed officers.

As the three of them approach the officers by the entrance door, one of the officers speaks up, "It's the music room. The first set of doors on the left."

Detective Taylor, Detective Simpson and Mr. Gibson enter the school and see more uniformed officers down the hallway near the two large doors of the music room.

As they walk down the hall, Mr. Gibson speaks up, "A music room, very slick."

Detective Simpson questions, "What do you mean?"

Mr. Gibson replies, "It is sound proof."

Detective Taylor speaks up, "No one could hear a thing, even if standing right outside in the hallway."

The three of them walk into the music room and see Kevin taking a picture by the door to the small office in the back of the room. The three of them walk around the edge of the room slowly and as they get closer to Kevin, they see Alicia's body on the floor, laid out and dressed like all the others.

As the two detectives and Mr. Gibson walk up, Kevin puts down his camera, "Well, as you can see, it appears the same as all the others. The victim's name is Alicia Hannigan, age 28. The only clue left is the writing on the stomach."

All of them look down and see the letter "N" written on Alicia's stomach.

Detective Simpson speaks up, "I just wish we knew what the killer has been trying to tell us with these writings."

Kevin nods, "My team has processed the scene so we will go ahead and move the body if that's okay."

Detective Taylor is just staring at the body, "Sure." She pauses, "Oh, by the way."

Kevin nods, "Jennifer already talked to the principal. The victim always came in here after any end of school assembly."

Detective Taylor shakes her head, "Even with the warnings, people still don't change things up."

Mr. Gibson speaks up, "Because everyone thinks that it can't happen to them. Not in a city this size."

Detective Taylor looks up at Kevin, "Okay, go ahead and head back. We are going to talk to some of the staff. We will meet you back in the office."

Kevin nods and motions for his team to get everything loaded up and get the body ready to transport. Detective Taylor, Detective Simpson and Mr. Gibson walk out to go find the other teachers and talk with them.

It has been a few days since the last victim, and Detective Taylor finds herself walking into the conference room in the office as the sun is coming up. She puts some food in the refrigerator and walks down to the cork board at the end of the table. She stares at the pictures of the eleven victims. Then, the door opens and Detective Simpson walks in. Detective Taylor turns around to see who it is.

Detective Taylor smiles, "Morning Natalie."

Detective Simpson returns the smile, "Morning Ashley."

Detective Simpson puts her food up as Mr. Gibson and Kevin walk in.

Mr. Gibson speaks up, "Good morning everyone."

Detective Taylor and Detective Simpson both reply, "Good morning."

Mr. Gibson and Kevin put their food in the refrigerator and join Detective Simpson sitting at the table. Detective Taylor walks over to her chair and sits down.

Detective Taylor looks at Kevin, "Has Jennifer found anything else from Seattle?"

Kevin shakes his head, "Nothing yet. With records that old and not being on the computer, it is talking some time."

Detective Taylor nods, "Okay. I want to change focus for now."

Kevin and the others look at her.

Mr. Gibson questions, "What do you have in mind?"

Detective Taylor grabs one of the evidence bags from the table in front of her. Inside the bag is the old picture of a man in his twenties and a young boy.

Detective Taylor holds up the bag, "In four more victims, we are going to get a copy of this picture. I want her to find out who this is. The first killer could very well be in this picture."

Kevin nods, "I'll have her get on it right away."

At that moment, the door opens and Captain Sutherland is standing there.

Captain Sutherland speaks up, "I hope I'm not interrupting anything important."

Detective Taylor replies, "No sir. What do you need?"

Captain Sutherland smiles, "One of the teachers from the high school is out here. She said she just remembered something last night and wanted to tell you about it."

Detective Taylor smiles, "Sure. Have her come in sir."

Captain Sutherland steps inside and motions out the door. A black woman in her forties walks in. All of them recognize her as the music teacher from the school.

Detective Taylor speaks up, "Good morning Mrs. Jackson. How can we help you?"

Mrs. Jackson speaks, "I don't know if it will help, but Alicia told me about a guy she ran into just a day or two before she was killed. She seemed pretty smitten with him."

Mr. Gibson speaks up, "Did she tell you his name or anything about him?"

Mrs. Jackson replies, "She said his name was Phillip. She did say he was a good looking man with short, spiky brown hair with blonde highlights."

Detective Simpson questions, "Did she say what color he was or how tall?"

Mrs. Jackson thinks for a second, "She just said he was about average build, but she did say he was white." She pauses, "I don't know if it has anything to do with what happened or if this even helps, but I thought you should know."

Detective Taylor asks another question, "Did she say where she met him?"

Mrs. Jackson nods, "She said she bumped into him on the sidewalk right before school one morning."

Detective Taylor immediately looks a Mr. Gibson and sees Mr. Gibson nodding his head.

Detective Taylor speaks up, "It has to be him."

Detective Simpson jumps in, "That would fit perfectly with the idea that he knows each victim's routine to a tee."

Detective Taylor looks back to Mrs. Jackson, "Thank you very much." She looks at Kevin, "Go ahead and get with Jennifer about the picture."

Captain Sutherland looks at Mrs. Jackson, "Thank you

for coming forward with this information."

Captain Sutherland walks Mrs. Jackson out of the room and shuts the door.

Detective Simpson speaks up, "So, now we have an idea of what the killer might look like, and a possible name."

Detective Taylor nods, "The description gives us a little more, but I don't know about the name."

Mr. Gibson speaks up, "I would guess he gave her a fake name." He pauses, "But you know something that I never thought about or had in the previous case. What if the killer bumps into all of his victims a day or two before he kills them and this just happened to be the first person to come forward with the information."

Detective Taylor nods slightly, "That is a very good possibility. Something we could have definitely overlooked with all the previous interviews we've done." She pauses, "Natalie, you take the files from 1950 and glance through some of the interview notes to see if anything like that is mentioned. I'll take our case files."

Mr. Gibson speaks up, "I'll start going back through my files from 1975."

As Kevin is on the phone with Jennifer, the others start digging through the paperwork on the table in front of them. Each one feeling that they may have taken one more step closer to finding the identity of the killer.

Chapter 13

THE NEW YORK CITY nights have started to warm up some causing more and more of the homeless to start wandering the streets. The killer walks among the poor, downtrodden and runaways without standing out. The killer makes his way around the streets of downtown, staying to the shadows as he appears to be looking for someone and not wanting to be recognized.

From out of an alley not far in front of the killer emerges a young girl. She can be no more than 16 years old. She stands around 5'6" tall and weighs a scant 115 pounds. She is wearing tight jeans, tennis shoes and a long sleeve shirt. She has blue eyes and darker blonde hair that hangs below her shoulders. She is very attractive which causes most men to look her way.

As the young girl slides some money into her front pocket, a man walks out of the alley behind her. The man appears to be in his thirties and dressed as if he doesn't belong in this area of town. He whispers in the girl's ear, then heads for a nice car parked across the street. The young girl starts off down the street, unaware of the killer following closely in the shadows.

The young girl walks about six blocks and steps inside an all night diner. She walks over to a booth and sits down. The killer stands in the shadows across the street, watching the young girl through the windows of the diner. After she eats, the young girl walks out of the diner and starts down the street towards an old, abandoned building that use to be low rent apartments before it burned.

The killer follows the young girl as she stops at a fence that surrounds the building. Warning and keep out signs hang all over the fence, but the young girl glances around and when she is sure no one is watching, she ducks through a hole in the fence and heads for the building. She gets to the front doorway and slides between some of the boards that are meant to keep people out.

The young girl walks by numerous other homeless people in the main lobby area as she heads for a doorway in the back. She walks through the doorway and down a long hallway. As she approaches another doorway, she hears a man speak.

The older man's voice, "Is that you Rachel?"

Rachel turns around and sees an older man in the hallway behind her, "It's me Carl."

Rachel smiles at Carl. She likes the older man as she can remember the time when she first ran away and he took her in and protected her.

Carl walks up to Rachel, "I was worried about you."

Rachel continues to smile, "I went to get something to eat. Now I think its time to get some sleep." She pauses, "But you're still taking me to the park tomorrow, right?"

Carl smiles, "Of course."

Rachel gives Carl a hug, "Good night, I'll see you in the morning."

Carl hugs her back, "Good night sweetheart."

Carl walks back to the main lobby as Rachel walks into the back room. The room has a table with a couple of chairs and a mattress on the floor with a blanket. The room is dimly lit up by the lantern next to the bed. Rachel crawls into bed and covers up. She lays on her side facing away from the doorway and tears come to her eyes as she thinks about what she did with the man earlier so she could get some money to eat.

As Rachel drifts off to sleep, hoping to dream of happier times, she is completely unaware of the figure of a man, the killer, standing in the shadows of the doorway watching her.

As the sun peeks the horizon, casting the morning light over the city, Mr. Gibson finds himself wandering through Central Park. Still unable to shake the past images from his mind, Mr. Gibson tries to focus on the cases and anything he might have overlooked. He continues to walk and breath in the morning air. His gaze scans the area around him as he wonders where the next victim will be. He knows that time is running short before the killer strikes again.

Mr. Gibson is brought back to reality as he hears a young, female voice behind him, "Hey mister, you got any change?"

Mr. Gibson turns around and sees Rachel standing there, "Excuse me?"

Rachel breaks a slight, yet almost embarrassing smile, "You got any change?"

Mr. Gibson robotically digs in his pocket, his mind still on the killer as he pulls out a few dollars, "Here you go."

Mr. Gibson hands the money to Rachel and she smiles at him, "Thanks mister."

Rachel starts to walk off as Mr. Gibson turns back around. Before he walks off, Mr. Gibson glances back and watches Rachel disappear around a corner in the path. Mr. Gibson turns back the way he was walking and starts off again.

Ashley, Natalie, Kevin and Mr. Gibson find themselves sitting at the conference table late into another night. Each one looking over pictures, papers and their own notes, trying to piece together anything that might give them a break in the case.

Kevin puts down one of the copies of the picture of the young man and the baby, "This picture is so old, Jennifer will be lucky to find anything on it."

Mr. Gibson speaks up as he rubs his tired eyes, "No doubt if we cracked a few of the clues, the picture would make more sense."

Detective Simpson sits back, "Just like the writings on the bodies. It could be any number of combinations. It could be names, addresses or just a distraction."

Detective Taylor speaks up, "Well, something ties it all together and once we find that common thread, everything is going to fall into place."

Kevin looks up at the clock, "Whatever that common thread is, we better discover it soon cause we just ran out of time on the next victim."

The other three look up at the clock to see it is just after midnight. A collective, heavy sigh fills the room as each of them realize that they missed the next victim's deadline. Each one of them knows that the next phone call will be coming soon enough.

In the predawn hours of the city, Rachel weaves her

way through the city streets on her way back to the abandoned building where she has been staying. She thinks about the family she left behind when she ran away. As she passes the last alley before the building, she hears a glass bottle shatter just down the alley. Rachel freezes as her eyes stare down the alley. She wants to move, but her legs don't seem to be listening to what her mind is telling her. She is unsure how long she has held her breath, but she can feel the strain on her lungs.

At that moment, a couple of cats appear out of the shadows. Rachel lets out a long, relaxing sigh. She turns back to the building and a man is standing right next to her. Rachel freezes, unable to even let out a scream. It takes her only a moment to see that it is her friend, Carl.

Rachel lets out a nervous chuckle, "You scared me to death Carl."

Carl smiles at the young girl, "You should get inside. A couple of us are going to check the park for William. He didn't come in earlier."

Rachel takes a deep breath, "I'll help you look."

Carl shakes his head, "You need to get some rest, you've been up long enough."

Rachel smiles at Carl, "Okay, I'll see you in a few hours."

Carl and another man heads off down the street as Rachel heads for the hole in the fence around the abandoned building. A few moments later, the killer steps out of the shadows of the alley and walks slowly after Rachel.

Rachel slips through the hole in the fence, completely unaware of the killer just yards behind her. Rachel makes her way into the lobby area of the abandoned building. The burning candles cast some light on the sleeping bodies of the other homeless that share the building. Rachel makes her way for her room in the back as the killer enters the lobby and watches her disappear into the hallway in the back. As Rachel approaches her doorway, she notices that the light in her room is out.

Rachel speaks softly to herself, "Carl must be really worried to have forgotten to light the lantern before he left."

Rachel steps through the doorway into the pitch black room. She inches her way across the room and when she feels the mattress against her foot, she kneels down and slides across the mattress. Her hand slowly reaches out and searches the area for the lantern. Once Rachel feels the lantern, she goes through the steps of lighting it.

As the dim light flickers on, it exposes the killer who is standing at the edge of the mattress right behind Rachel. As the light flickers again, the killer strikes. His body comes down on Rachel, pinning her to the bed as the cloth is placed firmly over her nose and mouth. The look of terror crosses Rachel's face. The fear paralyses her for a few moments, then she begins to struggle. Rachel's scrawny frame is just no match for the killer as tears swell up in her eyes.

Rachel's eyes catch the killer's gaze and she recognizes the face from the day before. Then, her eyelids start to grow heavy as the chemicals take effect. Her vision starts to fade in and out as she gets a heavy feeling in her head.

The killer leans in and whispers in Rachel's ear, "Relax my young runaway Rachel, relax."

Then, the sixteen year old runaway's world goes dark.

It is a familiar scene as a Ford Taurus pulls up in front of the abandoned building that Rachel called home. Detective Simpson parks the car next to the two CSI vans. Detective Taylor gets out of the passenger's seat, Mr.

Gibson gets out of the back seat and Detective Simpson gets out of the driver's seat. The three of them walk over to the two officers standing by the hole in the security fence.

Detective Taylor is first through the fence, followed by Detective Simpson and then Mr. Gibson. The three of them start for the open door, each wondering who the victim is this time. The three of them enter the lobby area where there is ten uniform officers talking to the homeless people who reside in the building.

As the three of them cross the lobby, they can hear the clicking of the camera from down the back hallway. As they approach the hallway, they see Jennifer talking to Carl and they see Kevin at the doorway to Rachel's room, taking pictures of a body on the floor.

Jennifer looks at Detective Simpson, "This is Carl. He was kind of the man that watched over the victim."

Carl speaks with a heartbroken voice, "I just don't understand why someone would do this. She was such a sweet girl."

Detective Simpson questions, "Is there anything you can remember that might help us find who did this?"

As Detective Simpson talks with Carl, Detective Taylor and Mr. Gibson walk down the hallway towards Kevin. The two of them stop a few feet from Rachel's body and they can tell right away that she is young.

Kevin speaks with a heavy heart, "Victim is Rachel Wood, age 16. The best we know is that she ran away some time ago. I have one of my guys tracking down her family. We have gone through the area, but with all the traffic in here, I doubt we will find anything useful." He pauses, "All I'm sure of is the writing on the body."

Detective Taylor and Mr. Gibson look down at Rachel's body which is laid out like all the others and they see the letter "T" written on her stomach.

Mr. Gibson swallows hard, "I've seen her before."

Detective Taylor looks at him, "What?"

Mr. Gibson sighs, "She bummed some money off me a few days ago in the park."

Detective Simpson walks up, "Carl couldn't give us anything that helped."

Kevin speaks up, "We'll get the body back to the lab and check it out. I'll link up with you back in the conference room."

Detective Taylor gives a quick nod, "Alright."

Kevin and his team get Rachel's body and the rest of the equipment and leave the scene. Detective Taylor, Detective Simpson and Mr. Gibson walk around the crime scene, hoping something will stand out.

Chapter 14

DETECTIVE TAYLOR, DETECTIVE SIMPSON, Mr. Gibson and Kevin are sitting in a booth at one of the city's many fast food places during the busy lunch rush. Each one felt like they needed to get out of the conference room for a little while, hoping the change of scene might clear their heads.

Detective Taylor puts down her drink, "Okay, we know that this guy has a set plan. He is going to give us twenty-seven bodies, each with a letter or number." She takes another drink, "We also know that the phone call came at the same time and the other physical clues are going to be the same and come at the same time."

Mr. Gibson takes the last bite of his burger, "All the clues are like a giant puzzle and once we find the common factor, all the pieces will no doubt fall into place."

Detective Simpson chimes in, "And give us the killer."

Kevin puts down his drink, "You would think the clues would lead us to an obvious place, but I just don't see it." He pauses, "The killer wants to be caught, but we just can't find the direction he is leading us in."

Detective Taylor sighs, "The answer to the killer's identity has to be linked to Seattle. All the dates point to that case, but without the information on a computer, its going to be near impossible to find the needle in the haystack that we need."

Kevin speaks up, "I've decided that I'm going to see if Captain Sutherland will let me send Jennifer to Seattle. I think if she can do some onsite research, she might be able to come up with something."

Detective Taylor nods, "That's not a bad idea."

Detective Simpson looks at her watch, "I think we should be getting back."

Detective Taylor nods and the four of them get up from the booth. The four of them start for the door through the busy lunch crowd.

Detective Taylor speaks to the others, "I'm going to get a refill, I'll meet you at the car."

Detective Taylor heads for the counter as the others walk out the door and head for the car. Detective Taylor steps up to the drink machine and fills her cup and places the lid back on. Detective Taylor turns around and bumps into a man standing behind her.

The man speaks in a calm, smooth voice, a voice that was the last thing twelve women heard, "Excuse me. I'm sorry."

Detective Taylor smiles, completely unaware she is now face-to-face with the killer she is trying so hard to find, "I'm sorry. I guess I should be more careful."

The killer returns the smile, "I think I'll be okay."

Detective Taylor chuckles slightly and walks off as the killer refills his drink and returns to the table not far from where the detectives were sitting.

The killer is sitting at his dimly lit desk, writing in his journal. He puts down his pen and picks up a picture on the edge of the desk.

The killer speaks to the picture, "I'm sorry to say that there is not much hope for you. They have everything they need and yet, they can't see what is right in front of them."

The killer puts down the picture and closes his journal. He sits back and looks at the older journals that sit on the corner of his desk and thinks about the lives before him that has brought him to this place in his life.

The killer smiles at the journals, "Maybe we've overestimated law enforcement. They try to analyze every little thing instead of sitting back and looking at the big picture." He pauses, "Well, I guess they are just not ready yet. Too bad, I had high hopes for Detective Taylor."

The killer stands up, turns off the lamp and walks out of the room.

It is a warm night in New York City. The hustle and bustle of the city echoes through the seedy, downtown environment of bars and strip clubs. Even though it is well past midnight, there are plenty of men and women still on the streets, completely oblivious to the mounting serial killer case going on in their city.

In one of the strip clubs, the intoxicated patrons hear the one thing that puts a cloud over their happy evening.

The DJ comes over the speakers, "Okay everyone, this is the last dance of the night. Thank you for coming out."

As the music starts, a petite blonde takes the stage. She is about 5'4" tall and weighs a very nice 120 pounds. She looks to be near thirty years old with piercing blue eyes. The attractive dancer goes through her routine as the men sit around the edge of the stage.

The dancer makes her way to each person sitting around the stage. She stops in front of a man holding a twenty dollar bill and dances for him for a moment. Unknown to the dancer, she just met the man that has her in his sights for his next target. After sliding the money in the strap of the dancer's g-string, the killer gets up from the stage and makes his way for the front door.

As the music finishes, the bouncers start to get the patrons moving towards the front door as the dancer walks off the stage and heads for the dressing room in the back. As the club empties of it's patrons, the four dancers left start to change into their street clothes.

An attractive brunette looks at the blonde that just finished the last dance, "So Michelle, another good night down."

Michelle slides her jeans on, "You bet. I especially like the twenty dollar tips."

Another dancer speaks up, "Yea, I saw that guy slip you a twenty there at the end."

Michelle puts her t-shirt on to finish covering her incredible body, "Hey, it pays the bills and I'm not going to complain."

The other dancers let out a nice laugh, as they hear a man's voice, "You ladies dressed?"

Michelle yells back, "Yes."

A well built man in his thirties walks into the dressing room, "You ladies ready to go."

The four dancers follow the man out of the dressing room and across the club to the staff door. The four dancers walk out the door into the darkness of the city night that covers the parking lot where all their cars are parked. The bouncer locks up the door and turns around.

The bouncer smiles, "You ladies be safe going home. I'll wait until you're in your cars."

The four dancers make their way to each of their cars across the dimly lit parking lot. The bouncer gets in his car and starts the engine. He watches as the four dancers get into their cars. As the dancers start their cars, the bouncer drives off. Michelle starts to back up when she feels something break under her back tire. She puts the car in park as the last of her friends pull off the parking lot.

Michelle gets out of her car and walks back and looks down at her rear driver's side tire. She sees a broken bottle under her car.

Michelle sighs, "Great."

Suddenly, Michelle feels her body shoved against the trunk of her car as an arm wraps around her waist and a hand holding a cloth is placed firmly over her nose and mouth. The killer uses his body to pin Michelle against her car. A look of complete fear crosses Michelle's face. Her firm, dancer's body tries to struggle, but the killer is just too strong for her and she starts to get physically weaker.

Michelle starts to sob, fearful of what this person is going to do to her if she passes out. Her vision starts to fade as she can no longer struggle. Tears stream down her face.

The killer whispers in Michelle's ear, "Relax Michelle, my beautiful private dancer."

Michelle's eyes are just too heavy for her to hold open and she quickly passes into darkness.

In the early city morning, just before sunrise, Ashley finds herself in the conference room alone. She has the physical clues spread out on the table in front of her. She knows the date and knows that a call will be coming soon. She appears in deep thought as her eyes pass from one clue to the next, trying to piece them together. Her eyes pass over the blank birth certificate and blank death certificate. Her eyes then pass over the 1949 pennies and the 10 ounce bag of dirt. Ashley's eyes next cross over the minute hand of the grandfather clock and the piece of adoption form paper.

Ashley picks up the transcript from the killer's phone call and reads it over. Her eyes narrow and she looks back at the clues on the table as if something might have clicked.

Ashley speaks to herself, "It all deals with a beginning and the inevitable end. Time is the key."

Ashley nearly jumps out of her skin as her cell phone on the table rings. She looks at her phone and recognizes Natalie's number immediately. She knows it is the call she has been waiting for.

Ashley picks up her phone, "Hello."

Natalie's voice, "Kevin called. I'm on my way to get Mr. Gibson, then I'll pick you up."

Ashley replies, "Okay, I'm already at the station. I'll be waiting for you."

Natalie replies again, "I'll be there shortly."

The two detectives hang up. Ashley looks back at the table and the clues, trying to pick up her train of thought before the phone call.

Ashley speaks to herself again, "Specific dates on everything. The word, clockwork, in all three calls. Time has to be the hidden key, but why time." She pauses, "What are you trying to tell us?"

Ashley lets out a deep sigh. She knows that time is running out for them and possibly for someone close to her as she remembers what Mr. Gibson told her about the last victim in each case.

Detective Simpson pulls the car up next to the crime scene tape that has the parking lot of the strip club taped off. She parks the car and gets out. Ashley gets out of the passenger's seat and Mr. Gibson gets out of the back seat.

The three of them see Kevin at the back of the parking lot by Michelle's car, taking pictures. They see the other CSI team members searching the entire parking lot for possible clues.

The three of them duck under the crime scene tape and start walking towards Kevin. They each know what is laying on the far side of the car and they each wonder if the writing on the body will be the letter or number that starts bringing everything together. However, the looks on their faces are not as enthusiastic as the thoughts in their minds.

As the three of them step around the back of the car, Kevin takes his last picture. All of them look down at Michelle's body, laid out and dressed like all the others. They all focus on the letter "R" written on her stomach.

Kevin speaks up, "Victim is Michelle Potter, age 29. The M.O. is the same as the others. Once again, the killer had a picture perfect setup to get her alone." He pauses, "A couple from my team are talking to the bouncer and other dancers that worked last night, but I'm sure you know what that will turn up."

Mr. Gibson walks over to the driver's door and looks inside the car, then looks back and sees the broken glass on the pavement, "She got in the car, ran over the bottle and got out. That's when he attacked." He pauses, "So, if she started moving the car, then got out, I doubt she turned it off. So why is the car off and where are the keys?"

Kevin shakes his head, "We haven't turned up anything in the entire area. The killer must have kept them."

Detective Simpson speaks up, "A trophy from the victim. I wonder if he has taken something each time and we just haven't caught it yet?"

Detective Taylor sighs, "I don't think it matters. The killer is all about making sure we see the clues he wants us to see. If he was taking a trophy from each victim, he would have made sure we knew about it."

Kevin changes the subject, "Jennifer is in Seattle now. I called her and informed her of what we have here."

Detective Taylor nods while looking around, "We are not going to get anything else here. Kevin, once your ready, go ahead and clear the scene. We will see you back at the office."

Kevin nods and walks off with his camera and gets his team together. The CSI team loads up Michelle's body and the two vans pull off. After talking to the other dancers and the bouncer for a few minutes, Detective Taylor, Detective Simpson and Mr. Gibson leave the crime scene.

Chapter 15

ASHLEY IS SITTING ON a nice couch in the living room of a very nice house. There are a few small kid toys on the floor. It is late in the evening, but Ashley just needed a break from the office so she decided to go see her sister. At that moment, a very attractive woman in her late twenties to early thirties walks in. She is a little over six feet tall with a nicely put together 150 pound body. She has medium length brown hair and very nice bluish-hazel colored eyes.

Ashley speaks up, "So Allison, where is Paul and the little man?"

Allison smiles, "This is the night they do a big guy, little guy bonding thing so they will be gone until tomorrow afternoon."

Ashley chuckles, "Man, we should have had a girls night out. I could use a little distraction right now."

Allison sits in the chair across from the couch, "Things not going well with the case?"

Ashley shakes her head, "I don't think it could get much worse. It's been five months and thirteen victims and we are no closer to this guy than day one."

Allison does her best to be supportive, "I'm sure you'll get a break in the case, but if you ever need a little break, just come on by."

Ashley smiles at her sister and looks at her watch, "Thanks Al. I guess I should get going. Tomorrow I'll be getting another bad wake up call."

Ashley gets up and so does Allison. Allison follows her sister to the front door.

Ashley steps outside, turns and gives her sister a hug, "Make sure you lock up and keep the phone close."

Allison smiles, "You worry too much, but you know I will." She steps back inside, "Goodnight Ash."

Ashley smiles back, "Goodnight sis."

Ashley walks off to her car. As Allison closes the door and locks it, Ashley drives off. Allison walks into the living room, picks up the glasses they were drinking from and walks into the kitchen. She puts the glasses in the sink, when suddenly an arm wraps around her waist and a white cloth is firmly placed over her nose and mouth. Allison's face is that of complete terror.

Allison manages a muffled scream, "Ashley!"

Suddenly, Ashley sits up in her bed at home, sweating and breathing heavily. She blinks her eyes back into focus as she does her best to slow her rapid breathing. She looks over at the alarm clock next to her bed and it shows 5 am. She throws her covers off to reveal her pajama pants that go with her tank top.

Ashley gets out of bed and walks into the bathroom. She turns on some warm water from the sink, bends down and splashes her face with the water. She looks up and stares into the mirror over the sink.

As Ashley's breathing returns to normal, she speaks to her image in the mirror, "I have to stop him."

Ashley wipes her face off and returns to her bedroom to get ready for the day.

It's a rainy night in the city. The old, yet beautiful downtown church is nearly empty. A woman in her early forties, standing 5'6" tall and weighing a nice looking 140 pounds with shoulder length brown hair and charming brown eyes is walking around the church putting out the prayer candles. She is very attractive, not looking her age. She is wearing loose fitting jeans and a sleeveless v-neck top. As she walks to the next set of candles near the large cross at the stage area of the church, she hears the door to the confessional booth open and close.

The woman puts out a few candles as a man steps up next to her. The man faces the large cross, lowers his head and crosses himself. The woman is completely unaware that she is a mere two feet from a serial killer.

The killer speaks to the woman while looking at the cross, "Good evening Miss. Be safe going home in this weather."

The woman replies while putting out another candle, "Good evening. You be safe as well."

The killer walks out of the church as the woman puts out the last candle. A few seconds later, the priest walks up to the woman. He is a tall man in his late fifties.

The priest speaks, "The last of the patrons has left so I'm going back to my office, then heading home. Be safe tonight Diane."

Diane smiles, "I will. I'll finish locking up and I'll see you Wednesday."

The priest returns the smile, "Well, goodnight."

Diane replies, "Goodnight."

The priest walks off to the back of the church. Diane walks around to ensure all the outer windows and doors are closed and locked. She walks over to the small foyer just off to the side of the main door. She grabs her jacket and umbrella. She puts her jacket on and walks to the main door. She opens the door, steps outside, locks the door and closes it.

After making sure the door is secure, Diane turns around and opens her umbrella. She starts down the twenty steps that lead to the sidewalk. She gets to the street and hails a taxi, completely oblivious to the man that watches her from only a few yards away.

The killer smiles to himself as he watches Diane get in the taxi and the taxi drives off. The killer walks up the stairs to the main door of the church. Once he is sure nobody is watching, the killer pulls a small device out of his pocket and in a matter of seconds, the lock clicks and the killer opens the door just enough to slip inside. The killer locks the door behind him. He scans the church with an evil smile and stare on his face.

It's early morning in the city as Detective Taylor, Detective Simpson, Mr. Gibson and Kevin are sitting around the table in the conference room. The paperwork has piled up even more than before from the addition of each new victim.

Detective Taylor looks at Kevin, "Have we got anything from Jennifer in Seattle?"

Kevin shakes his head, "Not yet. She has started with 1950 and she is working her way backwards. So far all she has that stands out is the two big cases that we already knew about. The serial killer and Michael Newman running away."

Detective Simpson sighs, "Nothing on the picture of the man and the kid?"

Kevin sits back, "Nope. Unfortunately, most of the records were either lost or destroyed during the depression so she is having trouble finding information from before the 1930's."

Mr. Gibson speaks up, "I just don't understand this one picture." He holds up the picture of the clearing in the woods, "Every other clue deals with time in some way or another."

Detective Simpson questions, "What do you mean?"

Mr. Gibson explains, "The first, a piece of adoption paper and the clock hand, it refers to beginning of new life and time directly. The second, bag of dirt, obviously a reference to death and burial. The third, pennies on the eyes, reference to the old myth of paying the boatman to cross the river after death." He pauses and continues, "The fourth, picture of man and child, I presume the beginning of a family. The fifth, blank birth and death certificates, obviously signifies the beginning and ending of life." He pauses once more and continues, "But this picture shows nothing. A grassy opening in some unknown wooded area. It just doesn't fit in with the others."

Kevin speaks up, "But we know it has to have some meaning. What doesn't make sense to me is the writings on the bodies. Is there a hidden clue about a certain time in the writings?"

Detective Simpson interjects, "No, not time. The last clue before the final note is a location, not a certain time." She pauses then continues as if it was obvious all along, "The numbers and letters are a location, an address."

Kevin looks at Detective Simpson, "An address, to what?"

Detective Taylor jumps in, "To the killer's location. The killer's house maybe."

Kevin speaks up, "Even just putting the writings in order of possible addresses, do you know how many possible combinations we are looking at?"

Mr. Gibson nods, "Enough combinations that would take well beyond this case to sort through, but what if one

of the addresses stands out and fits with the other clues."
He looks at Detective Taylor, "It's worth taking a shot."

Detective Taylor nods in agreement, "I'll take any
kind of possible progress right now." She looks at
Detective Simpson, "Get with the computer team and have
them focus the writings on just possible addresses."

Detective Simpson stands up, "I'm on it."

Detective Simpson walks out of the room.

Detective Taylor looks at Kevin, "Get with Jennifer
and let her know what we have come up with so far. Maybe
something will stand out in her research if she knows
where we are focusing."

Kevin stands up and walks out of the room to go call
Jennifer.

Detective Taylor looks up at the clock on the wall,
then looks at Mr. Gibson, "Speaking of time. Our next
victim is running out of time. I don't see us making it."

Mr. Gibson tries to stay enthusiastic, "Maybe not and
this may sound cold, but at least we are taking some
direction and forward steps."

Detective Taylor nods slightly, "But how many more
will be killed before we reach the answer?"

Mr. Gibson sighs and leaves the question unanswered.
However, the both of them have a look on their face that
says, at least one more victim, we know that for sure.

It is a surprisingly cool night in the city. Diane,
wearing loose fitting jeans and a long sleeve top, is
walking around putting out the prayer candles for the night.
As the last person leaves the church, the priest walks over
to Diane.

The priest smiles, "Goodnight Diane, be safe going
home."

Diane returns the smile, "I will. Have a good evening father."

The priest walks off towards the back. Diane puts out the last of the candles, assuming she is all alone now. As she walks by the confessional, she stops, and looks back over her shoulder as the dim light of one last glowing candle burns. She gets a puzzled look, sure she put all the candles out. Diane walks back over to the candle unaware of the figure moving slowly in the shadows towards the main door.

Diane puts the candle out and turns back around to leave. She walks for the main door. The inside of the church is mostly shadows now and Diane is completely unaware of the man she is walking almost directly towards. The killer quietly waits as his victim is seemingly walking straight to him. Diane walks over to the doorway to the foyer where her jacket is hanging. As she steps just inside the doorway and reaches out for her jacket, the killer appears right behind her.

The killer quickly wraps his left arm around Diane as his right hand places the cloth over her nose and mouth. As a shocked and horrified look crosses her face, the killer uses his weight to force Diane into the foyer and against the wall. Diane begins to struggle, but it is obvious that the killer is just too strong for her, especially with the chemicals on the cloth starting to take effect.

Diane starts to try and plead with the killer as her vision starts to blur. The killer seems oblivious to Diane's muffled pleading as he continues on with his work like an emotionless robot. Diane's head starts to feel heavy as she starts to fade in and out of consciousness.

The killer calmly whispers in her ear, "Relax my devoted Diane. You will see him soon enough."

As the killer finishes his words, Diane passes into the darkness.

Just as the sun starts to break through the morning sky, Ashley turns the first corner into her morning run. She has her hair pulled back into a ponytail. She is wearing sweatpants, t-shirt and running shoes. She has a waist pack on carrying her backup pistol and a bottle of water. She turns another corner and she hears a car approaching from behind, moving slowly.

Ashley knows that very few people are out on this road at this time of day. She moves her hand down slowly towards her pistol as she wonders if the car behind her is driven by the killer. As the car gets closer, Ashley quickly draws her pistol and spins around on the car. The car suddenly stops. Ashley lowers her pistol as she recognizes Natalie in the driver's seat and Mr. Gibson in the passenger's seat.

Ashley walks up to the driver's window as Natalie lowers the window.

Ashley puts her pistol away, "What's up?"

Natalie replies solemnly, "Kevin called me. The next victim has been found." She pauses, "I thought we agreed to change our normal routines. Is this not the same route you run every other day at this time."

Ashley lets out a slight smile, "I don't think the killer is targeting me, or you for that matter, but point well taken."

Ashley opens the back door on the driver's side and gets into the car. Natalie turns the car around and heads off down the road. As the car disappears, the killer steps out of the trees about two hundred feet up the road from where Ashley stopped running.

Chapter 16

NATALIE STOPS THE CAR next to Kevin's van that is parked in front of the church where Diane worked. Numerous police cars line the street as pedestrians start to gather to see what all the commotion is about. Natalie, Ashley and Mr. Gibson get out of the car and start up the steps towards the front door of the church. The three of them pass one of Kevin's investigators as they enter the church. They see Kevin standing by the large cross at the podium where the priest gives his sermons. They also see a police officer talking to the priest.

Natalie speaks up, "I'll go talk to the priest if you two want to get with Kevin."

Ashley nods, "Okay."

Ashley and Mr. Gibson walk towards Kevin as Natalie heads over to the priest.

As Ashley and Mr. Gibson draw closer to Kevin, they see Diane's body laying on the floor, dressed and laid out just like all the other victims. Ashley and Mr. Gibson stop next to Kevin.

Kevin starts to speak, "The victim is Diane Lewis, age 42. As you can see, she appears to have been killed just like all the others. The only clue that we could find is the letter written on the body."

Ashley and Mr. Gibson look down and see the letter "N" written on Diane's stomach.

Kevin continues, "I guess no place is sacred to this guy. A church for crying out loud."

At that time, Natalie walks up with the priest behind her.

The priest speaks obviously upset, "To do something like this in a house of the lord, this person is pure evil. No doubt hell has a place for him."

Ashley looks over to Kevin, "Better go ahead and move the body. The crowd is already starting to gather outside."

Kevin nods and starts motioning for his team to get everything together.

Ashley turns to the priest, "I'm sorry for your loss. Whoever did this, we will catch him."

The priest nods slightly, "I'll pray for you." He pauses, "I'll also ask God to send this person's soul straight into the fires of hell."

Mr. Gibson speaks up, "What about God's forgiveness."

The priest is quiet for a second, "Only if he repents and truly asks for forgiveness may his soul be saved, but tell me sir, do you think this person will do that?"

Mr. Gibson shakes his head slightly, "I know he won't."

Kevin and his team leaves. Ashley, Natalie and Mr. Gibson walk around the church for a little while and then they too leave the church.

In the early morning hours of the day, Ashley sits

quietly in the conference room by herself. She looks at the board at the end of the table and the pictures of the 14 victims. She knows that time is running out and they are not really any closer to the identity of the killer. A few minutes pass and Natalie walks into the room with Mr. Gibson behind her.

Ashley looks over to them, "Good morning."

Natalie replies still sounding tired, "Morning Ashley."

Mr. Gibson just nods and sits down next to Ashley. Natalie takes a seat across the table from the two of them. A quietness hangs over the room, mostly due to the lack of sleep over the months that the case has been going on.

Ashley finally starts, "We know everything is about starting, ending and time. I think that is the clues that will give us the answers we need."

Natalie nods slightly, "We have to find something to go along with the idea of the writings being an address. I stopped by the computer forensics office before leaving last night and the number of possibilities is overwhelming."

Mr. Gibson chimes in, "I think Ashley is right. Everything is so focused on time and dates." He pauses, "Maybe it's not the specific dates, but the concept of time and dates that is the clue."

Natalie questions, "What do you mean?"

Mr. Gibson explains, "We know that the killer has specific reasons for the dates and times that he has chosen, but what if it goes deeper than that." He pauses losing his train of thought, "I don't know."

Ashley speaks up, "Maybe you're onto something. Time, the beginning and end with the natural progression, just like someone's life." She pauses, "Maybe not the killer's life, but someone else important to the case."

Mr. Gibson looks puzzled, "What are you saying?"

Ashley explains her idea, "Maybe the clues are not about the killer, but someone else important to the case.

Maybe the clues focus on a person during that time that holds the answers to the case." She pauses, "Its pretty thin isn't it?"

Natalie chimes in, "No, I see where you're going with it. Someone else's life holds the answers to who the killer is, his identity. If we can figure out who the killer is pointing us to, then the clues might start piecing themselves together."

Mr. Gibson nods in agreement, "You know, as crazy as it sounds, that actually makes sense."

Ashley picks up the picture of the man and the young baby, "The next physical clue we are going to get is no doubt a picture of the person's name that we need."

Natalie sighs, "Well, lets start digging through the clues again and see if anything stands out more."

Ashley, Natalie and Mr. Gibson start shuffling through the mountain of papers on the table in front of them. Each one feels that they have made another discovery that is moving them closer to the killer.

It's a warm summer morning in a more lower income part of the city. A beautiful dark skinned young lady with blonde highlighted hair and deep brown eyes walks into a small, local coffee shop. She is wearing jeans, tennis shoes and a sleeveless tank top that covers her 5'6" 135 pound well fit body with nice curves.

The older man working behind the counter smiles when he sees the attractive young woman walk into the shop, "Good morning Jessica."

Jessica gives a heartwarming smile back, "Good morning Bill."

Bill starts to grab a cup, "The usual sweetheart?"

Jessica lets out a slight laugh, "You know me too well

Bill."

Bill starts to make the cup of coffee as the bell on the door rings. Both of them take no notice of the man that has just walked into the shop.

Bill continues to make the cup of coffee, "So, what's on the agenda for today Jess?"

Jessica digs in her purse for the money for the coffee, "It's my big sister day for the week."

Bill places the cup of coffee on the counter, "That's right. This old mind of mine doesn't work as good as it use to."

Jessica smiles and holds out the dollar bill, "Oh now Bill."

Bill slides the coffee towards her and shakes his head, "Jess, you know I'm not going to take that. You do too much for the community here."

Jessica puts the money away, leans over, kisses Bill on the cheek and grabs the cup of coffee, "Thanks Bill. You have a good day."

Bill smiles, "You too Jess."

As Jessica turns to leave, Bill looks at the man standing behind her, "What can I get for you sir?"

The serial killer glances over at Jessica as she walks out the front door, then turns back to Bill, "Coffee, black. I'm kind of in a hurry this morning."

As Bill makes the coffee, the serial killer puts a dollar bill on the counter.

It is a cool, rainy morning in the city of Seattle. Jennifer walks up to the doors of the city library. She closes her umbrella as she walks into the building. She wipes off her feet and walks towards the counter in the beautiful, old building.

Jennifer walks up to the older lady behind the counter, "Excuse me miss."

The older lady looks up at Jennifer, "Can I help you young lady?"

Jennifer holds up her badge, "I'm Detective Harris from New York. I've been working with the Seattle Police Department and the Sheriff's Office on a case and we are kind of stuck." She pauses, "I was wondering if you could help me?"

The older lady smiles, "I'll certainly try."

Jennifer reaches into the inside pocket of her jacket and pulls out the old picture of the young man and the little child, "I was wondering if you could tell me who this picture might be of?"

Jennifer hands the lady the picture. The lady looks at the picture closely.

After a minute, the lady hands the picture back, "It looks really old. I wish I could help, but I don't recognize it."

Jennifer takes the picture and sighs, "Thanks anyway."

Then the lady gives Jennifer a glimpse of hope, "There is someone who might be able to help you." She pauses, "Her name is Mrs. Littlefield. She is the lady that ran the library for many years and she just turned 100 years old and all of them were spent here in Seattle."

Jennifer questions, "Where can I find her?"

The older lady replies, "She lives out on Old Mill Road now. I think it is 10127. It's kind of the only house around so its hard to miss."

Jennifer smiles, "I'll find it. Thank you so much."

The older lady returns the smile, "No problem honey."

Jennifer heads for the main doors as she has a revitalized look on her face.

It's a warm New York City night as Jessica enters the six story, brick apartment building where she lives. As she gets on the elevator, she pulls out her cell phone and presses the speed dial number one.

Jessica presses the number five button on the elevator as she speaks into her phone, "Carrie, its Jess. I made it home okay." She smiles, "I swear you're like a mother to me, making sure I get home okay."

Jessica chuckles then continues, "Okay, I'll see you in the morning. Good night."

Jessica hangs up the phone and puts it back in her purse as the elevator door opens up to the fifth floor. The building is old, but not in too bad of a condition for this part of town. Jessica walks down the hallway towards her apartment door when the lights in the hallway flicker off, then come back on.

Jessica speaks to herself as she pulls her keys out and stops at the door marked number 512, "I guess they didn't get that fixed today."

Jessica unlocks the door and steps inside. She flips on the light switch next to the door and closes the door behind her. She locks the door handle, the deadbolt and then slides the chain lock on. She turns around and walks into the small living room of the apartment. Along one wall is a couch and chair with a coffee table and across the room from them is the entertainment center. On top of the entertainment center is a picture of a middle aged couple.

Jessica walks through the living room, placing her keys on the coffee table and she walks into the kitchen. She opens the refrigerator and pulls out the milk. She grabs a glass from the cabinet, pours her a glass of milk and returns the carton to the fridge. She turns around and walks towards the closed door across the kitchen from the fridge.

Jessica takes a drink as she opens the door and steps into her bedroom. A queen sized bed is across the room from the door with a nightstand next to it. Along the same wall as the door is a dresser. Just to her right as she walks into the bedroom is the bathroom door and it's closed as is the closet door in the far corner.

Jessica puts her glass on the dresser next to another picture of the middle aged couple in a picture frame that says "In Loving Memory" across the top of it. Jessica takes her shoes, jeans and tank top off, opens the dresser and pulls out her pajamas and puts them on. She leaves her clothes on the floor and walks back to the kitchen as she takes her last drink of milk. She washes out the glass and places it in the sink.

Jessica turns and walks back to her bedroom. She opens the bathroom door and turns on the light. She steps over to the sink in the decent sized bathroom. She grabs her toothbrush and turns on the water. She brushes her teeth and with the water running, she doesn't hear the faint noise of the closet door in her bedroom opening.

Jessica leans down and spits into the sink. When she looks back up, her eyes widen in horror as the image of a man, the serial killer, is in the mirror right behind her. Before she can move, the killer has his left arm around Jessica's waist and his right hand places the cloth firmly over her nose and mouth. She drops her toothbrush into the sink with the running water as the killer drags her into the bedroom.

Jessica struggles as tears come to her eyes. It quickly hits her that the man is just too strong and she can feel her body getting weaker.

Jessica manages a sobbing word muffled by the cloth, "Please."

The killer spins Jessica around and uses his weight to force her down onto the bed. Jessica feels the weight of the killer on top of her, but her head feels so heavy now and she can't hardly move any part of her body.

As Jessica's eyes start to glaze over, the killer whispers in her ear, "Relax beautiful Jessica, you will be seeing your mom and dad soon enough."

At that moment, Jessica passes out into the darkness.

Chapter 17

IN THE COOL, DAMP Seattle morning, a Sheriff's Deputy car slowly approaches the aging house on Old Mill Road. Jennifer sits quietly in the passenger's seat, holding the unknown picture tightly in her hands.

As they draw closer to the house, Jennifer speaks, "I hope Mrs. Littlefield will speak with us today. Each day that she lets this go on, the closer it gets to another victim in New York."

The male deputy replies, "Mrs. Littlefield is the longest living resident in Seattle, but her mind has been fading over the years and her health is not the best so she might not be able to help us if she is even up to speaking with us."

The car pulls into the driveway and stops. Jennifer and the deputy get out and make their way up to the stairs of the front porch to the front door. The deputy opens the screen door and knocks on the heavy wooden door. A minute passes and no one answers as the deputy knocks again. Jennifer's expression turns to that of rejection, just knowing that another day will slip away.

Then, as if an unanswered prayer was just granted,

they hear slow movement approach the front door from inside. A moment later, the door opens to reveal the elderly lady that Jennifer hopes can shed some light on the case.

The deputy speaks, "Mrs. Littlefield, how are you today?"

Mrs. Littlefield gives the young deputy a smile, "I'm okay. What can I do for you young man?"

The deputy explains, "I'm Deputy Cook and this is Detective Jennifer Harris from New York City. She was wondering if she could ask you a couple questions that involves some old history about Seattle."

Mrs. Littlefield seems excited to see someone think that she could be useful again after so many years, "Why sure, come in."

Mrs. Littlefield steps back and slowly walks into the living room as Deputy Cook and Jennifer follow her. Jennifer is in awe of all the old antiques in the house, and she especially takes notice of the grandfather clock.

Mrs. Littlefield sits in her chair by the couch, "Please have a seat."

Jennifer sits on the couch closest to Mrs. Littlefield and Deputy Cook sits next to her.

Jennifer smiles at the older lady, "Your antiques are amazing."

Mrs. Littlefield smiles, "Thank you young miss. Many years of collecting. So, what can I help you with?"

Jennifer explains, "I have a very old picture and we have been unable to find any information on it. I thought that maybe you might be able to give me an idea of who the picture is of."

Jennifer hands the picture to Mrs. Littlefield. The older lady puts on her glasses that hang around her neck.

Mrs. Littlefield speaks, "This is an old picture. I would guess from the 1920's or 1930's maybe."

Jennifer smiles, "That is what we also figure. Do you know who it might be of?"

Mrs. Littlefield is quiet again as she stares closer at the picture. Jennifer's smile leaves her face as the seconds pass and she can only figure that she has ran into another dead end.

Mrs. Littlefield finally speaks, "You know, I'm not absolutely certain, but the young man in the picture just might be Thomas Newman."

The name, Newman, instantly catches Jennifer's attention as she remembers the story of the missing child, Michael Newman.

Jennifer questions, "Thomas Newman?"

Mrs. Littlefield continues, "Yes. He started a very prominent clock making business here in Seattle back in 1920 and his wife started the O'Kelly adoption centers, opening the first one here in Seattle in 1924."

Jennifer's eyes widen as she instantly thinks about the first two clues left with the first body, the hand of a grandfather clock and the piece of adoption form paper. She knows Mrs. Littlefield must be right.

Jennifer smiles, "Do you think the child in the picture is their son, Michael?"

Mrs. Littlefield replies, "I'm not sure. Michael wasn't born until 1935. Thomas put such a terrible amount of pressure on that boy. No wonder the child ran away when he was 14. Then those horrible killings started and everyone forgot about Michael Newman running away."

Jennifer knows from the date testing that the picture is most likely from the 1920's, "So, if the picture was taken before Michael Newman was born, do you know who the young child might be?"

Mrs. Littlefield shakes her head, "I'm not sure. The Newman's took in a child many years before Michael was born, but no one in town knew anything about that child or whatever happened to him." She pauses, "I remember Thomas Newman commented only once about the child, saying that they sent the boy to boarding school. I'm afraid

I don't know much more than that."

Jennifer gives Mrs. Littlefield a huge smile, "Thank you so much. You have really helped me with this information."

Mrs. Littlefield hands the picture back, "If you need to talk to me again, just stop by."

Jennifer takes the picture and stands up, "Thank you."

Jennifer and Deputy Cook make their way out of the house.

As they walk to the car, Jennifer speaks, "We need to get back to the station so I can call New York and tell them that we might have a positive ID on one of the people in the picture. Then we research some more to verify the information."

Deputy Cook nods as the two of them get into the car and start on the way back to the city.

That very same morning across the country in New York City, a very familiar scene is unfolding at a six story, brick apartment building in a lower income part of the city. The apartment building where Jessica lives.

Police cars line the street and block the entrance to the apartment building. A few minutes later, Detective Taylor drives up with Detective Simpson and Mr. Gibson. The three of them get out of the unmarked car.

As they walk towards the building, Ashley speaks, "Well, this is the victim that should have the picture with it."

Natalie replies, "This sounds bad, but I hope so cause if the killer changes the pattern now that would really set us back."

Mr. Gibson chimes in, "He won't change."

The three of them enter the building and walk over to

the elevator. They all notice the lack of any kind of security for the building.

As the elevator doors close, Natalie comments, "This place has no security what so ever. The killer could easily get in and out unnoticed."

Ashley sighs and Mr. Gibson remains quiet, but nods in agreement. The elevator stops at the fifth floor and the doors open. The three of them can see Kevin at the far end of the hallway. They walk by numerous police officers and other crime scene investigators as they approach Kevin. The three of them also see Jessica's body laying on the floor in front of the apartment door. The body is dressed and laid out like all the others. Kevin nods at the three of them as they walk up.

Ashley gives a quick nod back, "So, what do we have?"

Kevin explains, "Victim is Jessica Adams, age 23. Everything appears to be the same as the other victims. She has the letter 'H' written on her stomach and we found the old picture of the young man and child next to her head, tucked under the corner of the pillow."

Kevin pulls out the evidence bag holding the picture from his case and hands it to Ashley. Ashley looks at the picture and shakes her head. She flips the picture over and sees a date written on the back in black marker. The date is 1924.

Ashley lets out a sigh, "Just like the others. The killer even wrote the 1924 date on the back of the picture."

As Ashley hands the picture to Natalie, Kevin's cell phone rings. Ashley squats next to the body and so does Mr. Gibson. Both of them are unaware of the phone conversation Kevin is having.

Ashley speaks to Mr. Gibson, "Something in the case has to turn for us."

Kevin hangs up his phone and looks over to Ashley, "Something just might have."

Natalie looks up at Kevin, "What?"

Kevin smiles, "That was Jennifer. She might have a possible ID of the young man in the picture. She said to call her when we get back to the station and she will tell us about it."

Ashley nods and stands up, "Have your team go ahead and move the body and finish processing the scene. We will go ahead and head back to the station."

Kevin nods and walks off.

Natalie looks at Ashley, "Finally, a break."

Ashley sighs, "It had to happen sooner or later."

Mr. Gibson brings them back to reality, "Lets not get too excited until we know what we have. Remember, this killer is very intelligent and may already have thought of this."

Ashley nods, "You're right. Lets get back and see what she found out."

The three of them head back out of the apartment building the same way they came in. Each one not wanting to get their hopes up, but each one also a little excited that they might have some vital information on the identity of the killer.

The killer sits at his dimly lit desk. He is writing in his personal journal. Another picture sits on the edge of the desk, no doubt the next victim.

As he writes, the killer speaks to himself, "I'm over halfway through the plan and they still have nothing. I expected more from Detective Taylor and the others." He pauses, "Maybe you both were right. Maybe they just can't see the hidden clues."

The killer writes a little more, then puts down the pen and closes the journal.

The killer sits back and talks to himself again, "I think they will figure out part of it, but the one hidden clue that they need, I just don't think they will figure it out. It is so subtle that I don't think they will see it."

The killer lets out a sigh, then picks up the picture on the edge of the desk, "Time to start working on the next piece to the puzzle."

The killer stands up, turns off the lamp and walks out of the dark room.

Ashley, Natalie, Kevin and Mr. Gibson are sitting in the conference room back at the police station. All four of them are excited to hear what Jennifer has found out. Kevin grabs the phone and drags it over to the table covered in papers and pictures and places the phone in the middle of the table. Kevin presses the speakerphone button and dials the phone number for Jennifer.

The phone rings twice, then Jennifer's voice, "Detective Harris."

Kevin speaks up, "Jennifer, it's Kevin. We are all here. What did you find out?"

Jennifer explains, "I met with someone and showed her the picture. She believes the man in the picture is Thomas Newman."

Ashley looks at the others and they all have the look of recognizing the name.

Jennifer continues, "I'm pretty sure the lady is right."

Natalie questions, "How certain are you?"

Jennifer replies, "I'm still looking into Thomas Newman, but given that he was a famous clockmaker and his wife dealt with adoptions, I'd say it's a real good chance."

Ashley nods, "It fits the first two physical clues

perfectly. Did she know who the child might be?"

Jennifer answers less confidently, "Not really. She mentioned their son, Michael, but the date on the back of the picture is far too early for it to be him." She pauses, "She mentioned that the Newman's adopted a child years before they had Michael, but she wasn't sure of the child's name."

Mr. Gibson questions, "Did she say what happened to that child?"

Jennifer replies, "All she said is that Thomas Newman commented only once that they sent the child to boarding school, then they never spoke of the child again."

Ashley comments, "So, Thomas Newman and this unknown child, but why is the picture important?"

Jennifer speaks, "I'm going back to the library to try and find out more information on Thomas Newman. Hopefully there is something that will stand out in his past."

Mr. Gibson speaks up, "No doubt the picture is meant to point us to Thomas Newman because he fits in with the clock clue and his wife fits with the adoption clue. But what about the other clues?"

Ashley speaks up, "We will have to try and figure out where they fit into all this while Jennifer finds out more about Thomas Newman and why the killer has directed us to him." She pauses, "Good work Jennifer, keep us posted on what you find out."

Jennifer responds proudly, "I will. Talk to you soon. Bye."

The line goes quiet and Kevin presses the speakerphone button to hang the phone up.

Natalie speaks up first, "I'll go get with the computer lab. Now that we know the killer is pointing us to Thomas Newman, maybe one of the addresses will point us to a house or location owned by him or someone named Newman."

Kevin comments, "It will still be a lot of options, but at least we are narrowing it down some. I'll give you a hand."

Ashley nods, "Okay. We will start back through the clues and see what might fit in with the Thomas Newman theory now and maybe find out why the other clues are so important now that we do know for a fact that these physical clues do have meaning and do point us to something."

Natalie and Kevin exit the room with haste as Mr. Gibson sits back in his chair and for the first time, he lets a smile come to his face.

Ashley looks at Mr. Gibson, "You're smiling. I didn't think that was possible."

Mr. Gibson replies, "Up until now, I knew everything about the case and was able to provide all the information to you. Now, I'm right there with you, in uncharted water. We've gone beyond the previous borders on this case." He pauses, "I'm excited, I feel like a new detective again. Like I've got another chance to stop this killer."

Ashley smiles, "That's exactly what we are going to do. Catch him and put an end to all this."

Ashley and Mr. Gibson both sit forward and get started in on the paperwork and clues, hoping that something will stand out more now that they have a name to go along with.

Chapter 18

THE WARM, MID-DAY SUN lights up the sky over New York City. The citizens continue on with their day as if not knowing anything has been going on in the city over the last few months. In one of the nicer neighborhoods of the city, two cars pull up in front of a beautiful, three bedroom, two story house on a nice corner lot.

A tall, short haired blonde gets out of the first car. She looks to be in her early thirties and is wearing a nice female suit that covers her near 5'10" tall 155 pound well figured body. She smiles at the young couple that gets out of the car behind hers.

The blonde lady speaks as she walks towards the house, passing by a realtor sign, "I told you it was nice."

The young man nods, "It's very nice Miss Edwards."

Miss Edwards smiles, "Please, call me Jenna. Shall we take a look inside?"

The young lady keeps walking towards the house, "Definitely."

Jenna looks at the young man, "I think someone likes it."

The three of them walk up the few steps to the large

porch. Jenna pulls out a key and unlocks the front door. As the three of them step inside, Jenna turns off the security alarm next to the front door.

Jenna starts her sales pitch, "As you can see, the house has a new alarm system which whoever buys the house can change the security code."

The young couple just looks around at the huge house in disbelief that something so nice could be in their price range.

Jenna continues to speak, "Shall we start in the living room?"

The young man nods, "Sure."

Jenna leads the couple into the living room and continues to pitch the house. She walks the young couple through each of the downstairs rooms and then the three of them walk upstairs. Jenna pitches each room they walk into, making sure to point out the two large bathrooms and the fact that each bedroom has large, walk-in closets.

As they walk out of the last bedroom and start for the stairs, Jenna speaks, "So, Tom, Mary, what do you think?"

Mary smiles with approval, "I really like it. It's in such good shape."

Tom nods in agreement, "It's the best house we've seen so far. I like the corner lot and the neighborhood."

Jenna smiles, "It's such a quiet neighborhood, nothing ever happens around here." She pauses, "Well, if you would like me to, I'll call you in a week when the finishing touches on the new bathrooms are complete."

Tom looks at Mary and nods, "Sure, that would be great."

Jenna smiles and the three of them walk down the stairs to the front door. Jenna opens the door. Tom and Mary walk outside as Jenna turns the alarm back on, locks the door, steps outside and closes the door. The three of them talk as they walk to their cars. All three are so excited that they don't even notice the figure of the killer looking at them from one of the bedroom windows on the second floor.

In the early morning hours of the new day, as the citizens of New York go about their usual day, Ashley sits in the conference room, looking over the massive amount of paperwork this case has brought. She sits in silence, waiting for the others to arrive. The long hours show on her face, but the information Mr. Gibson told her about the last victim keeps her going. The fact that the last victim is someone close to the detective and the dreams she has had about the killer targeting her sister drive her on. At that time, Mr. Gibson and Natalie walk in.

Ashley lets out a tired smile, "Good morning you two."

Mr. Gibson nods quickly, "Good morning."

Natalie smiles, "Good morning Ashley."

Ashley sits back in her seat as Kevin walks in. Mr. Gibson and Natalie sit down while Kevin puts his lunch in the small refrigerator.

Kevin walks over and takes his seat at the table, "Good morning everyone."

All three of them reply within moments of each other, "Good morning."

Ashley starts in, "I talked to Jennifer last night to see what she has come up with so far because we all know the date and what is coming." She pauses, "She told me that information is hard to come by, online and the old records in the library."

Mr. Gibson questions, "Has she got anything that will help so far?"

Ashley shakes her head, "Not really. Just some factual information. Thomas Newman was born in Atlanta in

1899. His family moved to Seattle in 1915 and he took over the family business of making clocks in 1920." She pauses, "He married Maureen O'Kelly in 1921. Then in 1924, the picture appears of him and the unknown child. After that, nothing until we know that Michael Newman was born in 1935. Then, nothing until Michael Newman runs away in 1949."

Ashley stops to take a drink and Kevin speaks up, "No, that doesn't really help much."

Ashley continues, "She did find something I thought was interesting."

Natalie quickly speaks up, "What was that?"

Ashley explains, "She said that Thomas Newman and his wife moved out of Seattle in 1974."

Kevin questions, "Why is that interesting?"

Ashley drops the information on them, "Because they moved to Kansas City."

Mr. Gibson immediately picks up what Ashley is talking about, "The killings started in Kansas City the very next year. Almost as if it followed them to my city from Seattle." He pauses, "What about New York?"

Ashley shakes her head, "Thomas Newman died in 1989."

Mr. Gibson sits back, "Still, it is not just by luck that the killer picked Kansas City the very next year after Thomas Newman moved there. That has to mean something."

Ashley nods, "That's what I'm thinking too." She looks at Natalie, "Have we got anything from the computer lab?"

Natalie dejectedly shakes her head, "Nothing yet. There is still too many variables involved. The options have narrowed, but not much."

Ashley lets out a sigh, "Unless something major breaks, we're not going to make it by the next victim."

Mr. Gibson speaks up, "All we can do is keep

plugging away at it. We know far more now than before and no telling what today might bring us."

Kevin nods, "He's right. We just keep pushing forward. Something is going to break for us eventually."

Ashley stares at Mr. Gibson and he can tell by the look on her face that she is thinking about the victims, especially the last victim being someone close to her.

Mr. Gibson nods slightly, "Well, shall we get started."

Ashley lets out a smile, "Absolutely."

The four of them start looking through the massive amount of papers that line the table in front of them, knowing the answer is there somewhere.

Jenna is sitting at her desk in her nice little corner office. She is looking over some of the prospective buyers for some of the houses she is selling. She takes a drink of coffee when the phone rings.

Jenna puts down the coffee and answers the phone, "Reynolds Real Estate, this is Jenna."

A man's voice replies, "This is Robert Billings with Billings Interior. I was calling to let you know that the work is done on the house you asked us to touch up if you wanted to check it out."

Jenna replies with a smile, "That's great. I'll go by and check it out tomorrow. The buyers will be so happy that it's ready."

Mr. Billings responds, "If you see anything else after you check on it tomorrow, just give my office a call."

Jenna sits back in her plush leather office chair, "I will. Thank you very much. Have a good day. Bye."

Jenna hangs up the phone and returns to shuffling through her papers. She knows she has one more sale done and wants to get started on the next.

In his dimly lit lair, the killer sits quietly writing in his journal. The scratching of the pen on the paper makes an eerie sound in the poorly lit room. The shadow of the killer that is cast by the desk lamp looks as if a ghost is sitting in the chair. As the scratching of the pen on the paper stops, the killer lets out a haunting sigh, almost deathlike.

The killer closes the journal and picks up the picture sitting on the edge of the desk and speaks in a very low, evil tone, "Too late detectives. You are too late to save this one."

The killer rises out of the chair almost as if rising like an apparition out of thin air. The killer turns off the desk lamp and slowly walks out of the dark room.

It's a warm, mid-morning day in New York City. The sun is bright and warm with a soft breeze blowing a few clouds across the suburban sky. A near perfect day for the selling of a house is what is going through Jenna's mind as she pulls up in front of the house she showed to Tom and Mary. Jenna gets out of the car and takes in the fresh, soft blowing breeze.

Jenna walks up to the front door and pulls out her keys for the house. She unlocks the door and walks inside. She turns and punches in the security code to turn off the security alarm. She closes the door behind her and locks it out of habit. She walks into the kitchen and smiles at the completed work. She knows that Tom and Mary are really going to like it. Jenna then walks upstairs to see how the bathrooms turned out. When she reaches the top of the stairs, she turns left and starts for the bedroom at the end of the hallway.

Thinking she heard something in the bedroom at the other end of the hallway, Jenna stops and turns around just before she walks into the bedroom she decided to check first. She shakes the puzzled look off her face and continues into the bedroom. She walks through the bedroom and into the bathroom on the far side of the room.

The big smile on Jenna's face shows how much she likes how the bathroom turned out. She walks back into the bedroom and passes the walk-in closet door as she digs in her purse for her cellular phone. She flips the phone open and starts to dial Tom and Mary's number. On the sixth digit, the right hand of the killer quickly wraps around Jenna from behind and places a cloth over her nose and mouth. At the same time, the killer wraps his strong left arm around Jenna's waist.

A look of panic and fear crosses Jenna's face. She instantly starts to struggle with the killer, but the killer's hold is just too strong for her. Jenna suddenly brings her right hand up and looks at the incompleted number she was going to dial. She does the only thing that comes to her mind, she presses the last number of Tom and Mary's phone number into the phone.

The killer realizes what Jenna is trying to do. The killer wraps his right leg around Jenna's legs and trips her forward. As her thumb moves towards the "talk" button, her body falls towards the floor. Just before her thumb presses the button, she lands hard on the floor with the killer on top of her. The force of the impact sends the air out of her body and her phone out of her hand. She whimpers, hoping the call was made and that someone might hear her.

Jenna sees her phone lying open just a foot from her right hand. Her teary eyes can see the phone number on the screen, but they display also shows the she never completed the call. As her strength fades, Jenna stretches her right hand out, but is well short of the phone. She can feel her head getting heavier and her vision starts to blur out the phone.

The killer whispers softly in her ear, "Relax, my real estate selling Jenna. This sale will be over soon."

The chemicals finally do their job and Jenna passes away into the darkness.

As the sun starts to break across the sky, Ashley is asleep on her couch still in her clothes from the day before. Papers from the case are laying all over the floor around the couch and beer cans cover the coffee table in front of the couch. Ashley is completely exhausted as her cellular phone starts ringing on the coffee table, but Ashley doesn't even move. The phone rings a few times, then the voice message answers the call.

The phone beeps to show a message was left. Ashley moves a little and in a few more seconds, the phone starts ringing again. Ashley's eyes slowly open and come into some kind of focus. Ashley reaches out and grabs the phone from the coffee table. Natalie's name appears on the caller identification.

Ashley opens the phone and answers in a tired voice, "Hello."

Natalie's voice comes over the phone, "The next victim was found just 30 minutes ago. Kevin is on his way. I'm going to get Mr. Gibson and we'll be there to pick you up shortly."

Ashley lets out a sigh, "I'll be ready."

Ashley hangs up the phone and slowly sits up on the couch. She looks down at all the pictures and papers on the floor.

In a frustrating swing, Ashley knocks some of the

empty beer cans off the coffee table, "Damn it!"

Ashley slowly stands and walks towards her bedroom to get ready for the new day with the all to familiar work that waits for her.

Chapter 19

IN THE WARM MORNING sun, the usually quiet suburban neighborhood's silence is shattered by the sirens of police cars, the hustle and bustle of news reporters and the curious public. Yellow police tape has the once beautiful house in the quiet neighborhood blocked off from the rest of the world. A familiar car pulls up in front of the house. Ashley gets out of the back seat, Mr. Gibson gets out of the passenger's seat and Natalie gets out of the driver's seat.

The three of them make their way through the news reporters to the police tape. They duck under the police tape and they can see Kevin standing on the porch snapping pictures. The three of them walk towards the porch, each one scanning the area as if they might catch a glimpse of the killer. As the three of them reach the top step of the porch, they see Jenna's body laying in front of the front door. The body is dressed and laid out just like all the others.

Kevin snaps one more picture, then turns to the others, "The victim is Jenna Edwards, age 34. As you can probably guess, she was killed just like the others. I've had my team going through the house, top to bottom, and so far, nothing." He pauses, "The only clue appears to be the letter written on the body."

Ashley walks around the body and steps inside the house. Natalie looks down at Jenna's body to see the letter "Y" written on her stomach. Mr. Gibson can see Ashley is thinking about something and follows her inside the house. Natalie and Kevin look at each other and follow the others into the house. Ashley is standing about ten feet inside the front door. Mr. Gibson is right behind her as Kevin and Natalie walk up.

Mr. Gibson questions, "What is it Ashley?"

Ashley glances around, "This house is for sale I would guess by the sign in the front yard."

Kevin nods, "Yes. One of my guys talked to her boss on the phone to see about the house. She was suppose to close on it today now that all the repairs were done."

Mr. Gibson looks at Kevin, "Someone was working on the house?"

Kevin nods, "Yes. An interior construction company."

Ashley's eyes lock on the security pad next to the front door, "We need to talk to everyone that did work on this house."

Natalie questions, "What are you getting at Ashley?"

Ashley replies with a slight smile, "Because someone had to know the security code to get in."

Kevin, Mr. Gibson and Natalie all look over and see what Ashley is staring at.

Mr. Gibson nods, "It's a long shot, but you're right. Maybe our killer was working here, or was at least around when the workers were here."

Natalie replies, "I'll call the real estate company and see who they contracted with."

Natalie walks out of the house.

Kevin speaks up, "I'm going to get the body to the lab."

Ashley questions, "Did any of your people find her personal belongings? I doubt she came here in just a white bra and panties."

Kevin shakes his head, "No. We figure the killer must have taken them."

Mr. Gibson pipes up, "She must have had a cell phone."

Natalie walks back up, "I got the name of the company."

Kevin questions, "What are you saying Mr. Gibson?"

Ashley chimes in knowing what Mr. Gibson is saying, "That is an idea worth a try."

Natalie gets a puzzled look, "Did I miss something?"

Mr. Gibson continues, "We call her cell phone and see if we can track it's location. Maybe we'll get lucky."

Ashley looks at Kevin, "Go ahead and wrap up the scene and move the body. Natalie, call the company and get her cell phone number. I'm going to contact our techs and get them going on the tracking equipment."

Kevin walks off and starts gathering up his team. Natalie and Ashley both get on the phone as Mr. Gibson starts slowly walking back towards the car. Natalie and Ashley walk up behind Mr. Gibson and they both hang up their phones at the same time.

Natalie speaks, "I've got the number."

Ashley nods, "The tech team will be ready in about fifteen minutes."

Ashley gets in the driver's seat. Natalie gets in the passenger's seat and Mr. Gibson gets in the back seat.

Ashley hands her phone to Mr. Gibson, "Use my phone to keep calling her cell phone. Natalie, you stay on the phone with the tech team and tell me where we need to go."

Mr. Gibson takes the phone and punches in the number that Natalie gives him. He waits for the word to start the call. Ashley starts up the car and slowly drives off down the street.

The killer is walking down an alley in a residential neighborhood. It is a nice neighborhood in a suburban area of the city. Suddenly, he hears a phone ringing and feels his jacket pocket vibrating. The killer reaches into the pocket and pulls out Jenna's cell phone. An evil smile comes to his face as he sees the number on the phone.

The killer shakes his head, "Awe, Detective Taylor."

The killer flips the phone open and presses the "talk" button.

Mr. Gibson is sitting in the backseat of the car with Ashley's cell phone in his hand. Natalie looks at Mr. Gibson when she hears him say something she did not expect.

Mr. Gibson speaks into the phone, "Hello." He pauses, "Hello."

Ashley also glances in the mirror to look at Mr. Gibson, not believing what she is hearing.

Natalie speaks into her phone, "Anything yet?"

Mr. Gibson continues, "I know you can hear me, even if you don't want to talk."

Ashley glances at Natalie in disbelief, "Did the killer answer the phone?"

Natalie shrugs, then nods, "Northeast Ashley."

Ashley nods, does a u-turn and heads back towards the freeway entrance.

Mr. Gibson continues to speak, "I hope you know that we are going to catch you. We know your clues."

Natalie shakes her head and looks at Ashley, "I can't

believe he made such a mistake of taking the phone, and then answering it."

Ashley's eyes narrow some, "Not this guy. He is up to something. He has to know we are tracking the call."

Natalie nods, "Okay." She glances at Ashley, "Keep going northeast, out in the suburbs."

Mr. Gibson speaks again, "It's going to end this year. Your luck is going to finally run out."

Ashley looks over at Natalie, "Have they got a lock on the location yet?"

Natalie's face loses all expression of excitement, "What was the address again?" She pauses, "Are you sure?"

Ashley looks at Natalie again, "What is it?"

Natalie looks at Ashley with disbelief, not able to say anything.

Ashley questions harder, "Natalie, what's the address?"

Natalie replies with a hollow voice, "It's your sister's house."

Ashley's face loses all expression quickly followed by a look of concern in her eyes, "Jesus."

Natalie continues, "The signal stopped at her house."

Ashley pushes the accelerator to the floor as the sirens have all the other traffic moving out of the way.

Natalie shuts her phone, "I'm going to call your sister's house."

Ashley looks into the mirror and sees the look on Mr. Gibson's face as he stares at her in the mirror.

Natalie shuts her phone, "It's busy."

Ashley pushes even harder on the accelerator as if it would make the car go faster. All she can think about is her sister, her brother-in-law and their little boy. Ashley pushes the car to it's limits through the neighborhood. What seems like an eternity since the drive started finally ends as Ashley brings the car to a screeching stop in front of her sister's house.

Ashley jumps out of the driver's seat, draws her pistol and runs for the front door. Natalie is right behind her with her pistol drawn. Mr. Gibson is a mere two steps behind with his revolver in one hand and the cell phone in his other.

Ashley mashes the doorbell and screams, "Allison! Allison!"

Ashley is breathing heavy as she digs her keys out of her pocket, then they hear a phone ringing. Natalie and Ashley both look at Mr. Gibson.

Mr. Gibson speaks, "I redialed the number."

The three of them can hear the phone ringing and they all start to look around the porch, but they don't see anything laying around. Then Ashley's eyes focus on the mailbox attached to the house next to the door. Ashley walks over to the mailbox opens the top and reaches inside. Ashley pulls out Jenna's cell phone as Mr. Gibson hangs up.

Natalie speaks, "This is crazy."

At that moment, the front door opens. Still jumpy, Ashley, Natalie and Mr. Gibson all turn to the door with their guns ready.

Allison is standing in the doorway, "What's going on?"

Ashley lets out a sigh and lowers her gun, quickly followed by Natalie and Mr. Gibson. Allison has a look of concern on her face.

Allison questions again, "What is it?"

Ashley, not wanting to scare her sister, comes up with a quick story, "We were in the area and dispatch told us of a possible fire set at your house by an arson." She pauses and smiles, "I can see it's just another prank call."

Allison looks at her sister like she is crazy, "Yea, everything here is fine. Since you're here, would you like to come in for a minute?"

Natalie picks up the story quickly, "Sure, we have a few minutes."

Ashley slides Jenna's cell phone into her pocket without her sister noticing. In all the excitement, none of them noticed the man standing in the trees across the street. The killer smiles to himself as he watches the four of them walk back into the house.

It is the predawn hours in New York City. As most citizens are getting ready for the day, Ashley walks into the police department conference room which has become more like her home. The tired look on her face shows the months of long hours and sleepless nights she has suffered since the case began. She puts her food in the small refrigerator and walks down to the end of the table where the pictures of all the victims hang on the board.

A few minutes pass, then the door opens and Captain Sutherland walks in. Ashley, deep in thought, doesn't even realize he is in the room.

Captain Sutherland walks up next to Ashley, "Detective Taylor, I heard about the cell phone left at your sister's house."

Ashley comes out of her trance and looks at Captain Sutherland, "I'm surprised it went a few days without you hearing about it."

Captain Sutherland gives a slight smile, "This guy is just trying to get in your head. He is trying to distract you. I think he is worried that you're getting closer to his identity."

Ashley slightly chuckles, "He didn't have to pull a stunt like that to get in my head. This case is like nothing I've ever dealt with before. It's become an obsession."

Captain Sutherland nods slightly, "Just keep at it. If

you want, I'll create some off duty overtime and have people watch your sister's house."

Ashley, not wanting to reveal what Mr. Gibson had told her, nods slightly, "It's just a mind game. I don't think she is in any danger right now." She pauses, "Thanks anyway Captain."

Captain Sutherland sighs and nods, "Let me know if there is anything I can do."

Ashley smiles slightly, "I will Captain."

Captain Sutherland walks out of the room and Ashley returns her stare to the board and the pictures of the victims. She knows deep down inside that if she doesn't do something to catch this killer, the last picture will be someone she loves.

In his dimly lit room, the killer sits with his journal open. The soft scratching of the pen on paper echoes in the darkness like an eerie, ghostly sound.

As the killer writes, he speaks to himself, "I'm in your head now Detective Taylor. I would even bet you're having nightmares about me."

The killer continues to scratch away in his journal. He stops briefly to glance over at the picture of his next victim that is laying on the edge of his desk.

The killer speaks to himself again, "But do you think I would show you my cards so soon when it comes to the person I'm targeting that is close to you. Surely you would know me better than that by now."

The killer scratches a couple more lines in his journal, then puts down his pen. He picks up the picture and sits back in his chair.

The killer lets out a hollow sigh, "Time for the next one Detective Taylor."

The killer rises out of the chair and turns off the light. He slowly walks out of the pitch black room.

Chapter 20

IT IS A HOT summer night in New York City. The outside air is filled with the noises of car engines and horns. The normal smells of the evening dinners being cooked in all the restaurants fills the air with the exhausts from the thousands of vehicles. Inside a small boxing gym in the old downtown area, the only noise is that of fists pounding away on a heavy bag and the only smell is that of sweat.

The old style gym has a boxing ring in the middle of the large room. Around the boxing ring are different workout stations including a heavy bag, speed bag, weight set and an open area for jumping rope and other aerobic exercises. The room is dimly lit and no outside lights are shining in.

At the heavy bag is a young woman looking to be in her early twenties. She is stands around 5'6" tall and weighs a trim and firm 130 pounds. She has long brown hair pulled back in a ponytail and brown eyes. She is wearing a tight fitting tank top, sweat pants, boxing shoes and boxing gloves.

She breathes heavy as she pounds away on the heavy bag. She appears to know something about boxing as her boxing form looks fairly good. She stops for a minute and she hears someone walking up behind her. She turns around and sees an older black gentleman with a smile on his face.

The man nods, "Looking good Miss George. The next champ."

Miss George returns the smile, "Ray, there is only one champ standing here."

The older man looks down a little embarrsed, "That was many lifetimes ago Miss George." He pauses, "You wanted to know when it was ten. I'm going to lock the doors and go on home."

Miss George nods, "Okay. I'll see you tomorrow Ray."

Ray turns to leave and Miss George takes her gloves off.

Ray turns back to Miss George, "If you don't mind me saying Miss George, your dad would be proud of you keeping the old gym going."

Miss George smiles and glances around, "Dad loved this place and it was the least I could do." She pauses, "Ray, you've known me since I was a baby. You can call me Summer."

Ray smiles and looks down, "That wouldn't be proper Miss George. You have a good night now."

Summer nods, "You too Ray."

Ray turns and walks off. Summer heads for the back of the gym and walks through an open doorway with the words, "locker room", painted over it. She tosses the gloves in a basket, grabs a towel that is hanging on the wall next to the basket and heads for the shower area.

In the mid-day heat of the city, Ashley, Natalie and

Mr. Gibson are sitting in a booth at a fast food restaurant. They are completely oblivious to the lunch rush of people around them. As they eat their food, they discuss the case that has caused so many sleepless nights.

Ashley is first to speak, "So, lets look at what we know about Thomas Newman again." She pauses, "Born in Atlanta in 1899. That would explain the dirt from Atlanta and also the clock hand."

Natalie speaks up, "He moved to Seattle in 1915 and took over the clock business in 1920. The obvious connection to Seattle."

Mr. Gibson takes his turn, "He married Maureen O'Kelly in 1921. She opened the adoption centers so that explains the piece of adoption paper."

Ashley nods, "Then in 1924, the picture of Thomas Newman and the unknown child is taken. We are not sure what the child has to do with anything, maybe nothing at all since Thomas Newman is the focus."

Natalie chimes in, "Then in 1935, Michael Newman is born, heir to the Thomas Newman empire. That would explain the upcoming clue of the blank birth certificate from 1935."

Mr. Gibson speaks up, "Michael Newman runs away due to intense pressure in 1949. That explains the pennies from 1949 and the twist of the upcoming blank death certificate from 1949." He pauses, "The death certificate could signal the death of the Thomas Newman empire and not specifically a person."

Ashley puts down her drink, "That would be the kind of twist this killer would throw at us. Then of course, the killings start in 1950." She pauses, "Then Thomas Newman moves to Kansas City and behold, the very next year, the killings start again."

Natalie lets out a sigh, "Think about this for a second. What if the original killer was Thomas Newman? He might have gone over the edge when his son abandoned him."

Mr. Gibson nods slightly, "You know, that is an idea. He could have done the killings in 1950 and found someone in Kansas City to carry on after him."

Ashley puts down her fries, "The only thing is that he dies in 1989. So, whoever is killing here in New York would have to have carried on from the killer in Kansas City." She pauses, "But then that would fit into our serial killer bloodline theory we have."

Natalie nods and puts down her drink, "The only thing that doesn't make sense is the picture of the grassy opening in the trees. It doesn't fit with anything we have so far."

Mr. Gibson puts down his fries, "Maybe that is the one thing that we just haven't discovered yet. The hidden clue to the identity of the killer or the location of the killer." He pauses, "Or it could just be mind games. The killers have all seemed good at that. The one little thing to throw you off."

Ashley sits back, "I just hope Jennifer can dig more up on Thomas Newman. We are running out of time before the next victim." She looks at her watch, "We better get back to the office."

The three of them gather up their things, get out of the booth and throw their trash away. They walk out of the busy fast food restaurant under the watchful eye of the killer.

It is another rainy afternoon in Seattle. The storm clouds and the rain have not deterred Jennifer from continuing on in her investigation. She pulls her rental car up in front of the Sheriff's Office. She gets out and jogs to the front doors. She walks in and looks around for Deputy Cook. Jennifer spots Deputy Cook and walks over to him.

Jennifer smiles, "Hey, wonderful day we are having."

Deputy Cook returns the smile, "Is there something I can help you with Detective Harris?"

Jennifer nods and lowers her voice, "I found out that the Newman mansion is abandoned, but still stands. I was wondering if I could get inside and take a look around?"

Deputy Cook stands up, "Let me get it cleared through the boss and we can head that way if he says it's okay."

Jennifer nods, "Okay."

Deputy Cook walks off and Jennifer glances around the office area. She knows she is being watched by some of the other officers. A few minutes pass and Deputy Cook walks back up.

Deputy Cook smiles, "You want to follow me or ride with me?"

Jennifer shows a heartwarming smile, "I'll just ride with you."

Jennifer follows Deputy Cook out of the office and through the rain to his car. The two of them get in the police car and head off north.

Ashley, Natalie and Mr. Gibson walk into the conference room back at the station. They see Kevin putting push pins into a map of New York City on another cork board next to the one with the pictures of the victims.

Kevin turns to the three of them, "I was thinking that maybe the locations of the bodies might form some kind of pattern on the map." He pauses, "I've also got a Seattle and Kansas City map."

Ashley nods and smiles, "Anything that might help, I'm open to."

Ashley, Natalie and Mr. Gibson walk around the table to start helping Kevin.

Kevin speaks while pushing in the next pin, "Jennifer

called. She is on the way to check out the abandoned house of Thomas Newman."

Natalie unrolls the map of Seattle, "Maybe she will find the prize that the final note mentions."

Mr. Gibson smiles, "If we could only get that lucky."

The four of them continue to plot the locations of all the victims on the three city maps. They each hope that Jennifer will turn something up to help them.

The ominous clouds slowly move across the rainy, afternoon sky in Seattle. Jennifer looks out the passenger window of Deputy Cook's car at the large mansion in the distance. The trees and grass has grown up and looks like it hasn't been cared for in awhile. Deputy Cook pulls off the main road into the beginning of a long driveway. About a hundred feet down the driveway is a large iron gate that is standing open.

The vegetation has grown up through the iron gate and covers the brick security wall surrounding the estate. Deputy Cook slowly drives up the driveway to the mansion. He parks the car near the front door and shuts the car off. Jennifer gets out of the passenger seat and closes the door behind her. Deputy Cook also gets out of the car.

Jennifer glances around, "It looks like a scene from a horror movie."

Deputy Cook walks up beside Jennifer, "Nobody's been up here in years."

Jennifer walks up on the huge front porch. Deputy Cook retrieves a crowbar from his trunk and joins Jennifer on the porch. The front door is big and has a few boards nailed over it. Deputy Cook pries a few of the boards off as Jennifer looks around. He grabs the door handle and turns it. The latch clicks open and he pushes the large door open.

The door creaks and moans from years of being closed.

Jennifer smiles at Deputy Cook, "That was a nice sound."

Jennifer reaches inside her jacket and pulls out a small flashlight from her belt. She turns on her flashlight and walks inside the mansion. Deputy Cook pulls out his flashlight and follows Jennifer inside. They find themselves in a large foyer with a staircase in front of them and an open doorway to both the right and left. Jennifer can tell that the now dark and melancholy scene must have looked very grand back in the days when the Newman's lived here.

Jennifer starts to slowly walk to her left and the floor moans under her feet as the sound of dripping water fills the air.

Jennifer inhales and quickly covers her nose, "It smells like something died in here."

Deputy Cook nods not nearly as affected by the smell, "Animals could get in here. There is probably a few dead ones around."

Jennifer walks into the room on the left and finds herself in a large room with a fireplace. She figures it must have been the living room. Deputy Cook is standing right behind her when they both hear a scratching noise.

Jennifer looks at Deputy Cook, "Do you hear that?"

Deputy Cook nods, "It sounds like its coming from over by the fireplace."

Deputy Cook hands Jennifer the crowbar and he pulls out his pistol. The two of them slowly walk towards the fireplace and the scratching noise gets louder. The two of them get a few feet from the fireplace. Both beams from the flashlights are pointed at the fireplace when a raccoon suddenly runs out of the fireplace. Jennifer and Deputy Cook both hop backwards as the raccoon runs by them and out the front door.

Jennifer lets out a deep sigh, "That was fun." She

pauses to catch her breath, "I don't know how much we will find here. The house looks like an empty shell."

Deputy Cook slows down his breathing, "It would make sense. I'm sure the Newman's took everything with them when they moved to Kansas City."

Jennifer nods slightly, "Lets see if we can get upstairs to the bedrooms, then we can head back."

Deputy Cook nods and follows Jennifer back into the main foyer. The two of them make their way up the very old and creaky staircase.

It is another hot night in New York City. As the thousands of citizens go about their nightly routine, so does Summer. The small, downtown boxing gym has the smell of sweat mixed with bleach in the air. Summer, dressed in her workout outfit, pounds away on the heavy bag. She stops for a minute and she hears the cleaning cart rolling across the floor behind her. Summer turns around and sees Ray pushing the cleaning cart over next to the wall. Summer turns and hits the heavy bag a few more times, then stops. Summer pulls her gloves off as she walks towards Ray.

Ray smiles at Summer, "I've finished cleaning so I'm going to lock up and head home Miss George, if it's okay?"

Summer returns the smile, "Of course Ray. I'll see you in the morning."

Ray nods slightly, "You have a good night Miss George."

Summer leans close and gives Ray a kiss on the cheek, "You too Ray."

Ray smiles and looks down, "Thank you Miss George."

Summer gives Ray a heartwarming smile as Ray turns

and walks off. Summer watches Ray lock the front door and close it behind him as he leaves. Summer walks for the locker room. She walks through the open doorway and tosses her gloves in the basket. She grabs a towel off the wall and heads for the showers in the back.

Summer steps inside the large, open shower room which is lined in white tile and has ten showerheads along the walls. She turns on one of the showers and walks back out of the shower. She walks over to the old metal, six foot tall lockers. She opens the locker on the end and some regular clothes are hanging inside.

Suddenly, Summer's head lunges forward with great force and slams into the inside of the metal locker door. The force is so great that the sound echoes through the entire gym. Summer's eyes look like someone who just got hit by a powerful punch. Already somewhat knocked out, Summer can do nothing to stop the killer from placing the cloth over her nose and mouth as his left arm wraps around her waist.

The killer uses his body weight to pin Summer up against the lockers. Summer struggles the best she can, but the blow to the head has taken a lot out of her as trickles of blood come down her face from her forehead. She can feel her head getting heavy and her vision starts to blur. As the killer pulls her back from the locker, Summer's eyes lock onto the picture of her dad that hangs on the inside of her locker door. Summer can feel her body getting weaker and she knows that she is about to pass out.

The killer leans in and whispers in Summer's ear, "Relax Summer, my boxing beauty, just relax."

It is the last thing Summer hears as she pass into the darkness.

Chapter 21

WITH THE SUN JUST breaking through the morning sky, police cars surround the downtown boxing gym owned by Summer. Two CSI vans are parked near the entrance to the gym. Yellow police tape separates the gruesome scene inside the gym from the people beginning to gather outside the gym to see what is happening.

At that time, the familiar car of Ashley and Natalie pulls up. Ashley gets out of the driver's seat, Natalie gets out of the passenger's seat and Mr. Gibson gets out of the back seat. The three of them make their way pass the couple of news crews that have already started setting up for the story. The three of them duck under the police tape and walk into the entrance of the gym. They see Kevin in the back near the doorway to the locker room.

Kevin snaps his last picture as Ashley, Natalie and Mr. Gibson walk up. Kevin puts his camera down on his suitcase. Summer's body is laid out and dressed just like all the others. They all see the letter "N" written on her stomach.

Kevin speaks to the others, "The victim's name is Summer George, age 22. So far everything appears to be the same. My team hasn't turned up anything. It appears that the only clue is the letter on the body." He pauses, "One of my guys talked to the janitor. He locks up and leaves every night at 10 pm. After he leaves, the victim is here alone."

Ashley squats down next to the body and whispers to herself, "What are you spelling?"

Ashley looks over the body. She sees the same marks around the wrists and ankles. She also sees the mark around the neck.

Ashley shakes her head and lets out a sigh, "I'm sorry Summer George."

Ashley stands back up, "Lets look around some, then we should get back to the station and contact Jennifer to see if she has anything new."

Natalie nods, "I'll talk to the janitor again while you two check things out."

Ashley nods and Natalie walks off. Ashley and Mr. Gibson walk into the locker room. Kevin motions for his team to get Summer's body ready for transport.

In the late morning day, Ashley, Natalie and Mr. Gibson walk into the conference room back at the station. The table is covered with pictures, case files and newspapers. The corkboards with the city maps and pictures of the victims surround the table. The three of them all take a seat and start looking through some of the pictures and case files. A few minutes later, Kevin walks in with the new photos.

Kevin sets the pictures on the table and grabs the phone, "Here are the new photos. I'm going to call Jennifer to see if she has anything new."

Natalie and Ashley start glancing through the pictures.

Kevin presses the speakerphone button and dials the number. The phone rings a couple of times.

Jennifer's voice answers the phone, "Detective Harris."

Kevin speaks, "Hey Jennifer, this is Kevin. The others are also here."

Jennifer replies, "So, was the calendar still correct? Did we get another victim this morning?"

Kevin replies a little upset, "Yes. All we got was another letter on the body."

Ashley speaks up, "Did your search of the old Newman house give you anything?"

Jennifer replies a little frustrated, "No. It was completely empty of personal effects. Deputy Cook told me that the Newman's reportedly took everything with them when they moved to Kansas City."

Natalie speaks up, "So, maybe their personal effects are in Kansas City."

Jennifer replies, "Most likely. I still have some things I'd like to look into here, then I thought I would head to Kansas City to see if I might be able to track down Thomas Newman's things." She pauses, "There just might be something in their personal belongings that could shed some light on the subject."

Mr. Gibson speaks up, "While you're still checking into things in Seattle, I'll make some phone calls and see if I can get some help in Kansas City."

Jennifer replies, "Sounds good to me."

Ashley speaks again, "Okay. We'll let you get back to it. Thanks Jennifer."

Jennifer replies, "I'll be talking to you soon. Bye."

Jennifer hangs up and Kevin pushes the speakerphone button to hang up the phone.

Kevin questions, "So, what now?"

Ashley shakes her head, "We keep digging. I also want to start another board of all articles and headlines that pertain to the case." She pauses, "Who knows, maybe something in one of the articles might spark an idea."

Natalie lets out a sigh, "I'll take anything right now."

Kevin nods, "I'll get my team to start pulling old news articles, starting with the Seattle and Kansas City cases."

Ashley nods, "Alright. The clock has started again until the next victim. Lets get at it."

Kevin picks up his cell phone. Mr. Gibson grabs the phone from the table while Ashley and Natalie start back through the new photos.

The killer sits in his dimly lit room listening to the rain hit the roof of his place. He is scratching away in his journal. The rain hitting the roof and the scratching of the pen on the paper makes an ominous sound that lightly echoes through the poorly lit room.

The killer stops writing for a second, "Detective Taylor, I thought you were better than this. How can you miss the obvious?"

The killer writes a couple more lines then stops again, "You're looking in the right direction, but not quite the right road."

The killer writes a few more lines and puts his pen down. He closes the journal, sits back and listens to the rain for a few seconds.

The killer sits forward and picks up the picture on the edge of the desk, "On to the next."

The killer stands up, turns off the light and slowly walks out of the room.

In the late evening hours, after everyone except for a

couple of people have already left the upstart record recording company, a woman looking to be in her late twenties, walks down the hallway towards the recording room inside the studio. She is around 5'6" tall and weighs a very nice 140 pounds. She is wearing a snug fitting, brown tank top, tight blue jeans, brown cowboy boots and a light brown cowboy hat. She has straight, soft brown hair that hangs a few inches below her shoulders and beautiful hazel colored eyes.

The woman walks up to a middle aged man wearing a blue suit and speaks with a country accent, "Zack, we going to do some more recording tonight?"

Zack smiles at the beautiful woman, "I figured we would get at least one track done tonight." He pauses, "The guitar is already in the studio. Whenever you get setup Sara, I'll be at the sound station."

Sara gives a warm smile, "I'll get ready."

Zack nods and walks off. Sara continues down the hallway and walks into the sound proof recording room. She grabs the stool and sets it next to the microphone. She grabs the guitar and slings it over her shoulder. Sara grabs the headphones from the stand next to the microphone, puts them on and sits down on the stool.

Sara speaks into the microphone, "I'm ready."

Sara hears Zack's voice in the headphones, "Okay, I'm starting the music."

Zack starts the music and turns on the recording machine. Once Sara hears the music, she starts playing the guitar and after a few seconds, she starts to sing with quite a nice country sounding voice.

It is early morning in New York City. The ground is still damp from the rain that stopped just an hour earlier.

Ashley, Natalie and Mr. Gibson walk into the conference room at the station. Kevin is already in the conference room.

Kevin nods to the three of them, "Good morning all."

Ashley, Natalie and Mr. Gibson can see all the boxes sitting around the table.

Kevin speaks, "I see you noticed as quickly as I did." He pauses, "All the articles from 1950 and 1975. As you can see, a lot."

Natalie shakes her head, "Jesus. This will take days. Days we don't have."

Mr. Gibson sighs, "Well, the sooner we get started, the sooner we get done."

Ashley speaks up, "Okay, 1950 on the left wall and 1975 on the right wall."

Natalie, Mr. Gibson and Kevin start opening boxes. Ashley moves the board with the Seattle map to the left side of the room and the board with the Kansas City map to the right side of the room, then Ashley starts helping the others sort through all the news articles.

It is another late night in New York City. Most everyone has turned in for the night to rest and relax. Only those that are still chasing a dream of breaking into the big time are still hard at work. Sara, dressed in a snug fitting black tank top, tight blue jeans, brown boots and a black cowboy hat, finishes the last cords of the song she is recording.

Zack switches off the recording equipment and speaks into a microphone, "Sara, that sounded great. I think we finally got it."

Sara smiles, "Awesome. We should be finished up by the end of the week."

Zack replies reassuringly, "Without a doubt." He pauses, "Okay, lets call it a night."

Sara lets out a tired sigh, "I'll put the guitar up and I'll see you tomorrow."

Zack replies, "Be safe going home."

Zack shuts off all the equipment and puts up the recording tape of Sara. Sara puts the headphones back on the stand and puts the stool back where it usually is. Zack turns off the lights and walks out of the recording room. He heads off down the hall and disappears into the elevator.

Sara walks out of the soundproof room, crosses the hallway and opens a door to another room. She turns on the lights and reveals a large open room with numerous instruments. She walks over to a table with an open guitar case on it. She puts the guitar in the case and closes it. Sara turns around and walks back over to the door. She turns off the light steps out into the hallway and shuts the door behind her.

Sara stops and stares at the door to the soundproof room she was in not just a minute ago. The door is standing open and the light is on. Sara gets a strange look on her face as she was sure that she closed the door and turned off the light. Sara walks back over, reaches her arm inside the doorway without entering the room and switches off the light.

Suddenly, a hand grabs her wrist and pulls her into the room. Out of sheer reaction, Sara grabs the door to try and keep from getting pulled into the room. The killer jerks her arm too hard and all the happens is Sara ends up in the dark room with the killer as the door closes behind her. The killer moves quickly and wraps his left arm around Sara's waist from the front. With the killer's body pressed against hers, Sara looks into the cold eyes of the killer.

The killer uses his right leg to trip Sara to the floor. Sara's hat comes off as she falls. She lands on her back, letting out a painful grunt, and the killer's body lands on top of her.

Sara instinctively yells as she begins to struggle, "Help! Someone help me!"

The killer holds Sara down and smiles, knowing she can scream as loud as she wants and no one will hear her through the soundproof walls. Tears come to Sara's eyes as the killer places the cloth over her nose and mouth. Sara's muffled pleas to the killer are lost in the silence of the room. Sara can feel her body getting weaker and tears roll down her cheeks as she fears what this man will do if she passes out.

The killer feels Sara's body squirming less so he leans in and whispers in her ear, "Relax my singing Sara. Your name will be known soon enough."

Sara's body can no longer struggle. Her head feels extremely heavy and in a few seconds, her world goes dark.

Chapter 22

IN THE EARLY MORNING hours, just after the sun breaks through the sky to light up the New York skyline, Ashley sits in the conference room, quiet and alone. She is looking at the city map of Seattle and all the push pins that mark where each body was found. Ashley tries to find any kind of pattern that might give a location based on where the bodies were located to a possible address.

Ashley rubs her eyes and becomes a little frustrated as she is unable to see a pattern with the Seattle map. She turns her attention to the Kansas City map. Again she looks over the locations of the bodies to see if any kind of pattern might emerge. After staring at the map for a few minutes, she lets out a sigh and shakes her head.

Ashley sits back and looks up at the ceiling, obviously frustrated, "What is it? What am I missing?"

At that moment, Ashley's cell phone rings, snapping her back to the moment at hand.

Ashley answers her phone, "Detective Taylor."

Kevin's voice comes on, "Hey, the next victim has been found. I'm already on the way with my team."

Ashley grabs a pen and a piece of paper, "What's the

address?"

Ashley writes down the location and hangs up. She puts the piece of paper in her pocket, grabs her phone and dials Natalie's number.

The killer sits quietly at his desk. The echoing of his pen scratching the paper fills the dimly lit room.

The killer stops writing for a moment, "It must be driving you crazy. There is a hidden clue that points you in the right direction and it is so obvious that you're over analyzing it."

The killer writes a couple more lines, then stops and puts down his pen. He closes the journal.

The killer sits back in his chair, "I had such high hopes for you Detective Taylor. I thought that this year might be the end." He pauses and lets out an evil and hollow sigh, "Look close detective, the answer is right in front of you."

The killer grabs another picture from the edge of his desk. He stands up as if rising out of the chair like a ghost. The killer turns off the desk lamp and walks quietly out of the room.

Kevin is standing over Sara's lifeless body. Her body is laying in the hallway right outside the door to the instrument room. Her body is dressed just like all the others. Her legs are straight, arms next to her body and a pillow holds up her head. On her stomach is written the letter "O". Kevin shakes his head. The scene is all too familiar for him. He raises up his camera and takes another picture.

The elevator opens and Ashley, Natalie and Mr.

Gibson walk out. Kevin sighs and lets out a weak smile when he sees them. Ashley, Natalie and Mr. Gibson walk by Zack and a police officer on their way to where Kevin and Sara's body awaits.

Ashley sighs and shakes her head when she looks down at Sara's body, "So, what do we have Kevin?"

Kevin speaks solemnly, "Victim is Sara Lang, age 29. I think it goes without saying that everything appears to match all the others. The only thing we have found so far is the writing on the stomach."

Ashley questions, "The letter 'O' or the number zero?"

Mr. Gibson speaks up, "No doubt the letter."

Kevin speaks, "That man that you passed was the last to see her alive."

Natalie nods, "I'll go talk to him."

Natalie walks off towards Zack.

Ashley looks at Mr. Gibson, "What makes you so sure it's the letter?"

Mr. Gibson replies, "This guy is so detailed that if he wanted us to know it was the number, he would have drawn a line through it. Just so we were not confused."

Ashley nods slightly and looks down the hallway at Natalie, "I'm sure you're right."

Natalie questions Zack, "So, when did you all leave last night?"

Zack replies shaken, "A little after 10 pm." He pauses, "I'm always gone first. She is usually just a few minutes after me."

Natalie nods, "So, why are you both here so late?"

Zack swallows, "We make song demo tapes using her voice. We send the demo tapes to established artists to sell songs."

Natalie nods again, "So, was she making an album?"

Zack shakes his head, "No, she just wanted to stay unnoticed and write songs. She wasn't interested in the spotlight." He pauses, "Why Sara, she was so talented and sweet?"

Natalie sighs, "Because she was quiet and wanted to stay out of the spotlight. The killer targets that type."

Natalie looks over as Ashley and Mr. Gibson walk up, both have an excited look on their face.

Natalie questions, "What is it?"

Ashley flips her cell phone closed, "Captain wants us back, now."

Natalie shakes her head slightly, "What?"

Ashley motions slightly for Natalie to head for the elevator. Ashley, Natalie and Mr. Gibson walk to the elevator.

When the elevator door shuts, Natalie questions again, "Ashley, what's going on?"

Ashley speaks like someone might hear her, "The computer kicked back a possible address from the writings we already have."

Natalie's eyes widen, "Are you serious?"

Ashley nods, "The address is a house owned by a single, white man, age 26." She pauses and excitedly continues, "His name is Charles Newman."

Natalie can only managed one stunned word, "Jesus."

The elevator opens on the first floor. Ashley, Natalie and Mr. Gibson hurry out the building to their car.

Captain Sutherland is standing at the podium at the front of a large meeting room. Twelve SWAT officers are sitting at the tables. The SWAT team commander is standing at the front of the room next to Captain Sutherland. The door opens and Ashley, Natalie and Mr. Gibson walk in.

Captain Sutherland nods to the three of them, "Okay,

everyone listen up. We have to move fast on this one." Captain Sutherland motions to the SWAT team commander, "Okay."

The SWAT team commander steps up to the podium as Ashley and Natalie walk up to the front of the room. Mr. Gibson remains by the door.

The SWAT team commander speaks, "On the board behind me is a quick layout of the house we are heading to. The target is Charles Newman. He is a 26 year old white male, around 5'10" tall and weighs about 170 pounds." He pauses, "This is not going to be an entry unless the detectives call for us. I want one team covering the front of the house and one covering the back of the house. The go word is crystal." He looks at Captain Sutherland, "Sir."

Captain Sutherland steps up to the podium, "Everyone understand, we do not have a warrant. Detective Taylor, Detective Simpson and Mr. Gibson will make contact with the target. They will attempt to gain entry into the house. If they need SWAT, they will call the go word over the radio." He pauses, "Now I will have Detective Taylor tell you what you might be up against." He looks at Ashley, "Detective."

Detective Taylor steps up to the podium, "What we have is a possible serial killer suspect. The killer has already killed 18 women by strangulation. He could also be linked to 54 prior murders dating back 50 years. This killer is very cold, calculating, highly intelligent and he will not hesitate to kill." She looks at Captain Sutherland, "Sir."

Captain Sutherland nods, "Alright, lets move fast while we know the possible suspect is still there." He pauses, "Be safe everyone."

The SWAT team commander barks out, "Lets move!"

The SWAT officers start moving like a well oiled machine.

Captain Sutherland hands a folder to Ashley, "We don't have much on him, but this is some information on

Charles Newman that might help you get in the door." He pauses, "Don't be a hero. You find something, call SWAT. You get a bad feeling, get out or call SWAT. Understood?"

Ashley nods, "Yes sir."

Ashley walks back over to Natalie and Mr. Gibson. They head out to their car, excited that they might have the killer in their sights soon.

The killer is sitting at his desk in his dimly lit room. He scratches away in his journal. The sound echoes through the room. It is an eerie sound and the contents that he writes about makes it even more ghostly.

The killer sits back and stops writing, "How close are you detective? Have you gotten any closer than your predecessors?"

The killer writes a couple more lines. He stops writing when he hears the slamming of car doors outside. The motion of his head and his posture gives notice that the sound is very uncommon for where he is at.

The killer turns the light off and stands up, "I wonder what is going on?"

The killer walks out of the room and starts towards the front of his house.

Ashley brings the car to a quick stop across the street from the Charles Newman house. The afternoon sun beats down adding to the already forming sweat on their excited faces. Ashley shuts off the car and gets out. Natalie and Mr. Gibson also quickly get out. The three of them start for the house while the two SWAT teams move into place.

Ashley speaks as the three of them walk, "I know we

don't have much info, but we need to think of something to get us in the house."

Natalie sighs, "I'm drawing a blank."

Ashley nods as the three of them walk up the stairs of the front porch, "I can't think of anything believable."

Mr. Gibson nods, "Just follow my lead."

Mr. Gibson knocks on the door causing a loud echo in the house. The three of them wait for Charles Newman to open the door. Ashley and Natalie both look at Mr. Gibson, hoping he has something up his sleeve.

The door opens and they see Charles Newman for the first time. Charles is 5'10" tall and looks to be about 175 pounds. He has short brown hair and brown eyes. He is wearing loose fitting jeans, a t-shirt and some black boots.

Charles speaks, "Can I help you?"

Mr. Gibson speaks as he holds up his old badge and brings it down quickly, "I'm Matthew. I'm a private investigator that was hired by someone to investigate possible theft from the appliance warehouse where you work." He pauses, "I was wondering if we might be able to come in and look at a few of your appliances and see if the numbers match the list I was given?"

Charles looks at the three of them closely.

Ashley holds up her badge, "I'm Detective Taylor with the NYPD and this is my partner. It would be best if you would let us take a look instead of making us get a warrant."

Charles nods slightly, "Okay. I don't have anything to hide. Come in."

Ashley, Natalie and Mr. Gibson walk into the house.

Charles questions, "What do you want to see?"

Mr. Gibson replies, "Washer and dryer will work for starters."

Ashley and Natalie let their eyes wander while Charles walks them to the back of the house. They notice a closed door in the hallway. They walk into the kitchen and to the left to the laundry room.

Charles speaks up, "Here you go?"

Mr. Gibson takes a flashlight from Natalie and starts looking around the washer and dryer until he finds the serial numbers. He pulls out a blank piece of paper and keeps it out of sight from Charles.

Natalie makes small talk, "So, this looks like it would be a quiet neighborhood."

Charles nods, still watching Mr. Gibson, "Yea. Not much happens around here. My neighbors will be wondering what is going on."

Ashley speaks up hoping to get more information, "Only if they're the nosey type. Are they?"

Charles shrugs, "I don't really know. I work nights and don't ever really talk to them."

Mr. Gibson gets up, "These two don't match." He looks at Charles, "How about your stove and refrigerator if you don't mind?"

Charles gives a smile, "No problem."

The four of them walk back into the kitchen and Mr. Gibson starts looking at the stove first.

Natalie questions, "Nights. Must be hard?"

Charles shakes his head, "Only during school time. Right now it's not too bad."

Ashley nods wanting more information, "What are you majoring in?"

Charles replies as he watches Mr. Gibson walk over to the refrigerator, "Forensic Science." He pauses, "Crime scene investigation is a big interest of mine."

Natalie replies, "Who knows, you might be working with us one day."

Charles replies, "I doubt it. I don't plan on staying in New York."

Ashley questions, "Do you have your eye on any place specifically?"

Charles nods, "Probably L.A." He pauses, "Anywhere

on the west coast will work though."

Ashley questions again, "Ever been to the west coast?"

Charles looks at Ashley, "I grew up in Portland, but I would prefer southern California."

Mr. Gibson speaks up, "Neither of these two match." He looks at Charles, "Do you have any other appliances in the house?"

Charles shakes his head, "Nothing that we have at the warehouse."

Mr. Gibson looks at Ashley and tries one more thing, "I've gotten some grease on my hands. Would you mind if I used your bathroom to wash up?"

Charles replies, "It's back up front, through the bedroom."

As the four of them start down the hallway, Natalie questions about the closed door, "Is this the bedroom?"

Charles shakes his head, "No, that was a bedroom I turned into a study. My bedroom is off the living room."

The four of them walk into the living room and Charles points to an open door on the right side of the room, "Through that door."

Mr. Gibson walks off for the bathroom. He looks around as he passes through the bedroom, not noticing anything out of the ordinary. He walks into the bathroom and quickly and quietly looks through the medicine cabinet. After a few seconds, he washes his hands and returns to the living room.

Mr. Gibson nods, "Thank you for your cooperation."

Charles smiles, "Any time."

Ashley, Natalie and Mr. Gibson walk out of the house. Charles shuts the door behind them.

Ashley speaks as they walk back to the car, "His voice didn't sound like the caller."

Natalie speaks up, "I think we should keep a car on him just in case. Some of his answers gives me suspicion."

Mr. Gibson sighs, "My gut says it's not him, but I agree, we don't want to take that chance."

The three of them get in the car. Natalie radios SWAT to tell them that they can stand down. Ashley drives off, not sure if they just met the killer or not.

Chapter 23

IN THE WARM AFTERNOON of the big city, a young woman looking to be around 19 years old, walks into a lobby of a modeling studio. She is around 5'3" tall and weighs a very beautiful 120 pounds. She has blonde hair that hangs to the bottom of her shoulder blades and sultry brown eyes. She is wearing tight fitting blue jeans, a pink spaghetti strap tank top and a pair of pink and white tennis shoes. She is holding a binder in her hands.

The lady sitting behind the reception desk looks up at the beautiful young woman, "Can I help you?"

The young woman shows her beautiful smile, "Yes. I'm Amanda Carson. I was asked by Sergio to bring my portfolio by so he could look at it."

The receptionist holds out her hands, "I'll make sure he gets it."

Amanda hands the lady the binder, "Thanks."

The receptionist puts the binder on her desk and starts scratching a note, "He will give you a call in the next few days whether he is interested or not."

Amanda smiles again, "Okay. Thanks again."

Amanda walks out of the office as the receptionist puts

the binder and note in the inbox mark with Sergio's name.

In the morning hours of a new day in the big city, Ashley, Natalie, Kevin and Mr. Gibson sit around the all too familiar table in the room that has become a second home to them. The four of them continue to look through the massive amounts of paperwork that covers the last fifty years.

Ashley looks up at Kevin, "Anything new from Jennifer?"

Kevin shakes his head, "No. She is still digging, but she can't seem to find much about Thomas Newman."

Ashley looks over to Natalie, "Anything else from the computer team?"

Natalie sighs, "Nothing yet."

Ashley sits back in her chair, "Our stakeout on Charles Newman hasn't turned anything up yet either."

Mr. Gibson speaks up, "I don't think he's involved. If he was the killer and knew we were on to him, he would play more cat and mouse games with us."

Kevin looks at Mr. Gibson, "Maybe he's worried about getting caught."

Mr. Gibson smiles at the comment, "If he was worried about that, he wouldn't give us clues to solve the case."

Ashley lets out a sigh, "Either way, we're back to the game of beat the clock. He no doubt has his next victim in his sights and if our stakeout team stays with Charles Newman and we get another victim, that's going to answer the question."

Natalie speaks up, "The bigger question we need answered is where is the hidden clue we've missed? The one clue that ties everything together."

Ashley looks at the board with the pictures of the

victims on it, "I don't know, but if we don't find it soon, we'll be adding another picture to that board."

The four of them are quiet after Ashley's comment. Each one thinking of who the next victim might be.

The killer sits quietly in his dimly lit room scratching away in his journal. The eerie sound of pen to paper echoes in the small room. Another picture sits at the edge of the desk, no doubt a picture of the next victim.

The killer stops for a few seconds, "Awe, Detective Taylor, is the case driving you crazy? Poor Charles Newman, he is just simply in the wrong place with the wrong name."

The killer writes a few more lines in his journal, then closes the notebook.

The killer sits back, "You were close. I heard all the commotion when you paid the poor guy a visit, but then again, so far away."

The killer picks up the picture and stands up, "Watch him close so that when the next clue is discovered, you will know it is not him."

The killer turns off the light and slowly walks out of the pitch black room.

It is fairly late in the evening as Amanda, dressed in tight fitting jeans, tank top and tennis shoes, is walking up the stairs of the apartment building where she lives. She is carrying a large manila envelope in her hands. The building is fairly old, but still livable for someone just trying to make it by. She reaches the fifth floor and starts down the long, dimly lit hallway to her apartment.

Amanda pulls her keys out of her pocket. She is staying steadily aware of her surroundings as she walks. She reaches the door to her apartment. She unlocks the two locks on the door and quickly steps inside. She closes the door behind her. She locks the door lock on the handle, the deadbolt and the chain lock.

Amanda reaches over and turns the light on. The light shows that she is standing in a small kitchen. Amanda starts across the kitchen when she hears movement in the living room which is the next room and has no lights on.

Amanda calls out, "Brewster, come here boy."

A couple seconds later, a small beagle puppy runs into the kitchen obviously happy to see Amanda. Amanda squats down and pets the puppy for a few seconds. She stands back up and walks into the dark living room. She flips the wall switch and the room is lit up. An entertainment center, couch, chair, coffee table and end table dot the small living room. On the right side of the room is a closed door that leads to the bedroom.

Amanda walks over to the coffee table and tosses down the manila envelope. She sits down on the couch. Brewster jumps up on the couch next to her.

Amanda speaks while petting Brewster, "I think this modeling job just might be the break I'm looking for little man."

Amanda takes off her shoes and socks. She stretches and pets Brewster a little more.

Amanda lets out a sigh, "I think it's time to call it a night buddy."

Amanda stands up and walks over to the bedroom door. She opens the door reaches in and turns on the light. A double bed and two dressers decorate the bedroom. The closed closet door is in the back right corner of the room and the closed bathroom door is in the back left corner of the room.

Amanda walks into the bedroom and over to the

dresser on the left side of the room. Brewster stops in the doorway and barks. The bark startles Amanda as she turns around quickly. With the bedroom door open, she is unable to see the figure behind the door waiting for her.

Amanda smiles at Brewster, "What is it buddy?"

Brewster barks again, but doesn't come into the bedroom.

Amanda starts back towards the bedroom door, "Well, you coming to bed buddy?"

When Amanda gets a few feet from the door, the killer explodes out from behind the door. The door swings shut and Brewster is stuck in the living room. Amanda's face is that of sheer terror at the sight of this strange man coming at her.

Amanda opens her mouth to scream, but the killer is already on her. His right hand forces the cloth over her nose and mouth as he wraps his left arm around her body. The killer uses his momentum and strength to force Amanda backwards. Amanda falls back on her bed and the killer lands on top of her. She tries to struggle, but it becomes obvious that the killer is too strong for her.

Amanda's eyes tear up and she manages a muffled word, "Don't."

The killer stares coldly into Amanda's eyes. The tears run down her cheeks as she can feel her head starting to get heavy. Amanda can tell that her body is getting weaker. She tries one more time to squirm free, but to no avail. Her vision starts to go blurry.

The killer whispers in Amanda's ear, "Relax my modeling Amanda. You will be known soon enough."

The killer's words are the last thing Amanda hears as she passes into the darkness.

In the warm morning hours of the city, an all too familiar scene is unfolding at Amanda's apartment building. The front of the building is blocked off with crime scene tape. Two CSI vans and a few police cars are parked in front of the building. Police officers do their best to keep the citizens from trying to wander into the scene.

At that time, the unmarked Ford pulls up and parks next to the CSI vans. Natalie gets out of the driver's seat. Ashley gets out of the passenger's seat and Mr. Gibson gets out of the back seat. The three of them walk towards the front of the building. Ashley is talking on her cell phone as the three of them enter the building.

Ashley hangs up her phone as the three of them start up the stairs, "I got the number for the two officers on the stakeout. I'm going to give them a call."

Ashley, Natalie and Mr. Gibson stop at Amanda's floor and they can see Kevin and his team down the hallway. They walk down the hallway as Ashley dials the number on her cell phone. Ashley stops about twenty feet from Kevin while Natalie and Mr. Gibson walk up next to Kevin. They see Amanda's body on the floor in front of her apartment door. She is dressed like all the other victims and her body is laid out like the others as well. On Amanda's stomach is written the letter "T".

Natalie shakes her head, "Well, what do we have Kevin?"

Kevin explains, "The victim's name is Amanda Carson, age 19. She has lived here since she turned 18. From what we have found out so far, she was trying to break into the modeling business. We found some pictures in an envelope on the coffee table. Everything appears to be the same as far as how she was killed. We'll run the tests anyway when we get the body back to the lab."

Mr. Gibson questions, "Anything inside the apartment?"

Kevin shakes his head, "Nothing. We know that the

attack took place in the bedroom, but that's about it." He pauses, "But as far as evidence, nothing."

Ashley walks up as she closes her phone, "Well, Charles Newman was at work all night long according to the officers on the stakeout."

Natalie shakes her head, "So it's not him, or he found a way to slip out of the warehouse unnoticed and get back without anyone seeing him."

Mr. Gibson speaks up, "I'm sure they have security cameras at the warehouse. If we watch them we can see if he shows up on them throughout the night."

Ashley nods, "I've already asked the Captain to send someone over to see if the warehouse will let us check out the tapes."

Kevin speaks up, "We've got everything here. I'll go ahead and move the body if that is okay?"

Ashley nods, "That's fine. We will look around some and get back with you at the station."

Kevin rounds up his team. They get Amanda's body and leave the scene as Ashley, Natalie and Mr. Gibson enter Amanda's apartment hoping to find something helpful.

The killer is sitting in his dimly lit room. His pen scratches away with his next journal entry. The sound seems to get more eerie and sinister as the coldly written lines of his evil deeds are applied to the paper. Seemingly uncaring of what he has done, the killer finishes his journal entry and puts down the pen. He reaches over and grabs an old notebook. He carefully opens the pages, taking care not to damage the aging paper.

The killer speaks to himself as he carefully turns the pages, "I don't know if they are going to get the answers.

They seem so close, but yet, they can't see what is right in front of them."

The killer stops at a certain page, "They want so badly to find the hidden clue and the one thing that ties all the victims together." He pauses, "The answer is so obvious and right in front of them that they just can't see it."

The killer reads a few pages of the old journal. He lets out a hollow sigh and closes the notebook.

The killer looks at a picture that is laying on top of two pieces of paper on the edge of the desk, "Time to start working on the next piece of the puzzle."

The killer switches off the light, stands and slowly walks out of the room.

Chapter 24

AS MOST PEOPLE IN the city enjoys their labor day, Ashley, Natalie, Mr. Gibson and Kevin find themselves laboring away in the conference room. The table is covered with even more papers and pictures. Another push pin is placed in the New York City map and another picture of the latest victim is pinned up on the cork board.

Ashley sits back, "There has to be a common factor amongst the victims. Something that the killer focuses on."

Natalie shakes her head, "We've checked into the backgrounds of all the victims. We can't find any common thread."

Kevin speaks up, "We know the killer picks certain victims. Each one is a loner for the most part, keeping a secret life." He pauses, "Easy targets."

Mr. Gibson lets out a sigh, "Maybe there is no common factor."

Ashley looks at Mr. Gibson, "What are you saying?"

Mr. Gibson speculates, "Maybe the only common factor is that they are all victims. The killer knows we are trying to find a pattern, something that we can focus on about the victims. It is textbook serial killer science."

Natalie nods slightly, "So he uses that knowledge to confuse us, knowing we will waste time looking for something that is not there."

Ashley ponders for a second, "I can accept that idea to a point. He didn't just randomly pick these women for no reason. He had a purpose for picking these women. He is trying to tell us something with these women that goes beyond the writings on the bodies."

At that moment, the phone rings. Kevin gets up and walks over to the phone.

Kevin answers the phone, "Detective Reynolds."

Kevin is quiet for a minute as he listens to the voice on the other end of the line tell him what he didn't want to hear.

Kevin shakes his head, "Okay, thanks."

Kevin hangs up the phone and turns to the others, "Well, my team finished looking through all the surveillance tapes from the warehouse."

Ashley knows the answer to the question before she asks it, "What did they find?"

Kevin sits back down, "Charles Newman was in the videos all throughout the night. Never out of sight long enough to get away, kill someone and get back."

Natalie shakes her head, "So, it's not Charles Newman, our first possible link to Thomas Newman."

Mr. Gibson sits back, "Maybe we're looking too hard at Thomas Newman. Maybe his name is just meant to point us in a certain direction."

Ashley looks up at the clock and then at the calendar on the wall, "Well, whatever direction that is, we better figure it out quick because the next victim is just a few days away."

A silence falls over the room like a death shroud. They all know that the killer has already put into motion the chain of events that will lead them to their next victim.

In the early evening hours, Jennifer is talking on the phone at her makeshift desk at the Sheriff's Office in Seattle. Deputy Cook sits quietly waiting for Jennifer to finish.

Jennifer has a dejected look, "Okay, thank you."

Jennifer hangs up the phone and Deputy Cook questions, knowing the answer can't be good, "Anything?"

Jennifer shakes her head, "The detectives in Kansas City checked on the Newman house, but it was empty of belongings as well."

Deputy Cook sits back, "So, what's the next move?"

Jennifer sighs, "I want to try and talk to Mrs. Littlefield again."

Deputy Cook nods, "Okay." He looks at his watch, "It's too late today, but we can see if she is up to it tomorrow."

Jennifer nods, "Okay." She stands up, "I guess I'll head back to my room. I'll see you tomorrow."

Deputy Cook nods, "Goodnight."

Jennifer walks off trying to think of what she might be able to learn from Mrs. Littlefield.

In the late hours of New York City, some students have made their way back to one of the college campuses to begin the new year. Walking towards the female dorms alone is a young woman that looks to be in her late teens or early twenties. She stands around 5'6" tall and weighs a nicely built 140 pounds. She has straight blonde hair and nice blue eyes. She is wearing tight jeans, white tank top, jean jacket and tennis shoes. She has a backpack slung over her right shoulder.

As the young woman approaches the front of the dorms, a flashlight beam hits her in the face. She is startled by the light and the person holding it.

She hears a male voice, "Can I help you miss?"

The young woman looks over and the light has impaired her vision, but she can make out a security uniform.

The young lady replies, "I have a room in these dorms."

The man raises up a clipboard with his other hand, "What's the name?"

The young lady looks puzzled, but figures this must be something new this year, "Bianca Upton."

The man looks down the clipboard for a few seconds and then replies, "Okay. Sorry to have startled you."

Bianca lets out a smile, "Goodnight."

Bianca heads off the all too familiar way to her old dorm room she has had for the last couple years.

The man turns off the flashlight and the face and voice of the killer becomes apparent, "I'll be seeing you soon my beautiful Bianca."

The killer turns and walks off into the darkness of the city night.

It is an overcast morning in Seattle. A Sheriff's car pulls up in front of Mrs. Littlefield's house. Jennifer gets out of the passenger's seat and Deputy Cook gets out of the driver's seat. The two of them walk up to the front door. Deputy Cook knocks on the door. A few moments pass when they hear movement on the other side of the door. The door opens and Mrs. Littlefield is standing there.

Mrs. Littlefield smiles, "Well good morning. Please come in."

Jennifer and Deputy Cook walk inside. Mrs. Littlefield closes the door and leads them into the living room. Mrs. Littlefield sits in her chair as Jennifer and Deputy Cook sit on the couch.

Mrs. Littlefield smiles, "What can I do for you young lady?"

Jennifer speaks dejected, "I can't seem to find enough information on Thomas Newman to find the connection he has to the serial killer."

Mrs. Littlefield replies, "Thomas Newman was a very private man. He really went into a hidden lifestyle when his son disappeared." She pauses, "Maureen held him together the best she could, but Thomas was devastated."

Jennifer sighs, "There is just not much of a paper trail to follow."

Mrs. Littlefield nods, "Well, you must remember, there was the Great Depression during some of those years. Being prominent, you had to be secretive. There was such a boom in homeless families and children being sent away to homes, following the rich was just not as important."

Jennifer questions, "And the Seattle police were absolutely sure that Michael Newman ran away. They are sure that Thomas Newman didn't do anything to him."

Mrs. Littlefield nods, "The police found no signs of foul play. After they talked to everyone, especially Maureen, it became rather obvious that the boy didn't care for his father." She pauses, "A massive search turned up nothing, but everyone knew that the boy ran away because he hated his father so much."

Deputy Cook interjects, "Have you thought about Michael Newman being responsible for the killings?"

Jennifer lets out a weak smile, "It's possible, but he was fairly young and it would have been quite hard for someone his age." She pauses, "We're thinking the link is Thomas Newman, maybe even him being the first killer."

Mrs. Littlefield speaks up, "So many people did not

like Thomas Newman because he kept his empire to himself. They loved Maureen because she gave back to the community by opening the O'Kelly adoption centers."

Jennifer speaks, "I just wish I could get a look at some of their personal things. Something just might stand out. But there is nothing here in Seattle and I also drew a dead end in Kansas City."

Mrs. Littlefield interjects, "I would think so."

Jennifer gets a puzzled look, "What do you mean?"

Mrs. Littlefield smiles, "After Thomas Newman died in 1989 in Kansas City, Maureen lived there for another ten years. She moved to New York City last year. If I had to guess, that is where all their belongings are."

Jennifer questions, "Why would she move to New York at such a point in her life."

Mrs. Littlefield replies, "Because that was what she did with Kansas City. They moved to Kansas City in 1974 and opened the center in New York that year. Last year she moved to New York and opened a center in her husband's home town of Atlanta."

Jennifer's eyes widen in disbelief. She realizes that even the adoption centers all follow the same city patterns of the killers giving more credence to the idea of a serial killer bloodline.

Jennifer smiles, "Thank you for everything."

Mrs. Littlefield smiles in return, "Any time my dear."

Jennifer stands up. Deputy Cook follows her out of the house.

One the way to the car, Deputy Cook questions, "What now?"

Jennifer replies, "I think it's time for me to head back to New York and follow the trail of their personal belongings."

The two of them get in the car. As Deputy Cook drives off, Jennifer thinks about everything she just learned about the Newman family.

Bianca is sitting in the school library. She has a couple of books open in front of her. She is writing notes in a notebook. After finishing the page, a young, attractive brunette woman walks up to the table.

The lady looks at Bianca, "So, you going to be at the party tonight?"

Bianca looks up at the young lady, "I don't think so Kelly. This professor is hitting us with a lot of homework early."

Kelly smiles, "You have all weekend to do that stuff. Come out and enjoy yourself for one night."

Bianca smiles, "That's okay. I'm just going to go back to the room. You have fun though."

Kelly nods slightly, "Okay. I guess I'll see you tomorrow. Call me if you change your mind."

Bianca closes her notebook, "Okay. Be safe."

Kelly walks off. Bianca closes her books and puts them in her backpack. She looks at her watch. She has the look that she can't believe it's already 9:30 pm. Bianca walks out of the library and starts back across campus towards her dorm.

The night breeze blows across Bianca's face. She looks around constantly, not liking to be walking alone at this time of night. She stays on the sidewalks which are fairly well lit up. She continues to glance around as she sees her dorm building. She starts to feel more at ease until she hears someone running on the sidewalk behind her and the person is getting closer awfully fast. Bianca looks over her shoulder at the moment a man runs by her. Bianca lets out a sigh of relief when she sees the man dressed in jogging clothes with headphones on.

Bianca walks into her dorm building lobby. She looks around and doesn't see anyone. She knows everyone will be at the big party across campus tonight. She smiles at the silence. Bianca walks up the two flights of stairs to her floor. She walks down the long hallway and turns left at the end. She passes two doors and stops at her room door.

Bianca unlocks the door and steps inside. She flips the light switch on and closes the door behind her. She locks the door and turns back around. Bianca walks over to the two beds and tosses her backpack on the bed on the right side of the room. She walks towards the closed bathroom door.

Bianca speaks to herself, "A nice bath, then more studying."

Bianca opens the bathroom door and turns on the bathroom light to reveal the small bathroom. She steps inside and turns on the bathwater as the image of the killer emerges from under the roommate's bed. Bianca tests the water and when she is satisfied with the temperature, she puts the stopper in the tub to let it start filling up.

As Bianca stands up, the killer brings his right arm around her body and places the cloth over her nose and mouth. The killer wraps his left arm around Bianca's body and squeezes her tightly against his body. A look of complete fear crosses Bianca's face. She starts to squirm her body left and right, but the killer's grip is strong. The killer drags Bianca into the room with the beds.

Bianca tries to scream, but only muffled noises come out. She can feel her body starting to get weaker. Bianca struggles some more. The killer can feel Bianca starting to slide loose so he uses his weight and shoves her against the wall. The killer adjusts his grip around her again. Bianca can feel the heaviness in her head and her vision starts to fade in and out. She gives one last effort to get free, but her body is just too weak now.

The killer presses his body against Bianca's and whispers in her ear, "Relax my beautiful and brainy Bianca. Study time is over now."

Bianca can't fight the chemicals any longer and she slips away into the darkness.

Chapter 25

IN THE EARLY MORNING hours of a new day in New York City, Ashley rolls over in her bed and looks at her alarm clock. She sighs as it reads 5:30 am and she knows that she just went through another restless night of sleep. She climbs out of the bed and shuts the alarm on the clock off.

Ashley walks into the bedroom and brushes her teeth. She looks at herself in the mirror. She almost doesn't recognize the face looking back at her. The sleepless nights and incredible stress has taken a toll on her. She grabs the bottom of the mirror and opens the medicine cabinet door. She grabs the bottle of aspirin, opens it, takes two tablets out and puts the bottle away. Ashley grabs the plastic cup on the sink and fills it with water. She takes the pills and puts the cup down.

Ashley stares at the sink for a second, then looks back up. She reaches up and closes the medicine cabinet door. Her eyes widen as the image of a man is behind her and a hand places a cloth over her nose and mouth.

Suddenly, an alarm goes off and Ashley sits up in her bed covered in a cold sweat. She tries to slow down her heavy breathing when her cell phone rings. Ashley turns off the alarm and grabs her phone. She knows what day it is and knows what this call is going to be about.

Ashley answers the phone in a tired voice, "Hello."

Kevin's voice comes on the line, "Detective Taylor, it's Kevin. We just got a call about the next victim."

Ashley grabs a pen and paper from the nightstand drawer, "Let me have the address."

Ashley writes down the location Kevin gives her and puts the pen down, "I'll be there as soon as I pick up Mr. Gibson and Natalie. Bye."

Ashley hangs up the phone. She gets out of bed and grabs her pistol from under the pillow next to hers. She walks into the bathroom and puts the pistol on the counter next to the plastic cup. Ashley gets cleaned up and ready for the new day and the next victim.

As the sun starts to brighten the morning sky over the college campus, Ashley pulls up in front of Bianca's dorm building. Many students have gathered around, but the police officers, campus police and crime scene tape keep them separated from the horrible scene inside the building.

Ashley, Natalie and Mr. Gibson get out of the car and start towards the front of the building. As they approach they see Jennifer standing in the main doorway to the building. The three of them walk up to Jennifer.

Ashley shakes Jennifer's hand, "When did you get in?"

Jennifer gives a tired smile, "Late last night." She pauses, "And it seems that I'm right back at it here, just like when I left."

Natalie smiles, "Don't let yourself down. Your research gave us insight that we might not have had if you didn't work so hard in Seattle."

Mr. Gibson sighs, "Shall we see what's waiting for us."

Jennifer nods, "Follow me."

The four of them head up the stairs to where Kevin and the rest of his team is at. As the four of them walk down the hallway, they can see Bianca's body laying in front of a room door. Kevin nods at the four of them when they walk up.

Ashley looks down at Bianca's body which is dressed and laid out like all the others. The number "5" is written on her stomach. All of them can see a piece of paper rolled up in each of Bianca's hands.

Ashley questions, "What do we have Kevin?"

Kevin explains, "The victim's name is Bianca Upton, age 20. She was drugged, tied up, then strangled. Everything appears to be the same as all the others." He pauses, "I was waiting for all of you before removing the papers from her hands."

Ashley pulls out some latex gloves and puts them on. Natalie also puts on some latex gloves as Kevin grabs two evidence bags from his case.

Mr. Gibson speaks up as Ashley and Natalie squat down next to Bianca's body, "One should be a blank birth certificate and the other should be a blank death certificate."

Natalie ever so gently removes the paper from Bianca's right hand and unrolls it, "It's a blank death certificate."

Ashley gently removes the paper from Bianca's left hand and unrolls it, "A blank birth certificate."

Natalie places the piece of paper in an evidence bag that Jennifer is now holding. Jennifer seals the bag and returns it to the case. Ashley places the piece of paper in the evidence bag Kevin is holding. Kevin seals the bag and places it back in the case.

Ashley and Natalie stand back up and Kevin speaks up, "Other than the writing and these two pieces of paper, as you can guess, we have found no other clues or evidence."

Ashley nods, "If you're ready, go ahead and move the body. We are going to look around some and talk to some of the other students."

Kevin nods and looks at Jennifer, "Lets get going."

Jennifer walks off to get the team moving. Kevin packs up his case and walks off. The rest of the CSI team removes Bianca's body. Ashley, Natalie and Mr. Gibson enter Bianca's room hoping to find something, but knowing deep inside that there won't be anything useful.

In his dimly lit study, the killer sits at his desk. With pen in hand, he scratches away at his next journal entry. The ghostly sound of the pen to paper echoes throughout the room.

The killer talks to himself while he writes, "How bad have the dreams gotten Detective Taylor?"

The killer writes a few more lines, then puts the pen down. A cold silence falls over the room.

The killer whispers as if someone might hear him, "The answer is easy detective. Connect the obvious and you will have your answers. You will solve the unsolvable case."

The killer picks up the picture from the edge of the desk. No doubt the picture of the next victim.

The killer coldly whispers again, "Let the clock start again."

The killer turns off the desk lamp and walks out of the pitch black room.

In the afternoon hours of the day, Kevin, Jennifer, Natalie and Mr. Gibson are sitting in the conference room. A few minutes pass when Ashley walks in. She is carrying a picture in her hand. She walks over to the corkboard and puts the picture of Bianca up next to the other victims. Ashley walks over to the New York City map and places a push pin in the map where Bianca's body was found.

Ashley turns to the others, "I think it's obvious that we have absolutely no pattern as to where the bodies are being found."

Natalie speaks up, "The computer team has been unable to come up with anything else with the writings on the bodies."

Jennifer sits back, "I got permission to look at the Newman estate and personal things. I'll be headed over there in the morning."

Mr. Gibson sits forward, "We've got seven victims left, then this guy goes into hiding for another 25 years." He pauses, "And the clock has already started on number 21."

Kevin shakes his head, "The date on the birth certificate was 1935 and the death certificate date was 1949. What do those date have to do with Thomas Newman?"

Jennifer speaks up, "His son was born in 1935, no doubt the high point of his life. In 1949, his son disappears, bringing about the death of the Newman empire, no doubt the lowest point of his life." She pauses, "Everything we know still points to Thomas Newman."

Ashley sits down, "The only thing missing is the clue that ties all these other clues together. I still think it's some common thing amongst all the victims that we just haven't seen yet."

Natalie sighs, "As far as we can tell through all our background checks, there is no common string that ties the victims together."

Ashley turns and stares at the board with the pictures of the victims on it, "There just has to be. I feel it in my gut."

The others look at the pictures of the victims and wonder if Ashley is right. Is there something that ties all the victims together and is that the piece of the puzzle that will bring everything else together.

Darkness has fallen over the city. The fall breeze has started to bring cooler temperatures. In a small office located in a nice part of town, a phone rings. A woman looking to be in her mid-forties walks into the nice office which consists of a desk and chair, another leather chair and a couch. Bookshelves line the outer walls of the office.

The woman has blonde hair that hangs just below her shoulders and blue eyes. She is about 5'4" tall and weighs a trim 115 pounds. She is wearing a pink, three quarter sleeve top, blue jeans and tennis shoes. The woman walks over to the phone on the desk.

The woman answers the phone, "Dr. Harrison."

A man's voice comes on the line, "What are you still doing in the office Marg?"

Marg smiles, "Getting more notes together for a book that both of us are suppose to be working on." She pauses, "How is the conference?"

The man replies, "Boring. To think, I have a whole week of this."

Marg chuckles, "That's what happens when you draw the short straw Tom."

Tom replies sarcastically, "Thanks for the support

partner."

Marg looks back up at her office door as if she heard something.

Tom speaks again, "Are you still there?"

Marg shrugs off the noise, "Yea, but I think I'm going to call it a night. Have fun tomorrow."

Tom chuckles, "Thanks. Be safe going home."

Marg smiles, "I will. Goodnight."

Marg hangs up the phone. She looks back up at her office door. She shakes her head and turns off the desk light. Marg walks out of the office and locks the door behind her. She walks into the small lobby and checks the office door to Tom's office to make sure it is locked. Satisfied everything is locked up, Marg walks out the front door and uses her key to lock it behind her.

A few minutes after she drives off, the killer emerges from under the receptionist's desk. He slowly walks towards the office door that leads to Marg's office. He pulls out a couple of small tools and takes only a couple of seconds to pick the lock.

The killer opens the office door, "Lets see what we've got."

The killer walks into Marg's office and over to her desk where her calendar is sitting.

Another early start to no doubt what everyone feels will be another frustrating day. Ashley, Natalie, Kevin and Mr. Gibson are sitting at the table in the conference room. Each one has a file covering one of the victims, trying to find a possible connection to the other victims. A few minutes pass and the door opens. Captain Sutherland walks in with the Mayor right behind him. The Mayor is carrying the morning newspaper in his hand. The four of them look up and they all get a dejected look when they see the Mayor.

The Mayor tosses the paper on the table, "Have you seen this mornings paper yet? I think you might like the headline on the front page."

Kevin grabs the paper and looks at it. The headline stands out, "SERIAL KILLER STILL AT LARGE".

The Mayor speaks with frustration, "Let me sum up the article. After twenty victims, the police still have no viable suspects and have made no arrests." He pauses, "Crime is bad enough without this. What are we doing about it?"

Ashley speaks up, "We are pursuing possible leads. We also had a potential suspect, but he turned out to be clean. We are killing ourselves trying to stop this guy."

Jennifer walks in the open door and glances at the others.

The Mayor's voice gets even louder, "That's it. We're working as hard as we can on it." His voice gets even louder, "That's not good enough. I want results, now!"

The Mayor storms out of the room

Captain Sutherland sighs, "Just keep at it. I know you're doing everything you can. I'll deal with the Mayor."

The Captain walks out of the room and shuts the door behind him. Kevin picks up a pair of scissors and cuts out the headline and article from the paper.

Jennifer walks over to a chair, "That sounded enjoyable."

Kevin gets up and walks over to the board where all the newspaper headlines remotely related to the case are pinned up. Kevin adds the new story to the already full board.

Ashley looks at Jennifer, "Anything yet on the personal belongings?"

Jennifer shakes her head, "Not much as far as their things."

Ashley and the others let out a collective sigh.

Jennifer speaks up, "However, I know that a paper trail of some kind exists on the child in the photo with Thomas Newman."

Natalie looks at Jennifer, "Are you serious?"

Jennifer nods, "Right now it's all tied up in litigation since Maureen died earlier this year, but I've been talking to the district attorney's office to see if I can get access to the paperwork." She pauses, "Maybe it will give us something that we didn't know before."

Ashley nods, "Keep on it hard. Any new information can only help us." She sighs, "Now, lets get back to the victim's files."

Natalie, Kevin, Mr. Gibson and Jennifer each grab another file and start looking through it. Ashley looks at the calendar on the wall. She knows that time is running short before they get the next victim.

Chapter 26

ANOTHER COOL NIGHT IN the city. Marg is sitting at her desk typing on her computer. She seems oblivious to everything around her. A few minutes pass and a man in his fifties, dressed in a blue suit, appears in the doorway to her office.

The man speaks, "It's late."

Marg blinks a few times and looks up, "I don't have too much more. I just want to get this down while it's fresh in my mind."

The man replies, "Would you like me to wait?"

Marg smiles and looks at her watch, "No, it's already nine. Your wife is probably wondering where you're at. Go ahead Tom, I won't be too much longer."

Tom smiles, "Alright, be safe going home. I'll see you in the morning."

Marg smiles and returns to typing, "Goodnight."

Tom walks off and locks the front door when he leaves. Marg continues to type her notes. After another twenty minutes, she stops typing.

Marg sits back in her plush leather chair, "Done. Thank God."

Marg puts a few papers in her desk and shuts down her computer. She stands up and stretches. She turns off the desk lamp and starts for the door to her office. She locks the door and pulls it closed behind her. She walks over to the main door to the lobby. As she reaches up to unlock the door, she hears something behind her.

As Marg starts to turn to her left, a strong arm wraps around her body and a cloth is placed firmly over her nose and mouth. Marg instinctively screams, but the sound is muffled by the cloth. Her eyes are wide and filled with terror. The killer turns Marg away from the front door. The killer uses his weight and forces Marg towards the wall by the receptionist's desk. The killer slams Marg with great force into the wall.

Marg lets out a moan and tries to struggle. The killer uses his body weight and strength to hold her in place. Marg can feel her head getting heavier as her vision starts to blur. Tears come to her eyes as she thinks about what this person is going to do to her after she passes out.

Marg manages a muffled plea, "Don't."

The killer leans close and whispers in her ear, "Relax my beautiful head doctor. It will be all over soon Marg."

The heaviness in Marg's head is too much for her and she passes out in the killer's arms.

As the sun starts to break through the New York City skyline, Ashley pulls her car up at a coffee shop on one of the many street corners near the police station. Ashley gets out of the car followed by Natalie and Mr. Gibson. The three of them walk over to the coffee vendor.

Ashley speaks to the clerk, "Three regular."

Mr. Gibson speaks, "You know, the more I think about it, the more I think you're right. There has to be a common factor amongst all the victims."

Natalie speaks up, "This guy is good, but 27 victims that all have something in common, something that we can't seem to find. That seems a little too much for me to accept."

Ashley looks at Natalie, "Who knows ..." She pauses for a second, "Maybe the connection is to the victims from the prior cases."

Mr. Gibson questions, "What are you saying?"

Ashley explains, "Maybe the number one victim has something in common with the first victim in each of the prior cases. So on and so forth with the corresponding victims."

Mr. Gibson nods, "That's an interesting idea worth looking into."

The counter person sets the coffee cups on the counter. Ashley pulls out some money when Natalie's phone rings.

Natalie answers her phone, "Detective Simpson." She pauses for a second, "What's up Kevin?"

Natalie nods as Ashley and Mr. Gibson look at her. Then it hits Mr. Gibson.

Mr. Gibson speaks softly to Ashley, "Today is the day for the next victim."

Ashley lets out a sigh, "You're right."

Natalie hangs up her phone, "Kevin and his team just got there. Lets go."

The three of them take their coffee, get in the car and head off to the next crime scene.

Ashley stops the car in front of the office where Marg and Tom work. Ashley, Natalie and Mr. Gibson get out of the car. They duck under the crime scene tape and walk in the front door to the office. They see Kevin standing over

Marg's body which is laying in front of her office door. Marg's body is dressed and laid out like all the other victims. Ashley, Natalie and Mr. Gibson walk up to Kevin. The four of them look down at Marg's body and see the letter "E" written on her stomach.

Kevin speaks, "The victim is Doctor Marg Harrison, age 46. So far, everything we can tell is the same as the other victims. My team hasn't found any other clues and of course, no evidence."

Natalie questions, "What kind of doctor was she?"

Kevin replies, "She was a psychologist. She and her partner were working on a book." He pauses, "It was a book about what makes serial killers tick."

Ashley looks at Kevin, "Are you serious?"

Kevin nods, "He's outside with Jennifer right now."

Natalie nods, "I'll go talk to him."

Natalie walks off.

Ashley looks back down, "We are going to look around some. You can go ahead and take the body."

Kevin nods, "I'll see you back at the office."

Kevin rounds his team up and they load up Marg's body as Ashley and Mr. Gibson walk into Marg's office.

The killer is sitting at his desk in his dimly lit study. A cold, deathly silence fills the room as the killer is reading one of the old journals. He slowly turns the worn page of the notebook and sits back.

The killer speaks to himself, "You're right. The detectives are always making it more complicated than it really is. They yearn for the common thread that ties the victims together." He lets out a ghostly sigh, "And yet it is so obvious and right in front of them that they just can't see it."

The killer carefully reads the next page of the old journal. Once he finishes the page, he carefully closes the journal.

The killer picks up the picture of the next victim from the edge of his desk and talks to the picture, "The clock starts again, but I don't think you're going to be saved."

The killer lets out an evil little chuckle as he turns off the lamp on the desk. He stands and walks out of the room.

In the early morning hours of the day, Ashley is sitting in the conference room all alone. She is flipping through the pictures from the last victim.

Ashley speaks to herself, "What are we missing?"

Ashley flips through a couple more pictures when the door opens. Natalie and Mr. Gibson walk in.

Ashley looks up at the two of them, "Good morning."

Natalie lets out a tired smile, "Good morning."

Mr. Gibson sits down at the table, "I don't think we are going to find a common thread of the victims between the cases. So far, nothing is matching up."

Natalie sits down, "Maybe Jennifer will be able to get those records today."

Ashley nods, "I know. I have a feeling that the child in the picture has more to do with this case than just pointing us to Thomas Newman."

Mr. Gibson speaks up, "My gut feeling has always been that the child in the picture is tied to the killings some how."

Ashley sighs and sits back, "I think we can stop looking into the backgrounds of the victims." She pauses, "Lets start looking at Thomas Newman's movements before and after the loss of his son."

Mr. Gibson speaks up, "We know he was born in

Atlanta in 1899 and moved to Seattle in 1915. He takes over the family business in 1920 and the business takes off creating the Newman empire. He then marries Maureen O'Kelly in 1921." He pauses, "Then this unknown child appears in 1924."

Natalie picks up the story, "Then nothing until 1935 when Michael Newman is born and this unknown child is sent off to school. After that, Michael Newman runs away in 1949. Which we all figure sent Thomas Newman over the edge with his only child, the heir to his empire, now gone."

Ashley nods, "Then not six months later, the killings in Seattle start. With no heir to his empire, Thomas Newman goes into seclusion, eventually moving to Kansas City in 1974."

Mr. Gibson speaks up, "Where the killings start again, the very next year. But then he dies in 1989, which to me, ends his involvement. So why New York in 2000?"

Natalie speaks up, "What I don't understand is why would his empire be over after Michael Newman ran away? He still had the other child that they took in, the one that they sent off to school." She pauses, "Why didn't that child return to take over the business?"

Mr. Gibson nods, "That child is what I think the link to New York is. Maybe the child was sent to a school here in New York."

Ashley lets out a sigh, "We need to get those records and find out what happened to that child." She looks at Mr. Gibson, "I think you're right. What happened to that kid holds some of the answers that we need."

Ashley looks up at the calendar on the wall and shakes her head, "We need them soon cause the next victim is running out of time."

Mr. Gibson lets out a sigh, "Until then, we keep digging into Thomas Newman to see if we can find anything else that helps."

The three of them look at the enormous mound of papers and pictures on the table in front of them. They each know that the answer is hiding in all that paperwork somewhere.

The curtain falls over the stage as the Broadway crowd erupts into a deafening applause. The stage actors all come out onto the stage behind the curtain. Amongst them is a beautiful young woman who appears to be of Hawaiian decent in her early twenties. She stands about 5'5" tall and weighs a nice 150 pounds. She has brown hair and dark brown, nearly black looking eyes. She has on an 18th Century period dress.

The curtain raises back up and the cheers and applause starts up again as the actors bow to the Broadway crowd. After a few seconds, the curtain comes down again and the lights come on. The actors walk off the stage as the crowd starts to leave.

The young woman walks into the female dressing room with the other female actors. Each of them start to get out of their costumes.

One of the other female actors looks at the young woman, "You did great tonight Debbie. Brought the house down."

Debbie smiles as she hangs up the costume and grabs her clothes, "Thanks Julie, but I definitely didn't do it alone."

Julie smiles, "Well, you were definitely the right person for the lead."

Debbie buttons up her jeans, "Thanks."

Debbie puts on a green, short sleeve, v-neck shirt and her black shoes, "I hope it goes this good tomorrow night."

Julie smiles, "I'm sure it will."

All the actresses start to leave the dressing room.

Debbie grabs her cell phone and puts it in her pocket.

Julie stands up after finishing getting dressed, "Well, I'll see you tomorrow night."

Debbie nods, "Goodnight."

Julie walks out of the dressing room leaving Debbie alone. Debbie walks out of the dressing room, but instead of heading out the back exit, she walks back to the stage. She walks out in front of the curtain and stares out into the empty chairs. She closes her eyes and takes in the silent applause.

A man's voice speaks from her left, "I wish everyone was as passionate about this as you are."

Debbie jumps slightly, startled by the person that just spoke. Debbie looks to her left and sees a man in his late forties dressed in a gray suit.

Debbie smiles, "Hey Robert. You scared me."

Robert walks up to Debbie, "Is this your after show ritual?"

Debbie chuckles slightly, "Yea." She pauses, "You know, it's not hard to be passionate about a well written show."

Robert smiles, "Well thank you. I'll leave you to your crowd. Be safe going home."

Debbie nods, "You too Robert."

Robert walks off and Debbie stands on the stage for a few more minutes. She smiles at the empty chairs and walks off the left side of the stage. As she walks out the back exit, the killer emerges from the shadows on the right side of the stage.

In the morning hours of the new day, Jennifer walks into the lobby of a very prominent lawyer's office. She sits down in one of the waiting chairs as the receptionist hangs up the phone.

The receptionist looks at Jennifer, "Can I help you?"

Jennifer stands up and holds up her badge, "I'm Detective Jennifer Harris. I'm here to see Mr. Williams."

The receptionist smiles and presses a button on the phone.

A man's voce comes on the line, "Yes."

The receptionist speaks, "Sir, there is a Detective Harris here to see you."

Mr. Williams replies, "Yes of course. Let her in."

The receptionist disconnects the line, "Through that door detective."

Jennifer walks over to the door the receptionist pointed at and opens it. She walks into a big office with a large desk across from the door. A leather couch is on the left side of the room and a closed door is on the right side of the room. Bookshelves line the walls. Two chairs sit in front of the desk. Behind the desk, in the plush leather chair, sits Mr. Williams.

Mr. Williams stands up. He is a distinguished looking man in his fifties. He is wearing an expensive blue suit.

Mr. Williams motions to the chairs, "Please detective, have a seat."

Jennifer sits down and so does Mr. Williams.

Mr. Williams questions, "What can I do for you detective?"

Jennifer replies, "You're the lawyer handling the Thomas Newman estate?"

Mr. Williams nods, "Yes."

Jennifer sits forward, "There is some paperwork that exists on a child that the Newman's took in back in 1924. I was wondering if I could look at those files to see what happened to that child."

Mr. Williams sits back, "I'm sorry detective, but there were very specific instructions left for those files. It specifically states that the information in those files are not to be revealed to anyone."

Jennifer nods, "I know that they wanted privacy, but those files could contain vital information in a serial killer case."

Mr. Williams shrugs, "It doesn't matter what the files might contain. I have to follow the instructions that were left by my client."

Jennifer gives a puzzled look, "Thomas Newman died in Kansas City in 1989."

Mr. Williams smiles, "I know and I still can't tell you what's in the files, nor can I tell you who left the instructions on keeping the files secret. I cannot violate the privilege." He pauses, "I'm sorry, but without a court order, I can't help you."

Jennifer shakes her head, "We only have a couple more days until the next victim. Those files could help save at least one life and you won't help us."

Mr. Williams sits forward, "Understand detective, it's not that I don't care, but I can't legally help you. If it's that important, get a court order."

Jennifer sighs and stands up, "Unfortunately, it's harder to get without any good probable cause."

Mr. Williams shrugs, "Well, that is a hurdle that you and the district attorney will just have to find a way to overcome."

Jennifer shakes her head in frustration, "Well, I hope you sleep well when you read about the serial killer's next victim."

Jennifer walks out of the office and slams the door behind her.

Chapter 27

IN THE LATE EVENING hours of the city, Debbie walks into the female dressing room with the other actresses. She has a huge smile on her face from another great show. They can hear the applause finally fading as the crowd starts to leave the theatre.

Julie starts to change into her regular cloths, "Debbie, your performance was incredible again."

Debbie hangs up her dress and grabs her regular cloths, "Thanks. I'm just glad that they decided tonight to extend the show for another week."

Julie finishes getting dressed as the others actresses start to leave, "I know, I'm so excited."

Debbie finishes getting dressed and gets a glass of water, "Well, I guess I'll see you in a couple of nights."

Julie smiles, "Goodnight, be safe going home."

Debbie returns the smile, "Goodnight."

Julie leaves and Debbie is now alone. Debbie finishes the water and puts the glass down. She walks out of the dressing room and walks back to the stage. Debbie stands on the stage and stares out at the empty chairs. She closes her eyes and takes in the silent applause. She loves acting and can't wait for her big break.

Debbie's eyes pop open as she hears a noise to her left. She turns her head and looks around, but doesn't see any one or any thing.

Debbie calls out with a nervous voice, "Hello. Anyone there?"

Debbie continues to glance around, but there is no answer. She finally figures she is just hearing things in the old building. After a few more seconds, Debbie walks off the left side of the stage. She walks down the five steps at the edge of the stage. She walks down a short hallway of about ten feet, then turns right around the corner into the shadowy dark hallway.

Debbie instantly freezes as the image of a man is standing right in front of her. Before she can do anything, the killer wraps his left arm around her body and firmly places the cloth over her nose and mouth with his right hand. Debbie's eyes widen in horror as the killer forces her backwards towards the wall. With a good amount of force, the killer slams Debbie into the wall.

Debbie lets out a painful grunt and she tries to squirm free from the strong grasp of the killer. She is unable to break free as the killer presses his body against her body to keep her from moving. The killer can feel Debbie shift to her left and the killer turns his lower body just in time to avoid Debbie's right knee hitting him in the groin.

The killer decides to take no more chances and uses his weight and left leg to trip Debbie to the floor. The two of them land hard and the killer hears the air leave Debbie's lungs. Debbie's vision starts to blur as her head feels like it is swimming in quicksand. She can't find the strength to struggle anymore. A few tears roll down her cheek as she knows that the struggle is over.

The killer leans in close and whispers in her ear, "Relax my darling Debbie. Your final curtain call is near."

As the killer finishes his words, Debbie slips away

into the darkness.

It's early morning in New York City, just before the fall sun breaks through the sky. Mr. Gibson is sitting on the couch in the apartment that the New York City Police have given him to stay in during the course of the investigation. He looks at his notes that are sitting on the coffee table in front of him. He then looks at the calendar next to his notepad. From the look on his face, he knows that the call will be coming soon.

Mr. Gibson sits back on the couch, "What are you trying to tell us? Where is the hidden clue?"

Mr. Gibson rubs his eyes, "Or is there a hidden clue? Maybe all this is just one big game that you don't intend on having anyone solve."

Mr. Gibson leans forward on the couch again. He picks up his notepad and looks over the timeline he has written on it about Thomas Newman's life.

Mr. Gibson sighs, "What are we missing?"

Suddenly, the phone on the stand next to the couch rings. Mr. Gibson swallows hard as the sound catches him off guard. He puts down the notepad, leans over and picks up the phone.

Mr. Gibson answers in a solemn tone, "Hello."

Natalie's voice comes on the line, "Hey, we just got the location of the next victim. I'll be there as soon as possible to pick you up."

Mr. Gibson sighs, "I'll be ready."

Mr. Gibson hangs up the phone and looks back at his notepad. He swings his hand in frustration, knocking the notepad off the coffee table and onto the floor. He stands up and walks into the bathroom to get ready for the new day of aggravation.

As the morning sun highlights the New York skyline, the all to familiar scene is taking place at one of the Broadway theatre buildings. Numerous police cars line the streets as crime scene tape holds back the onlookers and the news crews from the grisly scene inside. A couple more minutes pass when Natalie pulls the car up next to the two CSI vans.

Natalie, Ashley and Mr. Gibson get out of the car. News reporters try desperately to yell questions to the detectives, but Natalie and Ashley are oblivious to everything around them. The three of them duck under the crime scene tape and head in the front door of the building. They pass a couple more officers in the lobby as they make their way into the main hall.

As the three of them start down one of the aisles, Jennifer walks up towards them.

Ashley looks at Jennifer, "Where is Kevin?"

Jennifer replies in a hurry, "As you walk towards the stage, just head off to the right. You can't miss them."

Natalie questions, "Where are you going?"

Jennifer smiles, "The district attorney finally got a judge to hear our case about the sealed files. He wants me there to help talk to the judge."

Ashley smiles, "Then we won't keep you another second. Good luck."

Jennifer gives a quick nod and hurries off. The three of them continue on pass the stage and down the hallway like Jennifer told them. A few seconds later, they see Kevin standing by the victim's body which is laid out in front of the female dressing room. The three of them walk up to Kevin.

Debbie's body is dressed like all the other victims and

laid out just the same as the others. On her stomach is written the letter "N".

Kevin sighs, "Victim is Debbie Wilson, age 22. From our initial investigation, everything appears the same. It also appears that the only clue left is the letter on the body. I still have my team going through the building."

Ashley nods, "If you want to take half your team and get the body out of here, we will continue searching the building with the other half."

Kevin nods, "Okay."

Kevin gathers up his things and calls a couple of his people on the radio. A few minutes later, Debbie's body is taken away.

Ashley looks at Natalie and Mr. Gibson, "It's a big building, but it's worth a try. He may have just made a mistake this time."

Mr. Gibson and Natalie nod in return. The three of them walk off to start searching the building for any other clues or evidence.

The clear afternoon sky has brought warmer temperatures to the city as Jennifer walks into the lobby of the law offices of Mr. Williams. This time, one of the assistant district attorneys is with her. The assistant district attorney is a tall, heavy set white man in his mid-thirties with short balding hair. He is dressed in a nice gray suit and is carrying a piece of paper in his hands.

Jennifer walks over to the receptionist, "Can you inform Mr. Williams that myself and Assistant District Attorney Ryan Baker is here to see him?"

The receptionist swallows hard and presses the button on her phone. The line rings a couple of times.

Then, Mr. Williams voice comes on the line, "Yes."

The receptionist replies, "Sir, Detective Harris and ADA Baker are here to see you."

The line is quiet for a second, then Mr. Williams replies, "Show them in."

The receptionist hangs up the line.

Jennifer smiles, "I remember which door it is. Thank you."

Jennifer and Ryan walk into Mr. Williams office. Mr. Williams smiles when he sees the two of them.

Mr. Williams motions to the chairs by his desk, "Detective Harris and ADA Baker, please have a seat."

Ryan places the piece of paper on the desk, "This is a court order stating that you will turn over the personal files that are requested within."

Mr. Williams picks up the paper and reads it carefully. When he is done, he puts the paper back down on the desk.

Jennifer looks at Mr. Williams, "I need those files as soon as possible."

Mr. Williams smiles, opens one of his desk drawers and pulls out a large manila folder that is obviously packed with papers.

Mr. Williams sets the folder on the desk, "I've been expecting you."

Ryan looks at Mr. Williams, "You're not even going to try and fight us on this."

Mr. Williams chuckles slightly, "There was no guidance left to try and stop a court order on the files. Only simply to not turn them over without one."

Jennifer picks up the folder and opens it. The papers inside are very old and worn. She pulls the inch tall stack of papers out of the folder and glances through some of them.

Mr. Williams sits down, "You can take the folder with you, but I would like it returned when you are done." He pauses, "I'm expecting another client any moment if you don't mind."

Jennifer stops at a certain page as something catches

her eye. She looks closer and reads the worn paper.

Jennifer speaks in disbelief, "Incredible." She looks up at Ryan, "I have to get this back to the station immediately. They are not going to believe this."

Ryan looks at Mr. Williams, "Thanks for your help."

Mr. Williams nods, "Not a problem."

· Ryan and Jennifer walk out of the office. Ryan gets in his car and heads back to his office as Jennifer rushes to get back to the station.

In the evening hours of the day, Ashley, Natalie and Mr. Gibson are sitting in the break room at the police station just down the hallway from the room that has become their second home. The three of them are finishing up their dinner without conversation. Each one in deep thought about where to go next with the case.

The three of them take a few more minutes and finish their meals, then they make their way back to the conference room. The three of them walk in and sit down around the table. The three of them just stare at the mountain of paperwork and pictures sitting on the table in front of them. At that time, the door opens and Jennifer comes walking in with the manila folder she got from Mr. Williams.

Jennifer has a smile on her face, "So, do you want to know a little more about the child from the picture with Thomas Newman?"

Ashley gets a somewhat excited look, "Are you serious? You got the file."

Jennifer walks over to the table, "Oh yes, and it is quite a surprise."

Mr. Gibson speaks up, "I would just like to know if the boarding school they sent the kid off to was here in New

York."

Jennifer sits down, "No it wasn't."

Natalie lets out a sigh of frustration, "Then what tie do we have to New York."

Jennifer shakes her head, "I don't know that one."

Mr. Gibson questions, "So where was the child sent for school?"

Jennifer pulls the papers out of the folder, "That would be, nowhere."

Ashley looks puzzled, "What?"

Jennifer shuffles through the papers and speaks, "In 1935, a 13 year old boy going by the name of John Smith, was sent to the Seattle Boy's Shelter for runaways and abandoned children. The influential parents were listed as anonymous."

Natalie speaks up, "They didn't send the child away to school like everyone else thought. They sent the child to the children's home." She pauses, "But why?"

Mr. Gibson nods as the obvious answer comes to him, "Because in 1935 their biological son, Michael, was born." He speculates for a second, "The Newman empire was huge at that time so instead of having the kids fight over it, Thomas Newman sends the adopted child away leaving the empire to his biological son."

Ashley shakes her head, "Can you imagine being a 13 year old boy living a good life suddenly cast away to the children's shelter during the depression." She pauses, "That boy must have felt betrayed."

Jennifer pulls out the paper she was looking for, "That's what I was thinking."

Natalie adds, "Betrayed enough to want revenge or to simply go over the edge."

Mr. Gibson nods, "I would if it happened to me. That could definitely be the reason why the focus is around Thomas Newman."

Ashley sits back in her chair, "So, from what we think

now, we actually have a picture of the first killer with Thomas Newman when he was two years old going by the name John Smith." Ashley looks at Jennifer, "Is there any other names in the file that the child had or is John Smith it?"

Jennifer sighs, "I'm afraid we're stuck with John Smith from when he was adopted by the Newman family in 1924."

Natalie speaks up, "Do you know how hard it's going to be to track a John Smith over 65 years, not to mention if he had a family?" She pauses, "We've only got five victims left, there's no way."

Mr. Gibson sits forward and places his arms on the table, "But we have another angle to look at the clues from. Maybe hidden in the writings is something that relates to John Smith, or a children's shelter."

Ashley nods, "Okay. Natalie, you get with the computer team and see if the writings might correlate to John Smith or to the possibility of a children's shelter." She turns to Jennifer, "Jennifer, you hit the research hard on trying to track down what happened to John Smith after he was sent to the children's home. Mr. Gibson and I will start back through the files to see if we overlooked anything that might point us in this new direction."

Jennifer gathers up the file and walks out closely followed by Natalie.

Ashley looks at Mr. Gibson, "This is going to take some time unless it is something obvious that we missed."

Mr. Gibson sighs and smiles, "True, but doesn't it feel good knowing that we are almost absolutely sure we know who the first killer was that started all this?"

Ashley lets out a smile, "Yes it does."

The two of them sit forward and start shuffling through the papers on the desk hoping to find that elusive clue that will break the case.

Chapter 28

IN HIS DIMLY LIT room of death, the killer sits at his desk scratching away his next journal entry. The eerie sound of pen on paper could send a chill down even the toughest of spines. After a few lines, the killer stops writing and sits back.

The killer speaks to himself, "You don't think I know your most recent discovery, I know everything."

The killer writes a couple more lines, then stops again, "You have gotten a lot further than the last two investigations, but your still missing it just like the others did."

The killer writes a few more lines, then stops and puts down his pen. He closes his journal and sets it off to the side.

The killer lets out an evil sigh, "Discovering John Smith will help you with nothing. It will only add to the frustration you're already feeling."

The killer reaches over and picks up the picture of his next victim from the edge of his desk, "You're running out of time Detective Taylor." He gives a very evil smile to the picture, "And your time has already ran out."

The killer rises out of the chair like a ghostly figure rising out of thin air. The killer turns off the desk lamp and walks out of the room.

In the evening hours of the city, many of the newspapers are running around trying to get their final stories in for tomorrow's morning edition. In the copy room of one of the newspapers, the scene looks like organized chaos. People are running everywhere and trying to yell over each other.

Walking around among the other workers is a young woman looking to be in her mid-twenties. She is around 5'6" tall and weighs a nice looking 140 pounds. She has straight brown hair that hangs to just below her shoulder blades and pretty blue eyes. She is wearing a white t-shirt, blue jeans, tennis shoes and prescription glasses. Her hair is pulled back into a ponytail.

A young man pushing a mail cart stops by the young woman, "Tori, what are you doing here?"

Tori looks at the young man, "I'm just filling in tonight since Alan is out sick. Besides, one of my stories is going in the morning edition."

The young man smiles, "You're just way to dedicated for a place like this."

The young man pushes the cart off. Tori walks around the room giving advice to some of the others about what type and font to use, story placement and a few other things. After a short while, with the moon high in the sky, the room starts to clear out.

Tori walks over to the open door of the editor's office, "Everything is done sir."

A man in his late forties looks up at Tori, "Thank you Miss Harmon. You should be getting home. Another long day will be starting soon." He pauses, "By the way, great story on the serial killer."

Tori smiles, "Thanks. I'm going to go up to my office and type up a few notes, then head home."

Tori walks off to the elevator. She goes up a few stories and gets off the elevator on the empty floor where some of the offices are at. She walks down the hallway and turns to the left. She passes one office door and stops at the next. Tori unlocks the office door and goes inside. As she sits and prepares some notes for her next story, she is completely unaware of the killer standing in the shadows of the hallway outside her office, watching and waiting.

In the late night hours, Ashley is sitting on her couch looking over some of her personal notes. She is wearing jeans and a t-shirt, but no shoes. She has an open beer on the coffee table and a couple of empty cans in the trash already. She lets out a sigh and her face shows the frustration of months on a case she just can't solve.

Ashley sits forward on the couch when she hears a knock on her door. She reaches over and grabs her pistol off the end table and walks towards the front door. Another knock echoes as Ashley stops at the front door.

Ashley yells, "Who is it?!"

Natalie's voice is heard from the other side of the door, "It's Natalie and Mr. Gibson!"

Ashley opens the door and smiles at Natalie and Mr. Gibson.

Natalie smiles in return, "We couldn't sleep and figured you'd be awake also."

Ashley steps back and Natalie and Mr. Gibson walk inside. Ashley closes the door and locks it. Ashley and Natalie walk over by the couch and Mr. Gibson sits in the chair next to the couch.

Ashley questions, "Do you two want a beer?"

Natalie nods, "Sure."

Mr. Gibson answers just after Natalie, "Absolutely."

Ashley walks into the kitchen, grabs two beers from the refrigerator and walks back into the living room. She hands a beer to Natalie and one to Mr. Gibson.

Ashley sits on the couch next to Natalie, "So, I see I'm not the only one suffering from sleepless nights."

Mr. Gibson sighs, "I haven't slept good since 1975."

Natalie takes a drink, "I just can't figure this killer out. The clues have to mean something. I mean, the computer kicked back so many possibilities linked to John Smith that it would take months to track them all down."

Ashley puts down her beer, "And that's time we don't have."

Mr. Gibson takes a drink, "I've been thinking about this for 25 years. I know the clues are real. The killer is telling us how to solve the case, but I just can't see the clue that ties it all together."

Ashley lets out a sigh, "I know what you mean. I know the clue is here, but I just can't find it. How can this guy be so good? We've got technology and experience, yet he still eludes us."

Natalie takes another drink, "Yea, but look at how much time he's had to prepare all this. Plus, the knowledge from the two previous cases."

Mr. Gibson finishes off his beer, "He is intelligent, well prepared and methodical. That is a hard combination to crack."

Mr. Gibson retrieves three beers from the refrigerator and sits back down. He hands one to Natalie, one to Ashley and opens one for himself.

Ashley takes a big drink, "Ten months and twenty two victims. We are getting down to crunch time."

Natalie sits back, "We're going to catch this guy."

Mr. Gibson raises his beer as to a toast, "Amen to that sister."

Natalie raises her beer, "You better believe it."

Ashley smiles and raises her beer, "Hell yes we will."

The three of them chuckle and each take a drink. Then, they hear the bushes rustle by the front window. The three of them look at each other, all thinking the same thing. Before either of them can put down their beer, they hear footsteps running off down the sidewalk. Ashley is the first one up with her pistol. Right behind her is Natalie with her pistol, then Mr. Gibson with his revolver.

Ashley, in a rush, fumbles with trying to unlock the locks on the front door. When she gets the door open, the three of them rush outside, each looking a different direction. Their faces show the dejection of moving too slow as they see nothing.

Ashley speaks with some angry fire in her voice, "I'm getting real sick of this guy."

The three of them walk back inside and Ashley locks the door again.

In the cool morning hours of the city, Jennifer walks into the huge public library. She prepares herself for another long day of research which so far has turned up nothing on John Smith. She walks back to a more secluded area where some computer terminals and microfilm machines are located. She sits down at one of the computer terminals and logs in.

Jennifer speaks to herself while typing, "Lets see if we can find you today John Smith."

Jennifer pulls up a search based website and starts typing away. After twenty minutes of checking different websites, she gets up from the terminal and walks over to the coffee station set up for the patrons. She makes a cup of coffee and returns to the computer. She puts her coffee down and types some more.

Jennifer stares intently at the screen, "Where are you hiding?"

Jennifer starts to access the online files for the Seattle Children's Home in hopes that she might be able to discover some history about the place and people or a link to another site that might be of some help. She smiles as she finds some interesting information.

Jennifer takes a drink of coffee, "So that's how you kept the child a secret. Thomas Newman donated money to the home in exchange for privacy. Lots of money."

Jennifer types some more, then sits back and stretches while she waits for the information to show up on the computer screen. Once the information comes up, she looks through it all carefully. Her face turns to that of frustration as it becomes another dead end.

Jennifer sits back and rubs her eyes, "This is going to take forever."

Jennifer takes another drink of coffee and looks at the time and date on the computer. She knows by the date that they are running out of time for the next victim. She sits back and waits for another search to appear on the screen.

Jennifer sighs and looks around, "All this information. You can find anything on anyone." She looks back at the computer when it beeps, "So how can you hide so well?"

Jennifer gets a little smile on her face when she sees a glimpse of hope on the screen. She hears one of the custodians pushing a cart towards her. She motions to the custodian to come over to her station without looking at the person. Jennifer looks up at the custodian now standing beside her. She is now face to face with the very man they have been trying to find, the serial killer himself, and she doesn't even know it.

Jennifer questions, "Do you have this microfilm on

file?"

The killer looks at the screen and smiles, "Let me write down the number and I'll check for you."

The killer pulls out a pen, grabs a scratch piece of paper from next to the computer and writes down the number.

The killer smiles at Jennifer, "I'll be back in a few minutes."

Jennifer nods, "Thank you."

The killer walks off and Jennifer continues to look for more information that might help her.

In the late night hours of a city getting ready for Halloween, Tori sits at her computer in her office. She types away on her next story about the unknown serial killer that has turned the city into his own personal playground of death. She stares intently at the computer screen while she types, completely oblivious to everything else around her.

Tori jumps in her chair when she hears a man's voice at her open office door, "You should get some rest Tori."

Tori looks up and sees the senior editor of the paper, a man in his sixties, standing at her door.

Tori sits back, "I'm almost finished. I'm surprised to see you still here this late."

The senior editor smiles, "Halloween is going to be a big deal this year because of this nutcase. I'm just making sure everything is running as smooth as possible." He pauses, "I'll see you tomorrow, get some rest."

Tori chuckles slightly, "See you tomorrow."

The senior editor nods, "Goodnight."

The senior editor walks off and Tori returns to her typing.

Tori speaks while typing, "Maybe we can be alone now Mr. Killer so I can finish this story."

Tori continues to type, completely unaware that she is getting exactly what she just said. The floor is now completely empty except for her and the killer who stands in the shadows of the darkened hallway waiting for his next prey to come to him.

Tori stops typing and sits back, "There, done."

Tori saves the article and shuts down her computer. She gets up from the desk and turns off the desk lamp which shrouds her office in darkness.

Tori speaks as she walks towards the office door, "This is the story that is going to make me."

Tori locks the handle on the door, steps into the hallway and pulls the door closed. As she jiggles the door knob to make sure it is locked, the killer suddenly wraps his arm around her waist and places the cloth over her nose and mouth. Tori's eyes are as wide as they can be as her body stiffens in fear.

The killer pulls her back from the door, turns around in the middle of the hallway and uses his weight and strength to slam Tori's body into the wall directly across the hall from her office door. Tori lets out a moan of pain as she finally gets her body loose from the fear and starts to struggle. The killer holds her hard pressed against the wall and Tori is unable to break free.

Tori can feel her head starting to get real heavy as her vision starts to blur. Her eyes manage a couple of tears as she knows that this is going to be the end. Her vision blurs more and starts to fade as the heaviness in her head is unbearable.

The killer smoothly whispers in Tori's ear, "Relax beautiful Tori. Soon you will be the story."

The words echo in Tori's head for just another second before Tori finally passes into the killer's darkness.

Chapter 29

IN THE HOUR BEFORE a new sunrise over the city, Kevin stands in his bathroom brushing his teeth while his lovely wife still sleeps. He finishes brushing, then uses some mouthwash. He spits out the mouthwash and sighs. He walks as quietly as possible into the bedroom and grabs the rest of his clothes for the day.

Kevin walks into the living room and finishes getting dressed. He puts on his watch and looks at the time. It reads 5:45 am. He walks into the kitchen and drinks a glass of milk before starting the new day. As he walks back into the living room, his cell phone rings.

Kevin, knowing what day it is, answers the phone, "Detective Reynolds."

Kevin listens intently for a couple of seconds. He grabs a piece of paper and a pen.

Kevin sighs, "Give me the location again."

Kevin writes down the address and puts down the pen, "Contact the rest of the team. I'm on my way."

Kevin hangs up the phone and shakes his head. A tear comes to his eyes as he opens his cell phone and dials another number.

Ashley's tired voice comes on the line, "Detective Taylor."

Kevin speaks, "The next victim's been found."

Ashley's voice is solemn, "Where?"

Kevin gives her the address and hangs up. He walks quietly back into the bedroom. He ever so gently kisses his wife on the forehead, then leaves for another long and frustrating day.

In the cool fall morning, a good sized crowd has gathered around the front of the newspaper building where Tori works. Numerous police cars line the street. Ashley pulls the car up next to the two CSI vans. Ashley gets out of the driver's seat. Natalie gets out of the passenger's seat and Mr. Gibson gets out of the backseat. The three of them ignore the yells from the different news crews as they make their way to the crime scene tape.

Ashley looks over her shoulder to see where Natalie and Mr. Gibson are as they push their way through the crowd when she bumps into someone hard.

Ashley looks at the patron, "Sorry. Excuse me."

The patron, the elusive killer replies, "It's okay detective."

Ashley continues on through the crowd so focused on the next victim that she doesn't pay the words much mind. She gets to the crime scene tape, then stops and turns back to the crowd with a puzzled look on her face.

Natalie looks at her, "Ashley, what is it?"

Mr. Gibson can tell by the look on her face and questions, "Was it him?"

Ashley replies while glancing through the crowd, "I'm not sure. The voice just hit me as sounding familiar."

Natalie speaks quickly, "You two go inside, I'm going

to tell the officers to corral the crowd the best they can and start getting names."

Ashley nods and ducks under the crime scene tape followed by Mr. Gibson. Natalie rushes off to find the officer in charge of the uniformed officers stationed outside the building.

After following the directions to get to the floor where Tori's office is at, Ashley and Mr. Gibson walk off the elevator. They walk down the long hallway and look to the right. The two of them see Kevin standing next to Tori's body. Tori's body is laying in front of her office door. It is dressed and laid out like all the other victims. On her stomach is written the letter "H".

Ashley walks up to Kevin, "What do we have?"

Kevin replies, "The victim is Tori Harmon, age 26. I think it goes without saying that she was killed just like all the others. The only clue we've found is the writing on the stomach." He pauses and looks at Ashley, "What is it? You seem distracted."

Ashley lowers her voice, "I might have just had a close encounter with the killer coming through the crowd."

Kevin glances around as if someone might hear them, "Are you serious?"

Ashley nods slightly, "Something about the voice stood out."

Mr. Gibson looks at Ashley, "I don't think we're going to get much here."

Ashley nods in agreement, "Go ahead and take the body Kevin." She looks at Mr. Gibson, "We'll check through the office just in case."

Kevin rounds his team up and they remove Tori's body from the scene. Ashley and Mr. Gibson enter Tori's office to see if they can find anything. Natalie is still directing the officers out front who are going through the crowd getting everyone's name in hopes that the killer might be amongst them.

The killer sits quietly in his dimly lit lair of death. He puts the pen to paper, making his next journal entry. The horrifying sound echoes through the secluded room.

The killer stops for a second, "Nice try detective, but you have to be faster than that."

The killer writes a few more lines in his journal. He puts down his pen and closes his notebook.

The killer sets the notebook to the side, "It is so easy to avoid the police in a crowd that size Detective Taylor." He pulls out an old journal, "Have you gotten so desperate that you're now taking the names of everyone that shows up at the crime scene?"

The killer opens the old notebook and reads the page slowly. Once he finishes the page, he sits back in his chair.

The killer reaches over and picks up the picture of his next victim, "The clock starts again."

The killer closes the old notebook, turns off the light and gets up. He slowly walks out of the room to start the next hunt.

In the evening hours between dinner and bed time, the only light still on in one of the many small shopping centers is that of a hair salon. The all glass front window has a sign painted on it reading, "KRISTEN'S KUTS". Inside is an older lady sitting in a barber's chair as a man in his twenties is finishing up her hair. Another man is sitting in a waiting chair, reading the newspaper.

A beautiful young woman looking to be in her early twenties with a skin tone and features of a person with Oriental and European mixed descent walks in from the back of the salon. She has dark brown hair that hangs down below her shoulders with dark red highlights and she has captivating green eyes. She stands around 5'3" tall and weighs a trim 115 pounds. She is wearing a red, sleeveless v-neck top, light blue jeans and tennis shoes to match.

The young woman walks over to the man sitting in the waiting chair, "Hi, I'm Kristen. What can I do for you?"

The man lowers the newspaper to reveal the truth of who he is.

The killer smiles at Kristen, "I just need a quick trim."

Kristen smiles, "Right this way."

Kristen shows the killer over to one of the barber's chairs. The killer sits down.

Kristen questions, "What would you like done?"

The killer looks into the mirror, "Just a little off the top and take the sides down to about half the length it is now."

Kristen smiles, "We can do that."

Kristen wraps the barber's cape around the killer and pulls out her haircutting kit. Kristen starts cutting and talking to the man cutting hair next to her. The man finishes the older ladies hair, brushes her off and shows her over to the cash register.

The killer questions, "You look young to have your own salon."

Kristen replies, "Well, I worked at a nice salon, but once I inherited some money, I decided to give my own salon a try." She pauses, "So, what's your name?"

The killer smiles, "John."

Kristen finishes with the top and starts on the sides, "Nice to meet you. First time here?"

The killer replies, "Yes."

Kristen finishes cutting the killer's hair. The killer looks in the mirror and nods his approval.

Kristen brushes the hair off the killer, "Well, if you like it, I hope you become a regular."

The killer follows Kristen over to the cash register.

Kristen rings up the total.

The killer hands her the money, "I'm sure you'll see me again. Have a good night."

Kristen nods and smiles, "You too."

After the killer walks out, Kristen locks the front door. She walks over to the other man that was cutting the hair who is finishing up sweeping the floor.

The man smiles at Kristen, "Another regular customer?"

Kristen smiles, "Sure wouldn't hurt."

The man finishes cleaning up the floor as Kristen cleans the scissors and combs. She lays the cutting instruments out to dry. Kristen walks over to the register and takes out the drawer.

The man puts the broom up, "Well, I'm heading home. See you tomorrow."

Kristen smiles, "See you tomorrow Adam."

Adam walks through the door leading to the back of the salon. Kristen walks into the back room as Adam walks out the back door that leads to the parking lot. Kristen counts up the money at the desk next to the small safe. She pulls out her accounting book and enters the amount. She puts the money in a money bag. She opens the safe, puts the money inside and locks the safe. Kristen walks over and grabs her jacket. She walks out the back door which locks behind her when it closes and she heads across the parking lot to her car.

In the mid-morning hours of the new day, Ashley, Mr. Gibson and Kevin are sitting in the conference room shuffling through papers and pictures. Ashley looks up at the board and the picture of Tori's body added to all the others. She sighs and shakes her head. A heavy silence hangs over the room. The frustration is hanging so thick in the air that a person could cut it with a knife.

Ashley sits back and breaks the silence, "What are we not seeing?"

Mr. Gibson shakes his head, "Even with all the new discoveries since my case, I'm back to banging my head against the wall. I can't see where he is taking us."

Kevin speaks up, "That's the problem. We're following him. We have to figure out how to get ahead of this guy."

Ashley chuckles slightly, "A point that seems very elusive."

At that moment, the door opens and Natalie and Jennifer walk in. Both of them have a dejected look on their face. Natalie sits down next to Ashley and Jennifer sits by Kevin.

Kevin looks at Jennifer, "Anything?"

Jennifer sighs in frustration, "I can't find this guy. I can't track him down. He went to the Seattle Children's Home and just vanished into thin air."

Ashley shakes her head and looks at Natalie, "I hope your luck was better."

Natalie shakes her head in frustration, "We got nothing from the names in the crowd that day. He must have slipped past us."

Ashley stands up and walks over to the board where all the pictures of their victims are posted.

Ashley speaks while looking at the board, "We've got four victims left and the clock is running out on the next one."

Ashley turns her attention to the board with all the articles that have anything to do with the New York case posted on it, "Eleven months and hundreds of articles yet people still don't change their routines."

Natalie speaks up, "He has to love the publicity. We've got our own little shrine of articles. I wonder how many others do."

Mr. Gibson shakes his head, "I don't think he cares about the publicity. I think he gets off on being able to outsmart the police. Everything we have at our disposal and we can't catch him."

Kevin speaks up, "Maybe the clues are nothing more than a sick joke. He enjoys watching us not being able to solve the case."

Jennifer speaks up, "But the last clue talks about a prize in the letter."

Ashley turns back to the others, "No. The clues are going to lead us to an inevitable ending. We just have to find the missing piece that ties it all together."

Mr. Gibson nods, "I think we already have it and we just don't know what it is yet. The letters and numbers are going to give us something and the physical clues are helping to point a certain direction, we have to figure that out."

Natalie sighs, "But none of it so far is giving us a relation to Thomas Newman or John Smith. So, what are the clues and writings pointing us to?"

Ashley speaks up, "That's the piece that when we figure out what it is, everything is going to fall into place." She pauses, "Lets just pray that we find it soon."

Ashley walks back over to the table and sits back down. She starts shuffling through some papers on the table. Natalie, Mr. Gibson, Kevin and Jennifer follow suit. They each have the feeling that the hidden answer is somewhere amongst the hundreds of pictures and thousands of pieces of paper that is laid out in front of them.

Chapter 30

AS THE SUN GETS lower in the November sky, the killer sits at his desk in his dimly lit study. He is writing away on his next journal entry. The pen on paper is the only sound in the deathly silence hanging over the room.

The killer puts the pen down for a second, "I had such high hopes for you when all this started Detective Taylor. It now appears that you will fall victim to the case just like Detective Conners and your friend, Detective Gibson."

The killer writes a few more lines in his journal, then puts his pen down again. The killer closes the journal and sets it off to the side. The killer picks up the picture of Kristen from the edge of the desk.

The killer speaks to the picture, "Sorry, it's too late for you now."

The killer turns off the desk lamp, gets up and walks out of the room.

In the cooling darkness of the New York City night,

Kristen is cleaning up her salon as the last stylist walks out the back of the salon. Kristen sweeps up the salon, then cleans the haircutting instruments. Once she is done cleaning up, she walks over to double check that the front door is locked. After she checks the door, she goes over to the cash register and takes the drawer out.

Kristen switches off the light to the salon and now a little light shines in from the parking lot casting shadows all through the salon. Kristen walks to the door that leads to the back of the salon. Kristen opens the door and steps into the back area. The door swings shut behind her as she turns to her left and walks over to the desk and the safe. The refrigerator and coat rack are about forty feet behind her. Usually that is all, but tonight is different, tonight, the killer is also standing forty feet behind her.

Kristen sits down at the desk and starts to count the money. She is completely unaware of the killer moving slowly up behind her. The killer is so close now he can hear Kristen softly counting the bills. Kristen sets down one stack of bills and reaches for another stack. Suddenly, the killer firmly places the cloth over Kristen's nose and mouth.

The killer pulls her up out of the chair as Kristen's eyes show the surprise and horror of what is happening. Once Kristen clears the chair, the killer wraps his left arm around her waist and turns to the left. With great force, the killer slams Kristen's tiny body against the wall by the desk and safe. Kristen moans in pain. She tries to struggle, but the killer has too strong of a hold on her.

Kristen lets out a muffled plea, "Please, don't."

The killer holds the cloth firmly over her nose and mouth and keeps her pinned against the wall with his body. Kristen can feel her head getting heavy as her vision starts to fade in and out. The killer can feel Kristen's body getting weaker. A few tears run down Kristen's cheeks as she knows that it is hopeless.

The killer leans in close and whispers in Kristen's ear, "Relax beautiful Kristen, the last cut is done."

As the words fade in Kristen's ear, she passes into the eternal darkness that was waiting for her.

As the clock strikes 6 am on the new day in New York City, Jennifer is at the police station gym. She has her black hair pulled back into a ponytail. She is wearing a tight fitting, white tank top, gray sweatpants and tennis shoes. She is also wearing a wrist support on each wrist and 4 oz padded grappling gloves on each hand.

Jennifer is standing next to the heavy bag. She has some sweat rolling down her face and body from the morning workout. She takes a deep breath and resumes her fighting stance. She starts striking the heavy bag with various punches and kicks. After a couple of minutes, she stops again to catch her breath.

Jennifer resumes her stance when she hears her pager start beeping from her bag just a few feet away. Jennifer walks over and picks up her pager. She recognizes Kevin's phone number. She puts down her pager and picks up her cell phone. Jennifer presses the speed dial number one and the line starts ringing.

Kevin's voice comes on the line, "Detective Reynolds."

Jennifer speaks still catching her breath, "This is Jennifer. What's up?"

Kevin replies, "We just got our next victim."

Jennifer squats down and reaches into her gym bag. She pulls out a notepad and pen.

Jennifer replies, "What's the address?"

Jennifer writes down the address Kevin gives her. She puts the notepad and pen back in her bag.

Jennifer stands back up, "I'll get the rest of the team and head that way."

Jennifer hangs up. She tosses her phone back in the bag. She picks the gym bag up and hurries off.

The parking lot in front of Kristen's salon is covered with police cars, two CSI vans, a few news crews and other onlookers. Onto the parking lot pulls another familiar car and it stops next to the CSI vans. Ashley, Natalie and Mr. Gibson get out of the car. The three of them can see Kevin standing just inside the salon's front door.

As the three of them walk towards the front door, Ashley speaks, "What do you think the chances are that the killer is watching us right now?"

Mr. Gibson replies, "I would say, 100%."

The three of them make it to the front door and they see Kristen's petite body laying on the floor a few feet inside. Kristen's body is dressed and laid out just as all the other victims have been. Ashley walks up next to Kevin and looks down at Kristen's body. She sees the letter "A" written on Kristen's stomach.

Kevin goes ahead with the particulars, "Victim's name is Kristen Kruger, age 22. She was killed just like all the other victims. We talked to the other employees and none of them can offer us much help."

Jennifer walks up, "Well, the only possibility is that a new patron came in a few nights ago for a hair cut and seemed interested in Kristen. All the guy said was Kristen told him his name was, go figure, John."

Natalie shakes her head, "No doubt the killer."

Jennifer nods, "We asked the guy to come down to the station to get with a sketch artist. He's not sure how much it will help, he said he didn't see the man for very long."

Mr. Gibson sighs, "Anything will help at this point."

Ashley nods, "It definitely can't hurt." She pauses, "Any other clues or evidence found."

Kevin shakes his head, "Nothing."

Ashley replies as if she already knew that answer was coming, "Go ahead and get the body out of here. The three of us are going to look around some."

Kevin nods and looks at Jennifer, "Lets round them up."

Jennifer heads off to get the team together. As the CSI team loads up Kristen's body, Ashley, Natalie and Mr. Gibson walk around the salon looking for anything that might help them.

As the shroud of darkness falls over the city, the killer sits at his desk in his dimly lit study. He scratches away his next journal entry. The sound sends a cold chill through the room as the words are describing the death of a young woman.

The killer stops writing for a moment, "Is it eating you up inside Detective Taylor?"

The killer writes a couple more lines and sets his pen down. He closes the journal and puts it off to the side.

The killer sits back in his chair, "Is it killing you to know who the last victim will be? Who close to you will die?" He lets out an evil chuckle, "Continue the path you're on and you will soon find out Detective Taylor."

The killer reaches over and picks up the picture of his next victim. He stares at the picture for a moment.

The killer whispers to the picture, "You're almost too beautiful to kill." He pauses and lets go of an evil grin, "Almost."

The killer stands up and turns off the desk lamp. He

turns and heads off to start the stalk on his next victim.

Another late evening is underway in the conference room at the station. Kevin, Mr. Gibson, Natalie and Jennifer are all sitting around the table. A few minutes pass and Ashley walks in with a piece of paper in her hand. She walks over to the board with all the pictures of the victims on it. She grabs a push pin and pins the paper on the board under the victims. It is a sketch of the killer. A fairly close resemblance at that.

Ashley turns to the others, "This is John. He is a white male in his mid-twenties. He is approximately 5'9" to 5'10" tall and weighs around the 170 pound mark. He has brown hair and unknown eye color."

Natalie chuckles, "Well, that narrows it down to a few thousand suspects in the city."

Ashley nods, "Yea, doesn't help much, but burn the image in our minds. We know he shows up at the crime scenes."

Jennifer pauses for a second, "You know. That looks kind of like someone I saw working at the library when I was there doing my research."

Everyone else in the room looks at Jennifer. They each have a look of shock on their face.

Ashley questions, "Are you sure?"

Jennifer nods, "Yea. It looks like a guy that helped me find some microfilm once."

Natalie questions, "How many times have you seen him there?"

Jennifer thinks for a moment, "Just the once."

Ashley speaks to everyone, "First thing in the morning, we head to the library with this picture and start questioning everyone." She pauses, "We're going to stop for the night. I want everyone fresh for tomorrow."

The others nod at Ashley. Everyone gets up from the table. Ashley grabs the picture from the board and follows the others out of the conference room.

Just before midnight in a nice residential neighborhood, a small economy car pulls up to a one story brick house with an attached two car garage. Driving the car is a teenage girl, a very beautiful teenage girl. She has soft brown hair that hangs down to the middle of her back and captivating hazel eyes. She is around 5'5" tall and weighs a stunningly put together 130 pounds. She is wearing tight fitting, ripped blue jeans with a white belt, an orange tank top covered by a half zipped up purple jacket and designer shoes.

The garage door raises up and the girl pulls the car inside. As she parks the car, her cell phone rings.

The girl answers the phone, "Hello."

A teenage girl's voice comes on the line, "Jo, did you make it home before your curfew?"

Jo smiles, "Yea, just barely as always. I just like the fact that my parents trust me enough to get home in time and they go on to bed instead of waiting up for me."

The girl replies, "That's cause they know you're responsible."

Jo chuckles, "I guess that's it. I'll talk to you tomorrow."

Jo hangs up the phone and gets out of the car. From across the street in the shadows, the killer watches Jo walk through the door from the garage to the kitchen as the large garage door closes.

As the sun lights up the New York City skyline and the doors of the library open, two cars pull up in front of the library. Ashley, Natalie and Mr. Gibson get out of one car and Kevin and Jennifer get out of the other car.

Ashley hands a copy of the sketch to the others, "Okay, we split up and hit every worker and any patron we see." She pauses, "If you get a confirmation, radio and we will all meet up. If you see him, do not approach alone. Watch him and get us to your location quickly."

Everyone nods and heads up the stairs to the front doors. Once they enter the library, the five of them head off in different directions.

Mr. Gibson is the first to find someone and stops by a young lady, "Excuse me. I'm Detective Gibson and I was wondering if you've seen this man."

Mr. Gibson holds up the sketch so the lady can see it. The lady looks at it closely.

The lady replies, "He doesn't look familiar."

Mr. Gibson replies, "Are you sure, we think he works here."

The young lady replies, "I've only been here a month, but I don't recognize him. Sorry."

Mr. Gibson nods and walks off. Jennifer is the next to spot someone working. She walks up to a man in his thirties.

Jennifer speaks, "Excuse me sir. I'm Detective Harris and I was wondering if you recognize this man. He might be an employee here."

The man takes a minute to look at the picture, then shakes his head, "He doesn't look like anyone that I've seen working here. Sorry."

Jennifer nods, "Thanks."

Jennifer walks off to find someone else. Natalie is the next to find a library employee. Natalie walks up to a woman in her forties.

Natalie holds up the picture, "Excuse me miss. I'm Detective Simpson with the NYPD. I was wondering if you might have seen this man here? Possibly even working here."

The woman looks at the picture, "I'm sorry. I just started last week. He doesn't look familiar."

Natalie sighs, "Thank you for your time."

Natalie walks off. Ashley is the next one to happen across an employee. She walks up to a man in his twenties.

Ashley holds up the picture, "Excuse me sir. I'm Detective Taylor with the NYPD. I was wondering if you recognize this man? Possibly a fellow employee."

The man looks at the picture for a mere second, "I see guys that look like that every day."

The man looks away and Ashley speaks more firmly, "Look at the picture and tell me if you've seen him. It could save someone's life."

The man looks back at the picture, "Nope. Whoever that is, he doesn't work here."

Ashley nods, "Thank you."

Ashley walks off. Kevin walks up to an older lady in her sixties.

Kevin holds up the picture, "Excuse me madam. I'm Detective Reynolds. I was wondering if this man works here?"

The older lady looks at the picture, "Oh no."

Kevin sighs, then the lady speaks again, "It looks like someone that comes in here from time to time, but a lot of young men look like that."

Kevin re-questions, "He doesn't work here?"

The older lady smiles, "I've worked here for forty years and no one like that has ever worked here. I'm sorry."

Kevin smiles, "Thank you for your time."

Kevin walks off. Each one of them continues for another hour asking everyone they can find. The answers all seem to be the same.

Ashley grabs her radio, "Everyone meet me back at the front."

Ashley heads for the front doors. In a few minutes, the five of them are standing together at the front of the library.

Ashley questions, "Did anyone get anything helpful?"

Natalie is first, "Just that it possibly could be someone that comes here, but not an employee."

The others nods as that answer about sums it up for all of them.

Mr. Gibson speaks up, "I have no doubt Jennifer saw him and that he even helped her, pretending to work here just so he could see what she was up to."

Ashley nods, "That's what I'm thinking also." She pauses, "We will get an undercover detail to stakeout the place, just in case, but I don't think showing the picture is going to give us much more than what we have now."

Jennifer questions, "So, what now?"

Ashley replies, "We get back to the station and start back through the paperwork where we left off ."

The five of them walk out the front of the library to the cars. They get in the cars and drive off down the street. The killer smiles as he watches them leave from his hiding place across the street.

Chapter 31

AS THE LIGHTS OF the big city light up the night sky, the only light on in the killer's study is the desk lamp that dimly lights the room. The killer is sitting at his desk reading one of the old journals. He carefully turns the page and sits back in his chair.

The killer speaks, "Good work detective. I guess I'll have to do my research elsewhere now."

The killer reads another page, then pauses once again.

The killer sighs, "However, this new little break is not going to help the next victim."

The killer closes the old journal and sets it carefully off to the side.

The killer speaks again, "You're running out of time again Detective Taylor."

The killer stands up, turns off the light and walks out of the room.

In the late hours of the night, Ashley is sitting on her

couch in her pajamas. Her pistol is sitting on the coffee table next to an open beer can. She is sitting cross-legged with a large photo album in her lap and another one sitting on the couch next to her. She opens the photo album and slowly starts looking through the pictures. As she stares at each picture, she remembers the days that the pictures were taken.

Ashley flips through the pages of pictures of her, her sister, her mom and dad as well as other family and friends. A few tears come to her eyes as she knows that the last victim is going to be someone she cares a great deal about.

Ashley sniffles and talks to herself, "I have to stop him. I can't live with failing one of you."

Ashley continues to flip the pages of the album and taking drinks from her beer. She does her best to hold back the tears. Then, she hears a knock on her door. Ashley puts down the album, grabs her pistol and walks over to the front door.

Ashley yells, "Who is it?"

Natalie yells back, "It's Natalie and Mr. Gibson."

Ashley wipes her eyes and unlocks the front door. She smiles at Natalie and Mr. Gibson when she opens the door.

Ashley steps to the side, "Come in."

Natalie and Mr. Gibson walk in. Ashley closes the door and locks it. Ashley follows Natalie and Mr. Gibson over by the coffee table.

Natalie looks at Ashley, "We have one unmarked car at each end of the street, just in case."

Ashley smiles, "Beer?"

Natalie nods, "Sure."

Mr. Gibson pulls out a bottle of whiskey from the brown bag he his carrying, "I think it's a whiskey night for me."

Ashley walks off to the kitchen as Natalie sits on the couch and Mr. Gibson sits in the chair. Ashley returns with two beers and a glass. She hands one beer to Natalie and the glass to Mr. Gibson. Ashley sits on the couch and opens her beer. Natalie opens her beer as Mr. Gibson pours himself a glass of straight whiskey.

Mr. Gibson looks at the photo albums, "Doing some walking down memory lane?"

Ashley breaks a slight smile, "Yea."

Mr. Gibson replies after taking a drink, "You can't let yourself get distracted by who the last victim might be. You have to stay focused on the case at hand."

Natalie speaks up, "We still have time to solve this case and catch this guy before the last victim."

Ashley sighs, "I know, but it's hard not to think about it." She looks at Mr. Gibson, "How did you ever deal with it?"

Mr. Gibson holds up his glass, "With a lot of this." He pauses, "I never forgave myself for letting my sister down, but I can do something to help make it right."

Ashley takes a drink, "What's that?"

Mr. Gibson takes another big drink, "By putting a stop to it this time."

Natalie speaks reassuringly, "Something is going to break. It always does."

Ashley stares at the open page of pictures, "Yea, but how late will it be."

Mr. Gibson refills his glass, "Enough about the case tonight. Move over girl and show me some of those embarrassing pictures from your past."

Ashley smiles and slides over. Mr. Gibson sits down on the couch next to her and Natalie. Ashley grabs the photo album and starts telling them about the different pictures. As the time passes, the three of them at least have freed their minds of the serial killer for one night.

As the sun starts to set over the city, the killer sits quietly in his dimly lit room. He is carefully writing down his next journal entry as he prepares for the night ahead. The scratching of the pen on paper has an even more eerie feel to it knowing that by the morning the next entry will be about another dead female.

The killer stops writing for a moment, "You did your best again Detective Taylor, but it just wasn't good enough."

The killer writes a few more lines and puts his pen down. He closes the journal and sets it off to the side. He picks up the picture of Jo as well as another picture. It is a Polaroid of a grassy opening in some unknown wooded location.

The killer smiles, "Now it's time to give you the one physical clue that I know must have you the most confused." He pauses, "However, fit the pieces of the puzzle together and it will make perfect sense."

The killer stands up and turns off the light. He walks out of the room and into the darkness of the night.

As the clock reads a few minutes before midnight, Jo comes driving down the street towards her house, just like always. She hangs up her phone as she turns into the driveway and opens the garage door. She pulls the car inside and parks it. She gets out of the car and walks around the front of it over to the door that leads into the kitchen. She pushes the button and the large garage door closes.

Jo pulls out her keys, unlocks the door and walks into the kitchen. She turns around, closes the door and locks it. She walks over to the kitchen table and puts her purse and backpack on the table. She walks over to the refrigerator and opens it completely unaware of the figure that just emerged from the pantry behind her. She grabs a bottle of water and closes the refrigerator door.

Before Jo can turn around, the killer wraps his left arm around her body as his right arm places the cloth firmly over her nose and mouth. Jo tries to scream, but the cloth muffles the sound too much for the noise to wake up her parents on the other end of the house. The killer pulls her back away from the refrigerator to the middle of the kitchen where she can't kick anything to make noise.

Jo tries desperately to break free as a few tears come to her terrified eyes. The killer holds onto her and decides not to take the chance that Jo might squirm away so he uses his legs to trip her to the floor. Jo lands on her stomach and the killer is now laying on top of her. She starts to sob as her vision starts to blur. Tears stream down her face as she knows the end is near. Her head gets even heavier and her vision starts to fade in and out.

The killer leans close and whispers in Jo's ear, "Relax my most beautiful Joanna, no more worries about school and curfew."

Those are the last words Joanna hears as she passes out. The killer stands up and puts the cloth back in his jacket pocket.

The killer whispers to himself as he walks back to the pantry, "Time is against me now. Must finish before the parents get up."

The killer goes into the pantry and returns to the kitchen with a bag no doubt full of the things he needs to stage the body.

The alarm clock sounds loud at six in the morning. It wakes the mid forties couple from their restful sleep. The man rolls over and shuts off the alarm next to the bed. On the table next to the alarm is a picture of Joanna. The man gets out of bed and walks towards the bathroom door. The woman sits up in bed.

The woman speaks still sleepy, "I'm going to make some coffee."

The man nods still half asleep himself, "Okay."

The woman gets out of bed and puts her robe on as the man goes into the bathroom. The woman walks out of the bedroom and starts down the hallway as the man flushes the stool and walks over to the sink. The man washes his hands and grabs his toothbrush.

The woman stops by the front door first and gets the newspaper from outside, then locks the door back. The man finishes brushing his teeth, grabs the glass next to the sink and fills it. As the man takes a drink, he hears the most horrifying scream from his wife echo through the house. The noise causes the man to jump as he spits the water all over the mirror and he drops the glass causing it to break in the sink.

As the morning sun lights up the sky, the all to familiar scene is unfolding in front of Joanna's house. Police cars line the street along with two CSI vans. The yellow crime scene tape holds back the onlookers as well as the news. Then, the usual unmarked car pulls up next to the CSI vans. Ashley, Natalie and Mr. Gibson get out of the car and start for the crime scene tape. The three of them ignore the shouts from the news personnel.

The three of them duck under the tape and walk in the front door of the house. They pass Joanna's parents sitting on the couch in the living room as they head for the kitchen. The three of them walk in the kitchen and they see

Kevin standing over by the door leading to the garage. They also see Joanna's body on the floor in front of the door leading to the garage.

Joanna's perfect body is dressed and laid out like all the other victims. Ashley, Natalie and Mr. Gibson walk up to Kevin. The four of them look down at Joanna's body. They see the letter "K" written on her stomach, but they also see something in her right hand.

Kevin speaks solemnly, "Victim is Joanna Levens, age 17. She was killed just like the others. Her mother found her just after six this morning. Her dad said that she usually gets home around midnight." He pauses, "We have the writing on her stomach and ..."

Ashley jumps in, "What is that in her right hand?"

Mr. Gibson speaks up, "It should be a picture."

Ashley puts on some latex gloves and squats down next to Joanna's body as Kevin gets an evidence bag. Ashley carefully removes the picture from Joanna's hand. She holds up the picture of the grassy opening in the woods.

Ashley speaks as she puts the picture in the evidence bag, "The most baffling clue of them all. The picture that doesn't make any sense to the case."

Ashley stands back up, "Go ahead and get the body out of here. The parents don't need this dragged out any longer."

Kevin and his team get their things together and move Joanna's body as Ashley, Natalie and Mr. Gibson walk into the living room where Joanna's parents are sitting.

Ashley looks at Joanna's parents, "We're sorry for your loss Mr. and Mrs. Levens. I know this is hard, but we have a couple questions to ask."

Mr. Levens nods, "Okay."

Natalie pulls out the sketch of the killer, "Have you ever seen this man in the neighborhood or anywhere around Joanna?"

Mr. Levens looks at the picture for a minute, then shakes his head, "No."

Ashley, Natalie and Mr. Gibson look dejected, then Mrs. Levens speaks, "I've seen him."

Ashley gets a little more excited, "Where at Mrs. Levens?"

Mrs. Levens replies, "Two days ago. Joanna and I were grocery shopping and our carts bumped together as we turned into an aisle."

Mr. Gibson questions, "Which grocery store?"

Mrs. Levens answers, "The one just down the road a few blocks." She pauses and her eyes widen, "Oh my God. That's the man that killed her. He was watching her."

Natalie nods slightly, "The man who killed your daughter was watching her and we do believe this is the man."

Mr. Gibson questions, "She got home around midnight and was attacked in the kitchen. Did either of you two hear anything?"

Mr. Levens shakes his head, "No. We both take sleep medicine. Nothing short of the phone or alarm wakes us up."

Ashley nods, "Thank you. We'll contact you if we need anything else and please call us if you think of anything." She pauses, "Again, we're sorry for your loss."

Mr. and Mrs. Levens give a thankful nod. Ashley, Natalie and Mr. Gibson walk out of the house. They decide to stop by the grocery store just in case they get lucky and get an identification on their elusive killer.

The killer sits quietly at his desk in the dimly lit study. The heavy silence is broken as the killer's pen is put to paper. The killer writes about a page before stopping for a moment.

The killer sits back and stretches, "The last physical clue has been given. You're running out of time Detective Taylor."

The killer writes a couple more lines in his journal, then stops. He puts down the pen and closes the notebook. He sets the journal off to the side.

The killer sighs, "You have only one more month and two victims before the prize is lost for another 25 years."

The killer reaches over and picks up the picture of victim number 26.

The killer stands up, "Let the hunt begin." He pauses, "Good luck Detective Taylor."

The killer turns off the desk lamp and walks out of the room.

Chapter 32

AS THE MORNING SUN rises over the city giving light to a new day as well as starting the last month of the year, Ashley, Natalie and Mr. Gibson find themselves in the conference room once again, trying to find the elusive key that will bring the case to an end. The three of them shuffle through the massive amount of papers and pictures in front of them, knowing that the clock has already started on the next victim.

After a few more minutes, the door opens and Kevin and Jennifer walk in. They put their food in the small refrigerator and sit down at the table. The five of them continue looking through all the papers where they each feel that the hidden clue may be waiting for them to find.

Ashley finally breaks the cloud of silence hanging over the room, "Okay. As far as I'm concerned, we are out of time. We've gotten the final physical clue. The Polaroid picture that seems to have no connection to the rest of the clues."

At that moment, the door flies open and in walks the Mayor and Captain Sutherland. The five of them know that if it's this early in the morning, it can't be good.

The Mayor starts his tirade without shutting the door, "Do you know what I've discovered?!" He pauses, "You have a sketch of the killer and you haven't released it yet! You haven't alerted the public about what the killer looks like! Are you insane?!"

Ashley replies as calmly as possible, "We can't afford to scare the killer off without getting all the possible time we need to catch him. If he sees his picture in the paper, he might disappear without trying to complete his masterpiece."

The Mayor replies extremely heated, "Gambling with people's lives is a big decision for you to make all on your own Detective Taylor! If you don't catch this guy, more innocent people will die!"

Ashley's face starts to turn red and she stands up from her chair, "You don't think I know that! I don't need a politician telling me that people are dying. We're the ones standing over the bodies. We're the ones killing ourselves to track this killer down." She pauses, "Go make your political stand somewhere else! We're busy!"

The Mayor's face turns bright red, "Now listen here Detective Taylor!"

Captain Sutherland steps around in front of the Mayor, "If you have a problem with the way the case is being handled, you can talk to me about it. I made the decision to withhold the picture from the papers. All the decisions go through me first."

The Mayor takes a few deep breaths, "I want that picture in the paper, now." He pauses, "I would like to speak with you alone Captain Sutherland."

The Mayor storms out of the conference room. Captain Sutherland turns back to the others.

Captain Sutherland smiles and gives a thumbs up to Ashley, "That was good. I liked it."

Ashley takes a breath and sits back down, "Thanks Captain." She pauses, "Thanks for the support."

Captain Sutherland takes a deep breath, "Time for my next butt chewing." He pauses and smiles, "At least I will be able to get some smaller pants. Keep at it. I know you're going to get this guy."

Captain Sutherland walks out and closes the door behind him. The others return their eyes to the task at hand.

Natalie speaks up, "The Captain's butt and maybe his job is on the line because of all the heat he's taken for us. We can't let him down."

Ashley speaks up, "There are many reasons I want to stop this guy, but now I really want to just so I can walk into the Mayor's office and throw it in his face."

The others at the table get a good chuckle at Ashley's blow up at the Mayor. After a minute of refocusing, the five of them get back to the search for the elusive clue.

As night falls over the city, an incredibly beautiful young woman sits in a break room at one of the city's museums of history. She looks to be in her early twenties, standing about 5'5" tall and has one of the most incredible 130 pound bodies the world has seen. She has straight blonde hair that hangs down to her shoulder blades and the most captivating blue-green eyes. She is wearing a nice white tank top covered by a purple lace v-neck pullover, nice formfitting blue jeans and designer shoes.

The young woman is reading the paper on the table as she finishes her food. At that time, a man in his forties walks into the break room.

The man looks at the young woman, "How are you tonight Lauren?"

Lauren looks up and smiles, "Good. How are you doing Frank?"

Frank nods, "Not bad at all." He pauses, "How are the

classes going?"

Lauren replies, "Good thing I love history cause it's getting harder. I'm glad I got this job here to help." She stands up from the table, "So, how are the kids doing in school?"

Frank smiles, "So far, no bad grades."

Lauren tosses her trash in the trash can, "Well, I'll go see if there is one last tour before closing. See you later."

Frank nods, "Take it easy."

Lauren walks out of the break room and Frank sits down at the table. He looks at the newspaper article Lauren was reading. It is an article about the serial killer still at large in the city. He stares at the picture of the killer next to the article.

Lauren walks to the front of the museum to find the last tour of the day waiting for her. The group is a mix of men, women and kids totaling to about twenty. Too bad that Lauren didn't pay more attention to the article and picture of the killer. If she had, she would recognize the man, the killer, standing at the back of the tour group she is now walking through the museum.

Another sunset and another day ending in the city. The air has turned colder now that December has fallen on the city and the weather has also turned. However, neither has kept the five dedicated detectives from spending every waking moment trying to break the case. Ashley, Natalie, Mr. Gibson, Kevin and Jennifer are sitting around the conference table. Each has that very distinct look of frustration on their face. The frustration hangs so heavy in the air it could be cut with a knife.

Ashley stands up and breaks the silence, "What are we missing?!"

Natalie stares at the Polaroid picture, "I just can't figure out what this has to do with the case. It doesn't fit."

Mr. Gibson looks at Ashley, "The missing piece has to be in this room, somewhere."

Ashley walks over to the board where all the articles from the New York newspapers are pinned up.

Jennifer speaks up, "Well, we better find it quick."

Kevin shakes his head, "It's already too late for the next victim. All we can hope to save is the 27th victim."

The sound of the 27th victim triggers the anger building inside Ashley as she knows it is someone close to her.

Ashley swings her arms across the board with all the articles on it, "Who are you damn it?!"

Numerous articles and push pins fall to the floor. Ashley takes a couple of breaths as she looks at the board still covered with articles. An inquisitive look comes to her face as her eyes lock on a specific article. She reads the headline and the beginning of the article about Maureen O'Kelly, founder of the O'Kelly adoption centers and wife of Thomas Newman, passing away.

Ashley's eyes widen as everything hits her all at once. The images of the physical clues flash through her mind, the piece of adoption paper and clock hand, the bag of dirt, the pennies from 1949, the picture of Thomas Newman and the child, the blank birth and death certificates, it all makes sense now. Then, as if she was reliving each moment in her head, she sees herself standing over each victim again, each female victim.

Ashley spins around in excitement, "That's it!"

Natalie looks up at Ashley, "What is it?"

Ashley shakes her head and smiles, "We've been looking at the wrong person."

Jennifer questions, "What do you mean?"

Ashley explains, "We've been looking for the one clue, the common thing from all the victims, something that would give us what we were missing." She pauses, "Don't you see? The common factor to it all is that every victim is female, and that's it."

The four of them still look puzzled and Ashley continues, "Look closely. The victims are laid out like portraits. As if they are crying out, look at me." She pauses, "Look at the beautiful female."

Mr. Gibson nods, "Oh my God. You're right."

Kevin questions, "I still don't see it."

Ashley continues her thought, "All the clues pointed to someone and we thought it was Thomas Newman, but we were wrong. It wasn't Thomas we were suppose to look at, it was the female. It was Maureen that the killer was pointing us to. She's the key that ties everything together."

Mr. Gibson speaks up, "The piece of adoption form and clock hand signifies the start of a new life for an adopted child. The bags of dirt could signify the breaking ground on the new adoption centers that she opened."

Natalie nods, "And who was missing from the picture of Thomas Newman and the child? Maureen, the person who must have taken the picture."

Kevin catches on, "The 1949 pennies could be just as important to Maureen as they are to Thomas. Same as the blank birth and death certificates."

Jennifer nods, "All that leaves us is the Polaroid picture."

Ashley sighs, "That I'm still not sure of, but no doubt if we put the clues together, it will fit in somewhere." She turns to Natalie, "I want the computer team back in here tonight. We need all possible matches that the writings can give us in reference to Maureen O'Kelly."

Natalie gets up from the table, "I'm on it."

Natalie hurries out of the room.

Kevin speaks up, "You know what tomorrow is going to bring?"

Ashley nods slightly, "We might not stop him before

then, but he's not going to complete his masterpiece this time. This is the year it stops."

Mr. Gibson sits back and nods, "Good work Detective Taylor. You may have just found the one clue that could bring an end to fifty years of killing."

Ashley sits back down at the table, "Okay. While Natalie works with the computer team, lets recheck the pictures, clues and files to see if it all really does fit in with this theory."

The four of them return to the mountain of pictures and papers in front of them. Each has a renewed vigor as they feel that it is the killer who is now racing against the clock.

The killer sits in the dimly lit room as darkness falls over the city. The only sound in the room is the sound of his pen scratching away on his journal entry. The killer stops writing for a moment.

The killer sits back in his chair, "That was a fairly good picture of me in the paper."

The killer writes a few more lines, then stops again, "But how many men do you think looks like that and fits that description? It will do you no good."

The killer writes his last couple lines, then puts his pen down. He closes the journal and sets it off to the side.

The killer lets out a ghostly sigh, "Just put the clues together and it will all end. The nightmare will be over."

The killer picks up the picture of Lauren from the edge of the desk, "Unfortunately, your nightmare is about to become reality." He pauses, "Once again, they were too late."

The killer stands up, turns off the desk lamp and walks out of the room and into the night.

Chapter 33

IN THE COLD NEW York City night, Lauren walks into the break room just after the museum closes for the night. Frank walks into the break room a minute later as Lauren is getting her bottle of water from the refrigerator.

Frank grabs his jacket from the coat rack, "I guess I'll see you tomorrow Lauren. Bundle up, it's getting cold out there."

Lauren gives Frank a smile, "Okay dad, I will." She pauses, "I'll see you tomorrow."

Lauren sits down at the table as Frank walks out. She grabs a text book from her backpack next to the table and opens it. She looks at the few questions she has left on her homework.

A man's voice comes in from the break room door, "Homework tonight Miss Cross?"

Lauren looks over and sees the male security guard standing there, "Not much."

The security guard smiles, "I'll be at the security desk if you need anything before you leave Miss Cross."

Lauren nods and smiles, "Thanks Jack."

The security guard walks off and Lauren returns to her

homework. Jack shuts off the main lights and the museum is covered in darkness. Lauren takes about twenty minutes to finish her homework. Once she is done, she puts the book back in her backpack and gets up. She puts her jacket on and grabs her backpack. She slings her backpack over her shoulder and starts for the employees entrance in the back of the museum.

As Lauren walks, she is completely unaware of the killer following her in the shadows. The killer moves as if he knows where every security camera is located. Jack watches as Lauren passes by one of the cameras. Jack sits back and kicks up his feet. Once the killer sees Lauren walk into the area he wants her to be in, he quickly closes the distance.

The killer quickly wraps his left arm around Lauren's waist as his right hand places the cloth firmly over her nose and mouth. Not taking any chances, the killer steps around with his left leg and trips Lauren to the floor. Lauren lands hard and lets out a painful grunt as the air leaves her body and her backpack slides away from her.

Tears come to Lauren's eyes as she feels the killer's body pressing down on her from behind. She tries to struggle, but it becomes obvious that she is just not able to break free. She can feel her head getting heavier. She starts to sob.

Lauren manages to make a plea for her life through the cloth, "Please, don't do this."

The killer presses the cloth harder over her nose and mouth. Lauren's vision starts to blur. The tears start to run as she knows that once she passes out, this man can have his way with her. The killer can tell that Lauren's body is getting weaker.

The killer leans close and whispers in Lauren's ear, "Relax my beautiful Lauren. You are about to become a part of history."

Those words are the last thing Lauren hears as she

passes into the killer's darkness.

In the break room at the police station, Ashley, Natalie and Jennifer are sleeping on the foldout cots in the makeshift sleeping quarters. It is obvious that they spent the night at the station as they are still in their clothes from the day before. The three of them toss and turn from the restless sleep and uncomfortable conditions.

A few more minutes pass, then Mr. Gibson walks in. He goes to each one and wakes them up. As Ashley, Natalie and Jennifer start to move around and sit up, Mr. Gibson walks back over to the door.

Ashley looks at Mr. Gibson with tired eyes, "What time is it?"

Mr. Gibson replies, "It's 5:40 am." He pauses, "We just got a call. The next victim was found. We'll be waiting in the conference room."

Ashley nods, "We'll be right there."

Mr. Gibson walks out of the room. Ashley, Natalie and Jennifer each look at the other all thinking the same thing. Only one victim left. The three of them get up, get their things together and head off for the conference room.

In the cold morning of New York, numerous police cars surround the museum where Lauren works. Yellow crime scene tape keeps the crowd and news crews at bay. A few minutes pass until two CSI vans and an unmarked car pull up to the front of the museum. Kevin, Jennifer and the rest of the team get out of the vans as Ashley, Natalie and Mr. Gibson get out of the car. All of them duck under the tape and walk inside the museum.

Ashley speaks, "Natalie, Mr. Gibson and I will do some questioning while the CSI team gets their initial investigation and pictures done."

Kevin and his team walk off to the back as Ashley, Natalie and Mr. Gibson walk over to the people the police officers rounded up for questioning. As Kevin and his team work on Lauren's crime scene, Ashley and the others question all the security guards and other employees. After about thirty minutes, Ashley, Natalie and Mr. Gibson head to the back to find Kevin.

As the three of them approach Kevin, they see Lauren's body on the floor. Her body is dressed and laid out just like all the other victims. On her stomach is written the letter "Y".

Ashley walks up to Kevin, "Anything new?"

Kevin shakes his head, "No. Obviously putting the killer's picture in the paper didn't change anything." He pauses, "Find anything out?"

Ashley sighs, "Victim is Lauren Cross, age 21. She worked here while going to college majoring in history."

Natalie's phone rings. She walks off and answers it.

Kevin continues, "She was drugged, tied up and strangled, just like the others. What I don't get is how she wasn't found before now."

Mr. Gibson speaks up, "This is a dead spot in the cameras and the security is not real good about doing their rounds through the entire building."

Jennifer walks up, "We didn't turn up any other clues or evidence."

Ashley shakes her head, "Go ahead and move the body back to the station."

Natalie walks back up after just hanging up her phone, "We should all head back. The computer team got something very interesting."

Ashley nods, "Okay. Lets wrap this up and get back."

Kevin and his team gather up their things. They get

Lauren's body loaded in the van and drive off. Ashley gets in the driver's seat, Natalie gets in the passenger's seat and Mr. Gibson gets in the back seat.

Mr. Gibson questions, "What did they get?"

Natalie smiles, "An address on all three sets of writing. Addresses that have a direct connection to Maureen O'Kelly."

Ashley starts up the car and drives off.

In the mid-morning of the day, Ashley, Mr. Gibson, Kevin, Jennifer and Captain Sutherland are sitting around the table in the conference room. They each wait in anticipation for Natalie to bring what the computer team found. Ashley looks at Mr. Gibson and he is slightly bouncing in his chair.

Ashley smiles at Mr. Gibson, "Excited."

Mr. Gibson nods and smiles, "I've been waiting 25 years for what information might come through that door." He pauses, "It could be the end of the killings."

At that moment the door opens and Natalie walks in holding three pieces of paper.

Ashley questions, "What do we have?"

Natalie walks over to the dry erase board, "This is the address that the 1950 writings spell out."

Natalie writes the following line on the board: "1950 - 168 South Main Street Seattle WA".

Natalie flips to the next piece of paper, "This is what the writings from 1975 spell out."

Natalie writes the following line on the board: "1975 - 4816 Wornall Road Kansas City MO".

Natalie flips to the last piece of paper, "Even without the last victim, this is what the computer gave us."

Natalie writes the following line on the board: "2000 -

6815 North Manhattan New York NY".

Natalie turns back to the others.

Jennifer shakes her head, "Twenty seven victims each 25 years apart and they all spell out a valid 27 digit address." She pauses, "Now that's amazing."

Captain Sutherland can't hold back, "But what do those addresses mean?"

Natalie sighs, "Get ready for this." She pauses, "Each address is the location of the O'Kelly Adoption Center in the corresponding city."

Ashley speaks up, "Then that is definitely what those writings are suppose to spell."

Kevin questions, "Okay, but why point us to the O'Kelly Adoption Centers?"

It hits Mr. Gibson and he smiles, "The last clue. The prizes will be removed until the next time." He pauses, "The prizes, whatever they are, are at the adoption centers."

Jennifer questions, "Okay, we go there, then what? We search the entire building in hopes of finding something. We only have a couple of weeks."

Natalie shakes her head, "I don't think that's it. I think if we cracked the code, the killer has the prizes waiting for us."

Mr. Gibson nods, "I tend to agree. I bet if we go there and give them a name, we might get the prize."

Captain Sutherland speaks up, "Okay. You five go to the center. If you don't get the prize, call me. I'll have every officer available in the city there to search the building.

Ashley nods, "Lets go. The lunch traffic is going to slow us down some."

Ashley, Natalie, Kevin, Jennifer and Mr. Gibson rush out of the room as Captain Sutherland heads for his office. Everyone feels that they are getting closer to capturing the elusive serial killer.

The killer is enjoying a nice lunch at one of the fast food places on North Manhattan. As he puts down his fries and takes a drink, he hears sirens blaring in the distance. The killer puts down his drink and turns his attention to the window as the sirens get louder. In a few moments, two unmarked cars go by the fast food place. The killer recognizes the cars.

The killer turns back to his food, "Why in such a hurry detectives? You already have the 26th victim."

The killer continues to each his lunch and enjoy the cool day.

Chapter 34

THE TWO UNMARKED CARS screech to a stop in front of the O'Kelly Adoption Center in New York City. Ashley, Natalie and Mr. Gibson get out of one car and Kevin and Jennifer get out of the other car. The five of them start for the front door.

As they walk, Ashley questions, "Okay. What name do we give them to test the idea that they have the prize waiting for us?"

Kevin speaks up, "If I had to guess, Thomas Newman or perhaps Maureen O'Kelly."

Jennifer sighs, "It could be Michael Newman or John Smith."

Mr. Gibson shakes his head, "I don't think he'll make it tricky. He has focused on you. Give them your name and see what happens."

Natalie nods in agreement, "I think Mr. Gibson is right."

The five of them walk into the front of the center. They walk up to the receptionist sitting at the desk.

The receptionist looks at the five of them, "Can I help you?"

Ashley holds up her badge, "I'm Detective Ashley Taylor. I was wondering if you had something here for me?"

The receptionist looks down at the memos posted on the desk. She presses a button on the phone. Ashley looks at the others.

The receptionist speaks into the phone, "Yes sir. Ashley Taylor is here for her envelope." She pauses, "Okay."

The receptionist hangs up the phone, "Please have a seat. Mr. Jackson will be down in a minute with your envelope."

Ashley nods, "Thank you."

Ashley looks at the others as the five of them sit down in the waiting chairs. In a few minutes, a black man in his forties walks up holding a manila envelope and a piece of paper in his hand.

The man speaks, "Ashley Taylor?"

Ashley gets up and walks over to the man. Natalie and the others walk over behind her.

Ashley looks at the man, "I'm Ashley Taylor."

Mr. Jackson nods, "I'm afraid I'll need to see picture identification."

Ashley pulls out her badge and detective identification card, "What is this about?"

Mr. Jackson shrugs, "I don't know. We got this envelope on January 2nd. With it was a notarized letter stating only to release it to Ashley Taylor in person."

Mr. Jackson looks at her picture and name, "I'll just need you to sign this letter showing you received the envelope."

Ashley signs the bottom of the letter and Mr. Jackson hands her the envelope.

Ashley smiles, "Thanks."

Ashley and the others walk outside. Ashley carefully opens the envelope. She reaches inside and pulls out an old, worn piece of a map that looks like it was torn from a larger map. On the piece of map is a distinctive black "X" and a faded dotted line.

Kevin sighs, "This is the prize, a piece of an old map." He pauses, "Or another clue."

Mr. Gibson gets excited, "This is the prize. I bet there is a piece of map at the other two centers as well."

Jennifer questions, "But a map of where?"

Natalie speaks up, "I don't know, but I bet all three pieces will tell us where and how to get to the spot marked on this piece of map."

Ashley nods, "We need to get to those other centers, fast."

The five of them leave the center, jump in the cars and race off down the street.

As night falls over the city, the killer sits in his dimly lit study. The only sound in the room is the pen scratching on the paper as the killer writes his next journal entry. The killer stops writing for a moment.

The killer sighs, "The clock has started on the last victim. Are you going to make it in time?"

The killer writes another half a page in his journal, then puts his pen down. He closes the journal and sets it off to the side.

The killer sits back, "Time to start the next hunt."

The killer reaches over to the edge of the desk and picks up the picture of the last victim. It is a picture of Ashley's mother.

The killer stands up, "Sorry mom. I hope you have a lot of faith in your daughter."

The killer turns off the light and walks out of the room.

In the mid-day hours of the Midwest, a plane lands at the Kansas City airport. On the plane is Ashley, Natalie, Mr. Gibson, Kevin and Jennifer. They wait for the plane to park at the terminal, then they exit with the other passengers.

As they walk into the terminal, Ashley speaks, "A couple days for each flight. We are going to cut it close."

Mr. Gibson nods, "We are going to make it."

Mr. Gibson waves at a couple of men standing at the baggage claim belt. He walks over and shakes the two men's hands. Ashley and the others walk up.

Mr. Gibson speaks, "This is my old partner, now the big chief. I thought it would be faster if we had a police escort."

The man nods, "Nice to meet you." He turns to Mr. Gibson, "I haven't heard from you in twenty five years. What is this about bro?"

Mr. Gibson lowers his voice, "The serial killer. We've cracked his code and have one of the prizes he left."

The man looks stunned, "Oh my God." He breaks his stare, "Then lets get going."

They retrieve their bags from the belt and hurry off to the parking lot.

The two unmarked Kansas City police cars come to a screeching stop in front of the O'Kelly Adoption Center. Ashley and the others get out of the car and head for the front door.

As they walk Mr. Gibson speaks to his old partner, "That was some good driving. I never figured we would make it before they closed."

Ashley walks in with everyone behind her. She walks

up to the receptionist's desk while everyone else waits by the chairs.

The receptionist looks up, "Can I help you miss?"

Ashley nods, "I'm Ashley Taylor. I was wondering if you had an envelope for me?"

The receptionist looks over her desk and spots the same memo that was in New York. The receptionist presses a button on her phone. Ashley looks back over to the others and gives a slight nod.

The receptionist speaks into the phone, "Yes. Ashley Taylor is here for her envelope." She pauses, "Okay."

The receptionist hangs up the phone, "Mrs. Sawyer will be right down Miss Taylor."

Ashley walks back over to the others to wait. In about five minutes, they see a woman in her early fifties walk up to the desk holding a manila envelope and a piece of paper.

Ashley walks up to the woman, "Mrs. Sawyer?"

Mrs. Sawyer smiles, "Are you Ashley Taylor?"

Ashley nods, "Yes."

Mrs. Sawyer replies, "Can I see a picture ID Miss Taylor?"

Ashley pulls out her driver's license and hands it to Mrs. Sawyer. Mrs. Sawyer looks over the license and hands it back to Ashley.

Mrs. Sawyer speaks, "I'll just need you to sign this letter."

Ashley signs the letter and Mrs. Sawyer hands Ashley the envelope.

Ashley smiles, "Thank you."

Ashley walks back over to the others. She carefully opens the envelope as Natalie pulls the first map piece out of the envelope she is carrying. Ashley reaches inside the envelope and pulls out another old, worn piece of map with a faded dotted line on it that looks torn from the other pieces. Natalie holds the first piece up. It doesn't take them but a couple of seconds to fit the two pieces together.

Mr. Gibson's former partner sighs, "Will you look at that."

Ashley nods, "We need the third piece. No doubt it will give us the starting location."

Kevin nods, "Well, should we head to the hotel until our next flight?"

Natalie nods, "There is not much more we can do."

The two Kansas City officers lead them back out to the cars. They get in and head off for the hotel near the airport. They each have the same hope. They hope they stop the killer before the last victim.

In the night skies over a cold and overcast Seattle, a plane awaits it's turn to land. Ashley looks at the others sitting around her. She wonders where this map will lead them. About twenty minutes later, the plane is on the ground. The five of them sit patiently as the plane comes to a stop at the terminal. The five of them get up and follow the other passengers off the plane.

As they enter the terminal, Jennifer speaks, "Welcome to Seattle."

Jennifer looks around and spots Deputy Cook. The others follow Jennifer over to Deputy Cook and his partner.

Deputy Cook nods, "Good to see you again Detective Harris."

Jennifer smiles, "Good to see you too."

Jennifer introduces the others. After shaking hands with everyone, Deputy Cook steps back.

Deputy Cook explains, "We will have to take you to the hotel. The center wouldn't stay open late, no matter what we said and we had no legal way to make them."

Ashley looks at the date on her watch, "We're going to

be cutting it close."

Deputy Cook speaks, "If you'll follow us, we'll get going."

Ashley and the others retrieve their bags and meet the two deputies in the parking lot.

Later that night, as the rain falls, Ashley is sitting on her bed in the hotel room she is sharing with Natalie and Jennifer. She has the two pieces of the map sitting on the bed in front of her. Jennifer is sitting at the table in the room writing some notes as Natalie walks out of the bathroom after cleaning up for the night.

Ashley speaks up, "What I don't get is even if we get the third piece of the map. It looks like its taking us out in the middle of nowhere." She pauses, "What, is the killer going to be just waiting for us?"

Natalie shrugs, "Maybe the killer's house is in the middle of nowhere."

Jennifer looks up, "You know, that's a possibility." She pauses, "It better lead to something good cause we've only got seven days left."

Ashley nods, "I don't even want to think about that."

Natalie reassures her, "We're going to get him. You know that." She pauses, "We've cracked his code."

Jennifer sighs, "Not all of it."

The two of them look at Jennifer.

Jennifer continues, "We still don't know where the Polaroid picture fits into all this."

Ashley nods slightly, "I bet it will make sense once we find where this map is taking us."

Natalie looks at the clock, "We better get some rest. We are getting picked up in six hours."

Ashley nods and sets the pieces of the map on the end

table and stretches out. Natalie lays down in the other bed in the room. Jennifer shuts off the lights and walks over to the couch where a pillow and blanket wait for her. The three of them quickly fall asleep.

Chapter 35

IN THE DAMP, COLD, overcast Seattle morning, two Sheriff's deputy cars pull up in front of the O'Kelly Adoption Center in downtown Seattle. Ashley, Natalie and Mr. Gibson get out of one car as the deputy stays in the car. Jennifer, Kevin and Deputy Cook gets out of the other car. The six of them walk inside the front doors of the center. Ashley walks over to the receptionist's desk while the others wait by the chairs.

The receptionist looks up, "Can I help you?"

Ashley smiles, "I'm Ashley Taylor. I was wondering if you have something here for me, like an envelope."

The receptionist has a stunned look on her face, not expecting what she just heard.

It takes the receptionist a second to regain her composure, "Just a moment."

Ashley walks over to the others as the receptionist presses a button on her phone. After a short conversation, the receptionist hangs up the phone.

The receptionist looks over to Ashley, "Mr. Horton will be right with you."

Ashley nods, "Thanks."

Ashley and the others stand and wait. After about ten minutes, a man in his sixties walks up to the receptionist's desk. The receptionist points over to Ashley while talking to the man. Ashley walks back over to the desk.

Mr. Horton smiles, "Are you Ashley Taylor?"

Ashley nods, "Yes." She hands the man her drivers license, "Here you go."

Mr. Horton looks at her, "How did you know I needed a picture ID?"

Ashley smiles, "Just a guess."

Mr. Horton nods, "I'll need you to sign for the envelope."

Ashley signs the letter and Mr. Horton hands her the envelope.

Ashley nods, "Thank you."

Ashley walks over to the others that are waiting for her. She opens the envelope and pulls out the third piece of the map which has an "X" and a faded dotted line on it. Jennifer holds up the second piece and Natalie holds up the first piece. The six of them look at the now completed map.

Kevin shakes his head, "Okay. We have the whole map, but there is no writing on it. So where is this a map of?"

Deputy Cook looks closely at the map, "It's here."

The others look at Deputy Cook with a shocked look on their faces and Mr. Gibson questions, "Are you sure?"

Deputy Cook nods and points at the "X" on the piece of the map Ashley just got, "If I'm not mistaken, this is the old wood mill just down Old Mill Road from Mrs. Littlefield's house." He points at the "X" on the first piece of map they got, "This spot is somewhere in the woods past the end of Old Mill Road."

Ashley speaks up, "Lets get to this wood mill and follow the dotted lines to the final spot."

Deputy Cook nods and the six of them head back out to the cars.

In less than an hour, the two deputy cars are parked in front of the old wood mill on the dirt road that is mostly mud due to the recent string of bad weather. The sun has broken through the clouds and the temperature is still cold, but it is going up some.

Ashley turns to the deputy driving, "Okay. Looks like we head north until the road ends."

The two cars drive slowly down the muddy road. Ashley, Natalie and Mr. Gibson look around to make sure they don't miss a single thing. Jennifer and Kevin are looking all around as well from the car they are in. After about twenty minutes, the two cars come to a stop as the road ends and the woods begin.

The deputy turns off the car and looks at Ashley, "The end of the road. Now what?"

Ashley sighs, "We walk from here."

Ashley, Natalie, Mr. Gibson and the deputy get out of the car. Jennifer, Kevin and Deputy Cook gets out of their car.

Ashley looks at Deputy Cook, "I want you to come with us." She looks at the other deputy, "You stay with the cars. We might get out of handheld radio range and need you to relay for us."

The deputy nods and gets back in his car. Deputy Cook takes the lead with Ashley and they slowly make their way into the woods. They do their best to use the land features to follow the faded dotted line on the map.

Ashley speaks to Deputy Cook, "You seem pretty good at this."

Deputy Cook smiles, "I grew up hunting in these woods." He pauses, "I'm guessing in total we will go about five miles."

Mr. Gibson adds, "That is definitely in the middle of

nowhere."

The six of them continue through the woods as the trees get closer together and the underbrush gets thicker. Ashley keeps checking her watch. Deputy Cook stops every so often and makes sure he can still reach his partner waiting back on the road. It is a slow trek through the dense woods as the sun nears it's noon peak. Finally the woods start to get a little less dense.

Deputy Cook speaks, "It should be just a little ways over that hill in front of us."

Ashley and the others are all thinking the same thing, why are they being led way out here? They get over the hill and continue on. After another half mile, the woods open up into a grassy opening about twenty feet around. All five of them have a stunned look on their face. They immediately recognize the spot where they are now standing.

Natalie speaks still in shock, "This is the place in the Polaroid picture."

Mr. Gibson nods slightly, "That ties in the final clue."

Deputy Cook looks at the map, "If I had to guess. This is the spot marked on the map."

Jennifer nods, "This is definitely the spot."

Kevin sighs, "But why lead us here? I still don't get it."

Ashley takes a few steps forward and turns back to the others, "This is where the killer wants us. It all leads here. The answer is here." She pauses, "I'm guessing that whatever it is he wants us to find, it's buried in this opening."

Mr. Gibson nods, "I bet you're right." He pauses, "Everyone spread out and check over the ground thoroughly."

The six of them step into the opening and form a line. As they take a step, they each feel the ground under their feet. It is a slow process, but they don't want to miss anything. The six of them continue across the grassy opening. When they get about halfway across, Ashley stops. She pushes down with her foot a few times. The others stop as they notice what Ashley is doing.

Natalie questions, "What is it?"

Ashley looks puzzled, "I don't know. It's just that the ground feels a little different here."

Deputy Cook walks over and Ashley steps out of the way. Deputy Cook gets down on his knees and uses his hands to check the ground.

After a couple of minutes, Deputy Cook stands up, "I think she's right. Something could be buried here."

Deputy Cook radios his partner to get the Sheriff's Office CSI team started their way. The six of them get on their knees and start tearing at the ground. Because of the recent rain, the ground is soft. They claw the dirt away with their hands. After thirty minutes, the six of them have made some good progress. Suddenly, they all stop at the same time. All six of them stare at the ground in front of them where they have been digging with their hands.

Deputy Cook speaks first, "Is that what I think it is?"

Jennifer nods, "It's definitely bones." She looks at Kevin, "Human hand?"

Kevin leans in closer, "Yea. It's definitely a human hand."

Ashley sighs, "Okay. We're going to stop until the CSI team gets here. We don't want to disturb the site any more than we have."

The six of them stand up and walk a few feet away and wait.

In a couple of hours, the grassy opening is surrounded by crime scene tape. Ashley stands with the others by the entrance to the opening as they watch the Seattle CSI team work. The ground is almost completely excavated. Ashley and the others watch as bones are pulled out of the shallow grave and placed in a body bag.

Ashley turns to the others, "So, why did the killer lead us here?"

Natalie sighs, "It's obvious he wanted us to find this skeleton, but why?"

At that moment, one of the Seattle detectives walk up to Ashley. He is a man in his late fifties.

The detective speaks, "I'm Detective Morris."

Ashley nods, "I'm Detective Taylor. What do we have?"

Detective Morris explains, "It's a human skeleton. From what we can tell, probably a male in his early teenage years." He pauses, "So you're saying that your serial killer case is linked to the case from here in 1950 and Kansas City in 1975 and the clues led you here."

Ashley nods, "Yea."

Detective Morris looks puzzled, "Why?"

At that time, another detective walks up. It is a female in her early thirties.

The female detective holds up the head of an old claw hammer, "This was found next to the body sir. It's consistent with the two blows to the skull."

Natalie speaks up, "Maybe this was the first for our killer."

Detective Morris shakes his head, "If your killer is in his twenties, he didn't do this. Right now we're guessing this skeleton to have been here for about 50 years or so."

Jennifer sighs, "Well, we found this body that the killer led us to, but now what? We only have a few days until our next victim."

Mr. Gibson speaks up, "Whatever is next, we don't need to be in Seattle for it."

Ashley speaks up, "We need to get back to New York

right away. Maybe now that we found the body, the killer plans on giving himself up."

Kevin nods, "We did solve the clues. Maybe that's all he wanted."

Ashley replies, "Lets get out of here. I think they can take it from here."

Detective Morris nods, "I'll call you when we get an ID on the body. We will check our unsolved cases. Shouldn't take us long at all."

Ashley shakes his hand and the five of them walk off with Deputy Cook. Each one wondering why the killer led them to this spot.

As the mid-day sun bears down on New York City, Ashley walks into the conference room where the others are already sitting. She walks over and sits down next to Natalie. All five faces have a depressed look.

Kevin is the first to speak, "We get our next victim tomorrow and we haven't figured out why the killer led us to the shallow grave outside of Seattle."

Mr. Gibson speaks up, " I have a theory. It sounds a little crazy, but could be the reason behind all this."

Ashley sighs with an indifferent attitude, "What's that?"

Before Mr. Gibson can explain his idea, the door opens and Captain Sutherland walks in. He is holding a piece of paper and a white legal sized envelope in his hands.

Captain Sutherland speaks, "I just got the report from Seattle." He walks over to Ashley and hands her the envelope, "This certified letter came for you."

As Ashley opens the envelope, Natalie questions, "What did Seattle say?"

Captain Sutherland sits down, "Brace yourselves. We just solved one of the most high profile unsolved mysteries in the history of this country."

Jennifer questions, "What?"

Captain Sutherland continues, "The body found in the woods has been there since 1949. It is …"

Before Captain Sutherland can continue, it hits Mr. Gibson and he blurts out, "The body of Michael Newman."

Natalie, Kevin, and Jennifer look at Mr. Gibson as if they don't know what he is talking about.

Kevin shakes his head, "Michael Newman ran away."

Captain Sutherland speaks up, "The body is that of Michael Newman. He was killed with two blows to the head with a claw hammer."

Natalie has a shocked look, "So the killer led us to Michael Newman. He showed us the truth about what happened to Michael Newman."

Kevin shakes his head, "But why was that important and how does that help us in capturing the serial killer?"

It finally hits Natalie, Mr. Gibson, Kevin, Jennifer and Captain Sutherland that Ashley has been quiet through all of this. The five of them look over at Ashley who is just staring at the piece of paper in her hand.

Natalie questions, "What is it Ashley?"

Ashley shakes her head, "I believe this answers our questions. It's from the serial killer."

Mr. Gibson questions, "What does it say?"

Ashley reads the letter, "The truth has been discovered, now the killings will stop. You will never hear from me again. I will go on with my life and continue my grandfather's bloodline. It is unfortunate that the same cannot be said of the Newman family bloodline."

Ashley puts down the letter as a silence falls over the room. None of them can think of anything to say.

Mr. Gibson finally speaks, "So, all the killer, or killers over the last 50 years were trying to tell us is the truth about what happened to Michael Newman."

Ashley nods, "If I was a betting person, I would say that the child that was sent away, John Smith, murdered Michael Newman."

Mr. Gibson picks up the story, "Then he starts the serial killing to take the focus off of Michael Newman's disappearance, but leaving the clues for the police."

Natalie speaks up, "When Seattle couldn't solve it, he passed it on to his son and the killings followed Thomas and Maureen to Kansas City."

Jennifer jumps in, "And when that case ended, the information was passed down again and followed Maureen to New York."

Kevin shakes his head, "And all of it over the years was nothing more than clues to tell what happened about the murder of Michael Newman in 1949."

Ashley sits back and breathes a big sigh of relief, "It was just like Detective Conners thought and told Mr. Gibson back in 1975. The theory that Mr. Gibson shared with us at the beginning of this case. It really was a serial killer bloodline."

Captain Sutherland stands up, "Well, all that matters now is that we solved the case and put a stop to the serial killer." He pauses, "Time to go have a sit down with the Mayor."

Captain Sutherland walks out. The five of them look at each other still in disbelief.

Ashley stands up with a smile on her face, "Well, lets get everything together and filed away. I have to say, this is definitely the strangest case I've ever seen."

The others chuckle and start getting all the papers and pictures together. All of them can feel the weight lifted off their shoulders.

Epilogue

IT IS A COLD night in New York City. Snow covers the ground, but that hasn't kept the citizens from coming out on the biggest night of the year. The city is decorated for the new year's celebration. Also decorated for the new year holiday is the conference room that used to be decorated with some of the most horrible images in the history of law enforcement.

Food and drinks line the table in the conference room. Ashley, Natalie, Mr. Gibson, Kevin and Jennifer are standing around the table. The talk is about everything except for the serial killer. Each of them has tried to put the nightmares behind them.

Ashley kisses Mr. Gibson, "Happy New Year."

Mr. Gibson smiles, "In a few minutes, it will be. Happy New Year."

Jennifer and Natalie each give Mr. Gibson a new year's kiss. Then Ashley, Natalie and Jennifer give Kevin his new year's kisses.

Mr. Gibson looks at Natalie and Ashley, "So, any resolutions?"

Natalie smiles, "Get more sleep this year."

Ashley chuckles, "Amen to that sister."

Natalie questions Mr. Gibson, "How about you?"

Mr. Gibson nods, "I think I'll give up drinking. I don't think I'll need it any more."

Kevin walks up, "Where's the Captain?"

Jennifer walks up, "I haven't seen him."

The phone starts ringing. Jennifer walks over and answers it.

Jennifer looks over to Natalie, "It's for you Natalie."

Natalie walks over to the phone and takes the handle from Jennifer, "Hello."

A man's voice comes on the line, "Is this Detective Natalie Simpson?"

Natalie replies, "Yes it is."

The man replies in a cold, evil tone, "Then, let the game begin Detective Simpson."

The man hangs up before Natalie can say anything. Natalie hangs up the phone and turns to the others with a puzzled look on her face.

Ashley questions, "What is it Natalie?"

At that time, the door opens and Captain Sutherland walks in. All of them can tell by the look on his face something is very wrong.

Natalie looks at Captain Sutherland, "What is it?"

Captain Sutherland replies solemnly, "One of our officers just called in a homicide. The victim was shot and hung in a tree in Central Park. He said that there was a piece of paper pinned to the victim's shirt with some strange writings on it."

Ashley and Natalie look at each other. Ashley can tell by the look on Natalie's face that the phone call had something to do with what the Captain just told them. Without saying a word, Natalie, Ashley, Mr. Gibson, Kevin and Jennifer walk out of the conference room and head for their cars in the parking lot. Each one knowing that something bad has just started up in their city again.

Jody Slyman

THE END

www.ingramcontent.com/pod-product-compliance
Lightning Source LLC
Chambersburg PA
CBHW030243030726
47493CB00023B/564